I barely had time to gasp a few gulps of air before Mischa knocked Adam down and came after me. I backed down the aisle, pulling the apple-wood sticks from my hair. Behind Mischa, Adam went after Fatty in a blur of motion. I didn't have time to see the outcome of his attack, because just then Mischa produced nunchucks from her back pocket. With a self-satisfied grin, she swung them overhead like helicopter blades. Cans of Spam and packages of pork rinds flew to the floor as she advanced.

I retreated until I hit a dead end at the row of drink coolers at the back. The gunfire earlier had shattered the glass and most of the bottles and cans, but I managed to find a bottle of apple juice among the wreckage. I popped the top and tossed the contents in Mischa's face. She inhaled sharply out of surprise, forcing the forbidden fruit juice into her system. I ducked the flailing nunchucks and slammed a chopstick down at an angle behind her collarbone.

Mischa jerked back, falling into a display of Doritos. Her body ignited, and the chips went up in flames with her. The resulting odor was a bizarre mix of smoke, apple, and nacho cheese. In addition to the oddly pleasing scent of Mischa's death, I experienced the sweet taste of retribution on my tongue. Mischa might have tormented me for years with jokes about my shameful birth, but I'd just gotten the last laugh.

BY JAYE WELLS

Sabina Kane

Red-Headed Stepchild

The Mage in Black

Green-Eyed Demon

THE MAGE IN BLACK

Jaye Wells

www.orbitbooks.net

ORBIT

First published in Great Britain in 2010 by Orbit

A CIP catalogue record for this book
is available from the British Library.

ISBN 978-1-84149-757-0

Printed and bound in the UK by CPI Mackays, Chatham, ME5 8TD

Papers used by Orbit are natural, renewable and recyclable
products sourced from well-managed forests and certified
in accordance with the rules of the Forest Stewardship Council.

Mixed Sources
Product group from well-managed
forests and other controlled sources
www.fsc.org Cert no. SGS-COC-004081
© 1996 Forest Stewardship Council
FSC

Orbit
An imprint of
Little, Brown Book Group
100 Victoria Embankment
London EC4Y 0DY

An Hachette UK Company
www.hachette.co.uk

www.orbitbooks.net

For Spawn,
who is never allowed to read this book.

The Kum-N-Go's roadside-chic interior was bathed in a sickly fluorescent glow. The aroma of stale smoke, urinal cakes, and rotgut coffee had me breathing through my mouth on the way back to the ATM. It was my turn to pay for gas, so getting cash took priority over raiding the snack aisle for the moment.

While I entered my code and waited, Adam chatted with the attendant at the front of the store. He glanced over and raised his eyebrows. I lifted a finger and took a moment to admire the way his ass filled out his jeans. Even after sitting in a car for two days straight, he still looked hot with his stubble and road-weary smile. Too bad the mage part made him off-limits.

Before I got caught staring, I moved my gaze to the window. Adam's SUV and my cherry red Ducati provided the only scenery in the empty parking lot. The bike's 180 horses rested docilely on a trailer behind Adam's behemoth. Before we'd left California, he'd argued I wouldn't need wheels in New York, but I held my ground. That motorcycle was the only good thing left of my old, broken life. Leaving it behind wasn't an option.

A flash of white caught my attention as Stryx landed on the roof over the gas pumps. The red-eyed owl had followed us all the way from California, and I assumed he'd be joining us in New York. I'd gotten so used to seeing him, I no longer questioned his reason for following me. He never caused trouble, which was more than I could say for my other companions on this road trip from hell.

The headlights from a midnight-black Mercedes lit up the window. It pulled in on the other side of Adam's car, so I couldn't see the driver get out. I waited to see if he'd come inside to pay, but loud beeping from the ATM grabbed my attention.

I took the clump of twenties the machine spat out and stashed it in my pocket, relieved the account still worked. Registered under a false name through a bank in the Caymans, the account held the bulk of my savings. When I'd set it up, it was a better-safe-than-sorry measure, but now it was all I had left to my name.

I was turning toward the front of the store when the three redheads came around the back of Adam's car. My heart sputtered and then kicked into overdrive.

How'd they find me so fast?

"Adam! We've got company!" With one hand, I reached for my waistband and grabbed for my gun. I cursed, realizing I'd left it in Adam's center console along with a box of apple cider bullets. After a few days on the road with no sign of trouble, I'd grown complacent, and now I was about to fight three assassins armed with nothing but the pair of apple-wood chopsticks that held my hair back. Awesome.

The mortal male behind the counter wore a red smock with a nametag that read "Darrell."

"Go lock yourself in the storeroom," I told him.

"Huh?"

I flashed my fangs and pulled him bodily across the counter. "Get the hell out of here!"

Wetness spread across the front of his wrinkled khakis. He stammered for a moment, then turned tail and ran toward the back of the store.

Adam had already spotted the trouble. "Friends of yours?"

I turned toward the door, watching the three vampires make their way toward us. "The one on the left is Nick Konstantine. Likes to get stabby, so watch your back." Nick was the kind of vamp who gave the rest of us bad names. He liked to rape his prey before draining them. Nasty dude. "The big guy is Fatty Garza."

"What's his specialty? Eating his opponents whole?"

"Something like that."

"And the female?"

I narrowed my eyes and gripped my gun tighter. "Mischa Petrov." Just saying that bitch's name left a bad taste in my mouth.

Adam parted his lips to say more, but the assassins stopped about ten feet back from the door. Mischa's eyes met mine through the glass doors. She smiled snarkily and nodded. *You ready to die, bitch?*

I raised an eyebrow in return. *Bring it.*

Adam stood calmly at my side, waiting. He didn't waste time with unnecessary questions. I knew from experience he could hold his own in a fight, which meant I didn't have to worry about saving both our asses on my own.

Something shifted. Nothing obvious. No overt signal was given. But one second the whole world seemed to hold its breath, and the next, the air exploded with gunfire. I shoved Adam to our right, and we slid down the aisle in a tangle of limbs.

Bullets ripped through the store, turning it into swiss cheese. Sodas exploded in the refrigerated cases, coating us with cold, sticky wetness. Pulverized chocolate, salty snacks, and tampons rained down to create a PMS-themed collage on the floor.

"You got any weapons?" I yelled over the noise.

"Magic." I shot him a look. He smiled. "And a Glock." He pulled a Glock 20 from his waistband and handed it over. Releasing the magazine, I was relieved to find it full. That gave me fifteen rounds. Fifteen nonlethal bullets, considering we were fighting vampires, but I'd still be able to inflict some pain.

Finally, the hailstorm of bullets stopped.

"Yoo-hoo! Sabina?" Mischa called.

"What?" I shouted, and glanced at Adam. "Get ready to create a diversion."

"Just let me zap them out of here." I shook my head firmly. This was vampire business. I'd be damned before I let a mancy save me from my own kind. Besides, if anyone was going back to L.A., it was to take a message to my grandmother. And it wouldn't take three of them to deliver it. But Adam's magic could come in handy in other ways. I pointed to the fluorescent lights overhead. He nodded coolly and rose into a crouch.

Mischa sighed loudly. "I don't suppose you'd just surrender now and save us all some time, would you, Mutt?"

I gritted my teeth. Mischa never missed an opportunity to remind me and everyone in hearing distance of my mixed blood. "Riiight. Tell you what, if you're in such a hurry, why not just put that gun to your temple and squeeze the trigger? It'll save me the effort."

"And muss up my hair?" Mischa drawled. "You're just talking crazy now."

"Enough of this shit," Nick said, clearly unimpressed with our banter.

Boots crunched on broken glass, signaling the assassins were on the move. I nodded to Adam.

His lips moved with an incantation, and a zap of energy shot from his fingertips. The hair on the back of my neck stood on end as I peeked between cereal boxes. Two fluorescent lights exploded above Mischa and Nick, and the metal housings holding the bulbs broke loose and crashed on their heads. Mischa's gun skittered away, and Nick got knocked to the floor. Fatty, surprisingly agile given his size, jumped aside and started making his way to the back of the store.

With the shelves as cover, I opened fire on Mischa, who'd taken refuge behind a display of travel mugs. Taking aim at the bank of coffee machines behind her, I shot the carafes. Judging from her screams, the coffee shower that splashed on the bitch was roughly the temperature of magma.

One second, Adam crouched next to me, and the next, he inhaled sharply and cursed. I ripped my gaze off Mischa in time to see him pull a throwing star out of his thigh. He tossed it to the ground with an irritated grimace. "Okay," he said, his jaw tight. "Now I'm annoyed. Seriously—who uses a throwing star?"

I sensed movement behind me. Before Fatty could

get his hamhock hands on me, I back-kicked him in the stomach. My boot heel sank into the fleshy layers like I'd stepped into a pool of Jell-O before ricocheting back. Fatty's belly shook with laughter for a moment before cutting off suddenly. We all went still for a moment, and then everyone shifted into fast-forward.

Mischa, looking like a wet, pissed-off cat, jumped Adam from out of nowhere. As he fended off her claws and kicks, Fatty grabbed me from behind and started squeezing me like a fleshy boa constrictor. He shook me like a rag doll, and the gun fell from my fingers and sparks of light danced in my eyes. I reached back and poked his eye with my index finger. I had to jab a couple of times before he finally released me with a howl.

I barely had time to gasp a few gulps of air before Mischa knocked Adam down and came after me. I backed down the aisle, pulling the apple-wood sticks from my hair. Behind Mischa, Adam went after Fatty in a blur of motion. I didn't have time to see the outcome of his attack, because just then Mischa produced nunchucks from her back pocket. With a self-satisfied grin, she swung them overhead like helicopter blades. Cans of Spam and packages of pork rinds flew to the floor as she advanced.

I retreated until I hit a dead end at the row of drink coolers at the back. The gunfire earlier had shattered the glass and most of the bottles and cans, but I managed to find a bottle of apple juice among the wreckage. I popped the top and tossed the contents in Mischa's face. She inhaled sharply out of surprise, forcing the forbidden fruit juice into her system. I ducked the flailing nunchucks and slammed a chopstick down at an angle behind her collarbone.

Mischa jerked back, falling into a display of Doritos.

Her body ignited, and the chips went up in flames with her. The resulting odor was a bizarre mix of smoke, apple, and nacho cheese. In addition to the oddly pleasing scent of Mischa's death, I experienced the sweet taste of retribution on my tongue. Mischa might have tormented me for years with jokes about my shameful birth, but I'd just gotten the last laugh.

A bellow near the front of the store got my attention. Fatty bent over at the waist, his hands cupping his crotch. Apparently, Adam wasn't afraid to fight dirty. I smiled and mentally added that to my list of favorite things about him.

I moved to join the mage up front, but right then Nick performed an over-the-counter somersault, landing a foot away from Adam. My scalp tingled as Adam shot the vamp with a bolt of magical energy. Nick flew backward, his head crashing the counter before he collapsed on the floor.

I came up behind Adam and shot Nick a few times for good measure. The wounds wouldn't kill him. To do that, I'd need to inject a dose of the forbidden fruit into his system first, to strip away his immortality. But I had other plans for Nick.

I crouched next to his limp body. He groaned, his eyes fluttering. Whatever Adam hit him with had scrambled him good. His labored breath had a wheeze to it that made me suspect I'd clipped a lung.

Behind me, I heard the crack of knuckles against skin. Sounded like Fatty had come back for more from Adam. I needed to make this quick so I could help him finish off the obese vamp.

I leaned in close to Nick's ear. "Tonight's your lucky night, Nick. I'm going to let you live. But in return you're going to do something for me."

His head jerked and his mouth moved, but no sound came out.

"Sabina," Adam yelled. "A little help here." A grunt followed his plea.

I held up a finger over my shoulder. "Listen up, 'cause I have to go kill your partner in a sec. Are you listening, Nick?" I pressed a thumb into the wound in Nick's leg to make sure I had his attention. He moaned in response. I took that for a yes.

"I want you to give my grandmother a message. I want you to tell her what happened here. I want you to look her in the eye." I grabbed Nick by the chin and forced his gaze to mine. "And then I want you to tell Lavinia I'm coming back for her real soon."

My job done, I lifted the Glock and coldcocked Nick. His head fell to the side and his mouth went slack. Given the extent of his wounds, he'd probably be down for the count long enough for Adam and me to get the hell out of Dodge. I wasn't worried he'd give chase. He'd know better.

Another grunt echoed through the store. I rose and saw Adam and Fatty grappling near the magazine rack. I was relieved to see Adam looking relatively uninjured despite being trapped in Fatty's headlock. Even with Adam's height and impressive physique, the mage had nothing on four hundred pounds of vampire flesh. I wondered why the mage hadn't spelled the vamp into submission, but then I saw the brass knuckles glinting on Fatty's massive hand. Brass is like Kryptonite for mages, which explained why Fatty had survived this long.

I grabbed a bottle of aerosol hairspray from the sundries aisle and ran toward them.

"Hey!" I yelled. When Fatty turned, I blasted him in the

eyes with the hairspray. He dropped Adam and shrieked, swiping at his eyes with a huge paw. He ran at me blindly. I backpedaled, raising the gun. But my heel was sticky from the apple juice and slipped out from under me. As I fell, the shot went wide and clipped Fatty's shoulder instead of his head.

Adam came up from the rear and stabbed the big guy with a stake. Fatty roared in pain but still didn't explode. I scrambled up, trying to avoid his flailing arms. I ducked, barely avoiding one of his fists.

Adam's eyes widened. "The stake isn't big enough to reach his heart," he whispered loudly.

Roaring from pain, Fatty took off for the front doors. He crashed through and ran blindly toward the pumps. Adam and I looked at each other for a beat before hauling ass after him. We couldn't risk some mortal pulling into the station and seeing a huge, bloodied vampire lumbering through the parking lot. We skidded to a halt as Fatty crashed into Adam's Escalade. He bounced off the rear door and fell to the ground. The SUV rocked from the impact before going still again.

I raised the gun, determined to put an end to Fatty once and for all.

Adam grabbed my arm. "If you miss, you might hit a pump."

I shot him a glare. "I won't miss."

"Well, Miss Sharpshooter, did you think about what'll happen if you hit him and he ignites close to four gas pumps?"

"Oh." I lowered the gun. "So what now?"

Adam opened his mouth to answer but stopped when the back door to the Escalade opened. A hoof emerged, followed by a scaly green leg clad in too-short black sweatpants. Fatty heard the sound and cocked his head, like an animal sensing unseen danger. Giguhl emerged fully, raising his arms high above his seven-foot frame in an exaggerated stretch. His poison green *Got Evil?* T-shirt complemented his black horns nicely.

With a scowl, he focused on the large, groaning vampire to his right. Fatty seemed to have regained some of his sight. His eyes squinted and then widened. He moved surprisingly fast then, jerking to his feet and lumbering away.

Fatty got as far as the air and water station before he tripped. He scrambled to grab a hose and pointed it at us. A pathetic stream of water trickled out.

"What are you going to do?" Giguhl said. "Moisten us?"

Now that we were safely away from the gas pumps, it was time to end this charade. I calmly raised my gun and put my last bullet between Fatty's eyes. Since the wooden stake had already injected the forbidden fruit into his system and removed his immortality, his girth went up in flames immediately.

"Well, that's that, then," Adam said. "I guess I'll go fill up." He walked off toward the pumps like he was taking a Sunday stroll. The only sign he'd just survived an assassin attack was the slight limp courtesy of Nick's throwing star. How he could deal so calmly with the aftermath of such chaos escaped me.

My own body strained for action. Something to work off the residual adrenaline. My gaze strayed to Adam's retreating form. Something to release the tension. I admired the way his sweat-dampened shirt clung to his muscled torso. Something strenuous and sweaty. I took a step forward.

"Um, Sabina?" Giguhl tugged on my arm.

"What?" I stopped, dragging my eyes from Adam. Giguhl was dancing from hoof to hoof. "What are you doing?"

"I need to see a man about a unicorn."

And with that, all thoughts of ravaging Adam screeched to a halt. "Oh, for fuck's sake, Giguhl."

"It's not my fault. You know I have a small bladder."

"Okay, fine, little girl. Go tinkle. But make it quick."

He ran off toward the doors on the side of the building.

With one last look at the charred mass that used to be Fatty, I turned to walk toward the car. I was almost there when a faint sound made me stop in my tracks. "Gods-dammit," I cursed under my breath. "Look alive, mancy."

He looked over from the windshield he'd been cleaning. "What's up?"

"Sirens."

Adam cocked his head to listen. "I don't hear them."

My vampire hearing caught the sound long before human or mage ears would. "We've got about ten minutes. It's time to go."

I turned to go tell Giguhl to shake a leg, but a move-ment inside the store brought me up short. I'd forgotten all about the human, but the shotgun he held told me he hadn't forgotten about us. I ran back toward the car.

Before Adam could ask why I was running, the shot-gun barked. Luckily, the human had no idea how to handle such a powerful weapon. The shot went wide and took a chunk out of the tin roof over our heads.

"What the fuck was that?" Adam yelled.

"The human! I'll take care of him."

"Sabina, no! He's innocent. You can't kill him."

Another blast, closer this time. I ducked behind the SUV next to Adam. "You're fucking kidding me, right?"

Adam's expression told me he'd been serious. "He can identify us and the car to the police. Unless you want to play Smokey and the Bandit all the way to New York, he's got to go."

I moved before he could stop me, pulling the Glock out of my waistband as I went. Behind me, Adam cursed and moved to stop me. Speeding up before he could accomplish his goal, I raised the gun just as Darrell pumped the barrel again.

But before either of us could shoot, a dark figure exploded out of the store. Nick's second wind hit at exactly the worst moment possible. He grabbed the human, breaking his neck like it was nothing more than a matchstick.

"No!" Adam yelled behind me.

Nick grabbed the shotgun as the human fell. In Darrell's hands, the shotgun had been troublesome. In Nick's hands, the same gun scared the shit out of me.

In slow motion, I pivoted and ran toward the bathroom. Two reasons. One, I needed to warn Giguhl and somehow get both of us out alive. Two, the movement turned Nick's attention away from Adam. I had a better chance at surviving a shotgun blast than the mage.

Bam! The brick wall six inches above and just ahead of me exploded. I zigzagged toward the restroom and pounded twice.

"Time to go, G!"

"Jeez, give me a minute!"

"Now!"

"Can't a demon take a leak without being disturbed?"

he grumbled. The door opened as he was pulling his pants up. "What?"

"What happens if you get shot?"

His goat eyes widened. "It hurts."

"But you won't die or get sent back to Irkalla, right?"

"Nope."

"Good. Run!"

We hauled ass across the parking lot just as Nick pumped the shotgun again. Adam accelerated to meet us. Giguhl wrenched the SUV's back door open and dove in just as another blast ripped through the air. I heard the demon yelp, but I was too busy trying to get my own door open. When the latch finally gave way, Adam was already accelerating. I jumped in and grabbed my gun from the console. A click of a button lowered the window, and I ducked through the opening to take care of Nick.

A shot hit somewhere near the rear of the SUV. The car fishtailed as Adam struggled to maintain control. Sparks and a hunk of red, twisted metal appeared in the road behind us.

"That bastard killed my Ducati!" I yelled. With steely resolve, I rested my forearms on the top of the Escalade.

I'm a good shot, but even I have trouble aiming at moving targets from a speeding car. It took three shots. The first hit the Kum-N-Go sign, which exploded in a hail of sparks. The second nicked a gas tank, which bled fuel like a wound. The third punched Nick in the chest. His body ignited instantly and fell right into the puddle of gas.

A huge fireball lit up the night sky, bringing with it a wave of heat that seared my face. I watched the fireworks for a second before ducking back inside.

Adam watched the show through the rearview mirror.

A muscle worked in his jaw. "You should have killed Nick when you had the chance."

"Um, guys?" Giguhl's voice came from the back seat.

I ignored the demon and jerked my head toward Adam. "Excuse me?"

He turned accusing eyes on me. "You were ready to let the vampire live but couldn't wait to kill that innocent mortal. Why is that, Sabina?"

"Sabina?" Giguhl moaned.

I narrowed my eyes on the mage. "I had my reasons, and I don't appreciate your tone, mancy."

"You had reasons, huh? Well, guess what, your *reasons* almost got all of us killed."

"Adam?" Giguhl panted.

I crossed my arms. Adam's judgey tone pissed me off. He needed to get off that high horse before I knocked him off. "Yeah, you're right," I said. "It's okay for me to kill a vampire, but a human life is precious. I should have given the mortal a hug and then let him blow my head off, right? Gods, you're such a hypocrite."

His hands squeezed the steering wheel like he wished it was my neck instead. "I'm saying there is a bigger picture here. Nick was an assassin. The human was an innocent bystander. I know morality is a fluid concept for you, Sabina, but I abide by a code that says you protect the innocent."

I leaned forward, ready to tell Adam where he could shove his morality.

"Guys!" Giguhl shouted.

Adam and I spun around together and yelled. "What?"

"I've been shot in the ass!"

2

*T*wo nights later, the Escalade emerged from the Lincoln Tunnel. Seeing New York's skyscrapers looming ahead, I let out a relieved breath. We'd made it to New York without another appearance from the Dominae's death squads. Being on mage turf didn't make another attack impossible, but it made it a hell of a lot less likely.

"How much longer?" Giguhl asked from the backseat.

Adam shifted and looked in the rearview. "Few minutes. Fifteen tops."

It was the longest conversation any of us had had since Iowa. Adam was still pissed at me for not killing Nick when I'd had the chance and getting the human killed. I was pissed he'd taken such a holier-than-thou attitude. We'd killed three vampires, but one lousy human he had an issue with? As for Giguhl, he'd easily expelled the bullet and healed quickly, but he'd still spent most of the trip sulking over his ass wound.

Giguhl leaned up between our seats, watching through

the windshield. His claws tapped incessantly on the arm-rest. I turned to glare at him. "Do you mind?"

He stopped tapping. "Well, excuse me. Just because you're nervous doesn't mean you have to be bitchy, you know."

I rubbed my sweaty palms on my jeans. "What's there to be nervous about?"

Adam shot me a glance but kept his mouth shut.

"Come on," Giguhl continued. "After your grandmother turned out to be a lying, vindictive bitch, it's totally normal to be worried about meeting new family members. I mean, what if your sister hates you?"

"Oh, that's a big help, thanks."

He shrugged. "I'm just sayin'."

Truth was, I hadn't given much thought to how well I'd get along with my sister. I mean, sure, I was curious about her. It's not every day a girl finds out she has a twin she never knew about. I had to imagine it was even more rare when vampires had raised one twin while the other was raised by mages—two races who'd been enemies for centuries.

But I'd been so focused on getting the hell out of L.A. and finding a way to make my grandmother pay for her be-trayal that I figured allying myself with her enemies would be a good place to start. And after the fiasco at the Kum-N-Go, I was more determined than ever to throw myself into learning everything about magic so I'd have the upper hand when Granny and I had our showdown.

Adam maneuvered through traffic for a few minutes be-fore he spoke. When he did, he addressed Giguhl. "Maisie won't hate her."

I perked up but refused to be the one to break our

stalemate. Luckily, Giguhl spoke for me. "How do you know?"

"Maisie doesn't hate easily. As long as I've known her, she's never said a bad thing about anyone."

"And how long is that?" Giguhl said.

"A long time." He smiled fondly. "We were practically raised together."

The fondness in his tone gave me pause. He'd spoken of her before, but I never really asked much about their relationship. This was the first I'd heard they'd grown up together. I wanted to ask if the affection was of the brotherly sort or something more but decided I'd rather rip out my own fingernails than give voice to my curiosity on that matter.

"What's Maisie like?" Giguhl asked. Probably more to fill the silence than out of real curiosity.

Adam seemed to relax a bit, warming up to the topic. "She looks like Sabina, of course, only there are subtle differences."

"Like what?" Giguhl asked.

"Her hair's shorter. And where Sabina's hair is red with black streaks, hers is more black with red streaks, if that makes sense."

"Not really, but go on," Giguhl prodded. I shot the demon a grateful look. He winked back.

"Well, she loves to paint and has a knack for hedge magic."

"Hedge magic? Is that like landscape design or something?"

Adam chuckled at the demon's lame joke. "Not exactly. Hedge mages use herbs and plants to make potions. She used to bug the faeries visiting from the Seelie Court to teach her about plants." A fond smile spread on his face, as if he was picturing a memory. "This one time she broke into the greenhouse so she could make a potion to change her hair. She said she wanted it to be all black so she'd be all mage. Only the potion ended up turning her hair green temporarily."

He turned left onto a street teeming with billboards, flashing lights, and people milling about like ants on a hill. "Welcome to Times Square," he said. I spared the scenery a glance, but I was more interested in what he'd just said about Maisie.

"Why did she want to get rid of the red?" I asked, despite my promise to keep my mouth shut. Red hair is the hallmark of being a vampire. It's a trait we inherited from Cain, the male who fathered the first of our race. "Did the mage kids make fun of her for being mixed-blood?"

Adam paused and shot me a glance. "No, nothing like that," he began slowly, as if readjusting to speaking to me again. "It wasn't like she was an outcast or anything. I think she just considered herself fully mage and wanted to get rid of the symbol that marked her as being only half."

I could relate to that feeling, although for me it was the opposite. Being raised among vampires, who had no qualms about treating me like an outcast, I'd prayed and prayed to the Great Mother that I'd wake up one morning with solid red hair. Knowing Maisie had struggled with similar issues made me relax a bit. Maybe I'd finally have someone who understood what it was like to never really belong.

"Well, if she's anything like Sabina, I'm sure she's delightful," Giguhl said, his voice full of irony.

"Bite me, demon."

Adam turned onto a circle and followed it around to an exit for Central Park West.

A few minutes later, he slowed near a large apartment building and put on his blinker. In the dark, it loomed like something out of a horror film. With its Germanic spires and gables, it was the kind of building you might expect to see covered in gargoyles. Before I could fully process the strange architecture, Adam turned into a port cochere on the side of the building.

Inside the covered driveway, a wrought-iron gate with a Hekate's Wheel design in the center barred the entrance to an interior courtyard. Adam punched some codes into the keypad and waved at the cameras perched on top of the gates. In a few moments, the wrought-iron behemoths yawned open.

"Pretty wimpy security for the home of the Hekate Council," I commented. A system like that? I'd be in before he could say 'abracadabra.' "

Adam frowned at me. "Do you consider thermal scanners wimpy, too? Because there's one checking you out right now and identifying you as a vampire. If I hadn't cleared you, there'd already be a group of guards surrounding us."

I laughed. "Fat lot of good that'll do you. I could have a bomb hidden in the car. Boom, the whole building goes bye-bye."

"The metal plate we rolled over at the entrance scans the undercarriage for bombs," Adam explained. "You wouldn't have gotten inside with it."

I leaned toward him. "I could climb up the side of the building and shoot my target through a window."

He leaned over the center console, his eyes sparking

with challenge. He smiled slowly, deliberately, bringing my attention to his lips. "Bulletproof glass."

I chuckled and leaned back, impressed and not a little turned on by the exchange. "Touché."

Adam's trademark grin returned for the first time in days. I enjoyed seeing it, but I needed to change the subject before I jumped him. Something about a man with tactical prowess always gets me. But something else tickled the back of my mind. Adam's knowledge of weapons and security seemed advanced for someone who could just zap an enemy with a spell.

"What exactly is it you do for the council?"

He accelerated through the portico and into an open courtyard. On all four sides, the building's walls rose ten stories into the inky night sky. "I'm part of a group called the Pythian Guard. We were formed back in ancient Greece to protect the mages who acted as oracles. But since the oracles don't really serve the public anymore, our role has evolved over the years. These days, we're more like the council's private guards. We also do special projects as needed."

"Special projects? You mean like retrieving the long-lost sister of the council's leader?"

He cracked a smile. "Among other things."

I smiled at his evasion. "Are we going to meet your family here?"

His expression became closed. "Just an aunt. My parents died when I was young."

"I'm sorry," I said quietly.

He shrugged. "No need. It's old news. Aunt Rhea raised me. She and Ameritat were close friends, so Maisie and I spent a lot of time together."

"So does that mean we're the same age?"

Adam smiled. "Nope. Maisie came along when I was six."

My mouth fell open. Damn. He looked good for sixty. His magic must have been even stronger than I thought. Mages aren't immortal like vampires. Their magic allows them to live extremely long lives, though. Adam had told me in California that Ameritat, my father's mother, lived to be one thousand. Still, I'd figured Adam for midthirties at most. I guess I had a lot more to learn about mages—this one in particular—than I thought.

I opened my mouth to ask more, but Giguhl interrupted. "Hold the phone. Isn't this where they filmed that romantic comedy?"

Adam squinted at the demon through the rearview. "No, the Hekate Council has never allowed cameras inside."

Giguhl nudged my shoulder. "You know, the one with Mia Farrow? I saw it in L.A. one night."

I turned to look at the demon. "Wait, are you talking about *Rosemary's Baby*?"

Giguhl snapped his fingers. "That's it! I loved that movie."

Adam and I exchanged a look. "G, I think that was filmed down the street at the Dakota," Adam said. "This is Prytania Place."

Giguhl frowned. "Hmm, I could have sworn it's the same building."

"Common mistake." Adam shrugged. "Anyway, we're here. You ready to meet your sister?"

I looked around the interior of the courtyard. Even inside the car, I could feel the magic buzzing around like static electricity. But under that hum, I could feel something else, something stronger that I recognized instantly. Like the pull of a magnet in my diaphragm, Maisie's blood called out to me. I took a deep breath. It was time.

"Giguhl, change into cat form," I said over my shoulder. A puff of smoke signaled the demon's transformation. Angry feline cursing echoed from the back seat. I glanced back, and my eyes widened. Back in California, my first attempt at magic had ended in Giguhl's cat form going bald. I'd thought Adam had fixed that mistake, but I hadn't seen Giguhl in cat form since I summoned him from Irkalla and asked him if he wanted to come with me to New York. Now his pale, naked skin glistened in the car's dim light. Without fur, his ears resembled a bat's, and his wrinkled skin and grumpy face made him resemble a shriveled old man.

"Nice," he said, looking down at his skin. "Remind me to piss on your clothes later."

I ignored the demon's whining and turned to Adam. "Take me to your leader."

In the elevator, Adam used a retinal scanner and voice recognition program to gain access to Maisie's penthouse apartment.

On the way up, he told me Prytania Place served as headquarters for the mages in the city. In addition to holding apartments for all the council members and other high-ranking mages, it was the seat of their government, with meeting rooms and offices throughout.

"There's also an estate up north, near Sleepy Hollow. It's used for all the important magic rites and festivals. I'm sure you'll see it soon enough."

I nodded, only half listening. Instead, my eyes watched the rapid display of floor numbers. Too soon and not soon enough, the elevator dumped us into a foyer outside Maisie's front door. Adam had a key and let himself in without knocking.

Given the old-world, old-money feel of the building, I'd expected the decor to be sedate and snooty. But the apartment we entered was an eclectic mix of colors and textures. From the worn wooden floors to the eggplant paint on the walls to the rainbow of sheer fabrics fluttering around the windows, the place had a definite bohemian feel.

"Maisie?" Adam called.

My stomach dipped in both anticipation and anxiety. It's not every day a girl is introduced to her twin. But this re-union had the added complexity of two sisters being raised by opposing races. Even Giguhl seemed to sense the weight of this moment, as he remained uncharacteristically silent in my arms.

We continued into the apartment when no one re-sponded to Adam's greeting. Sandalwood permeated the air. Just as humans smell like dirt and vampires smell of copper, all mages smell like sandalwood. But in addition to the sandalwood, the sharp tang of turpentine and the oily aroma of paint scented the air.

Heading down a hall, we passed an altar of sorts cov-ered in fertility goddess statues clustered around a lit white candle. Just beyond it, a door painted apple green was covered with symbols written in gold paint. I wasn't sure what they meant, but I assumed they were protection spells of some sort.

Adam paused before knocking and shot me a reassur-ing smile. But before he could apply knuckles to wood, the sound of a woman singing drifted through the door. The hair on my arms rose.

That's my sister.

Adam knocked twice but, hearing no response other than more singing, pushed the door open after a moment. She stood with her back to the door in front of a large canvas set on an easel. She didn't stop singing when we entered. Instead, she slapped red paint on the canvas in time to music we couldn't hear. I was too shocked to see her at first to register the words. But slowly they became clear: "Could you be looooved, and be lo-oved?"

Her Bob Marley impression was lacking, but I had to give her points for enthusiasm.

I choked on a laugh, too shocked to hold it in. Just as she belted out, "Don't let them change ya, oh!" Adam touched her shoulder.

She yelped and spun around. "Dammit, Adam. You scared the shit out of me!"

"Yep, they're definitely related," Giguhl said.

Maisie pulled the headphones off her ears when she saw me. A slow flush crept up her neck and pinkened her cheeks. "Sabina?" she whispered.

I started to nod, but suddenly a blur of pink rushed toward me. I had just enough time to brace myself before she slammed into me and wrapped her arms around me in a fierce hug. Giguhl hissed and jumped from between us. Maisie didn't seem to notice the pissed-off cat. My hair muffled her voice, but I made out the words, "Excited . . . sister . . . here."

I looked at Adam for help, but he shrugged and grinned. She pulled back with a beatific smile. Her features were all the same as mine, except, like Adam had said, her hair was shorter and layered so it fell softly around her face.

But there were other differences, too—ones that might not register with the casual observer. Looking at Maisie was like looking through a mirror at an alternate version of me, a happier version. It wasn't just her smile. She seemed completely comfortable in her skin, and warm, earthy energy radiated from every pore.

An odd feeling of déjà vu washed over me. Something told me this warm, happy person was who I might have been if things had been different. If I'd been raised among the mages instead of given to the Dominae. Out of nowhere, resentment rose like bile, and I tried to pull away.

She let me go reluctantly. Her eyes glistened prettily with tears. My own felt dry and brittle. The defensive shields I'd carefully cultivated over the years locked back into place. I knew this was a significant moment in both of our lives, but I felt removed from it, an observer instead of a participant.

Knowing I needed to say something, I waved and said, "Hey." Lame.

"Hi there." She laughed and went in for another hug. "Thanks be to the Goddess for bringing you home, sister."

Adam, who'd obviously understood my discomfort at her easy affection, cleared his throat. "Give her a chance to breathe, Maze."

She pulled away and looked at me. A flush spread up on her cheeks. "Oh, I'm sorry. I'm just so"—she took a deep breath and exhaled it—"excited."

"You mentioned that," Adam said. Affection and humor laced his tone.

"Ahem! Can I change back now?"

Maisie's eyes widened at the bald cat sitting at Adam's feet. I sighed. One of these days, I needed to teach Giguhl about manners. I glanced at Adam, not sure how much he'd told Maisie about the Giguhl situation. But Maisie answered the unspoken question by approaching the cat.

"And this must be Giguhl. Adam told me all about your unusual familiar. May I pick him up?" She shot me a hesitant look.

"Why don't you ask him?" Giguhl said.

Maisie drew back, looking worried she'd offended him.

"Ignore him. He's always a bit surly when he's in cat form," I said. "Behave yourself, Mr. Giggles."

"You try behaving with your bald balls exposed to the world, *trampire*."

Maisie laughed, a musical sound that inspired images of fairy-tale princesses. She squatted down to look the cat in the eyes. Giguhl, recognizing a potential ally, widened his eyes to give her the saccharine-sweet kitty look. She rubbed him behind his bat-like ears. "He's just precious."

The cat cocked his head and purred. Still petting him, she lifted him and cradled him against her chest. Maisie looked at me with a smile. "You're so lucky. I wish I had such a sweet familiar."

Giguhl shot me a smug look. "Can we keep her?"

I rolled my eyes. But the truth was, a spark of jealousy went through me. He was my minion, dammit. "Whatever you do, don't give him your credit card number."

Maisie frowned. "Huh?"

"Never mind her," Giguhl said quickly. "If you like me in cat form, wait till you get a load of me in my demon form."

Maisie's eyes widened. "Oh, I'd like that."

An image of Giguhl naked popped into my head. "Trust me, you wouldn't. At least not until we have some clothes handy for him to put on."

Adam cleared his throat. "Speaking of, I better get our things so we can freshen up before Sabina meets the council."

"Oh," Maisie said, looking at me. "Do you need to borrow some clothes?"

I eyed her long skirt tie-dyed in rainbow colors and the pink peasant blouse. Apparently, our genetic similarities didn't extend to fashion sense. "No, it's okay. I've got clothes in the car."

"It's really no problem," she said. "In fact, I insist."

I started to protest again, but she pushed me toward the door. I looked back over my shoulder for help, but Adam nodded encouragingly. "I'll go tell the rest of the council to assemble for the rites."

"Rites?" I said, suddenly feeling like I'd gotten in way over my head. Maisie was now pulling me down the hall.

"Don't worry," she said. "It's just a basic cleansing ritual to rid you of the bad vampire karma."

"Vampire karma?"

She ignored the question in my voice and stopped at a door to another room. This door was sky blue with billowy white clouds painted all over it.

Maisie opened the door and I caught my breath. Multicolored murals filled every available inch of wall space—even the ceiling. There seemed to be no unifying theme to any of the images. Instead, it was like looking at schizophrenia in paint form.

"Wow," I said, not sure what else to say. It's not that I

didn't like it. I just couldn't figure out what this said about my sister's mental state.

"It's a bit busy, huh?"

"I think it's beautiful," Giguhl said, looking up at Maisie with adoring cat eyes.

I ignored the little bald traitor and turned slowly to take in the whole room. "This must have taken you a long time."

She chuckled. "You have no idea. This mural is based on a vision I had several years ago."

I turned to look at her. "What does it mean?"

She shrugged, rubbing Giguhl under the chin. "I'm still trying to figure it out." She touched an area depicting a cardinal and blue jay flying together. "Painting helps me decipher the messages of my visions. Sometimes they're straightforward images of future events. Other times they're like riddles I have to solve. But this one has been harder to translate than most."

I looked around at the swirls of color and the images of clocks, birds, golden lotuses, and dozens of other random symbols. When no meaning jumped out at me, I changed the subject. "The painting you were working on when I arrived, was that from a dream, too?"

She smiled. "No. That was your portrait."

I frowned at her, recalling that the painting in question was nothing but a bunch of red swirls and splotches mixed with some black and white in places. "I thought portraits usually involved, you know, faces."

She smiled as if about to explain something to a child. "No, I mean a portrait of your essence."

"Huh?"

"One of my strengths is color magic. Everyone has a

dominant color influencing their lives. It represents several things about their true selves. I use paint to show the true nature of people."

"And my essence color is red?"

"Definitely. Red represents boldness, aggression, impulsiveness, high energy, and extremes of opinion."

The cat snorted. "That's her, all right. Although you forgot stubborn."

I glared at the cat, promising retribution with my eyes. "What color are you?" I asked Maisie.

"I'm a blue." Before I could ask what that meant, she changed the subject. "Allrighty." She looked me over and tapped a finger against her lips. "I'm thinking red."

She set Giguhl on the bed gently. He stretched before curling up in a ball on her pillow and falling asleep. Maisie turned back to me and mumbled a few foreign-sounding words.

My skin started tingling like I was covered in static electricity. I looked down and gaped. The blue jeans and leather jacket were gone, and a long red dress took their place. I turned to look in a mirror on the back of Maisie's door. The straps of the gown were twisted and fell into a deep V-neck. The fabric fell away in loose folds under another twisted band of fabric at the Empire waist.

"I can't wear this," I said, panicking a little at the sight of me looking so . . . feminine. I didn't do dresses as a rule. Not only did the skirts trip me up during a fight, but dresses also tended to make weapon concealment an issue.

"Sure you can. Everyone wears chitons to meetings, it's a tradition from our days back in Athens."

"But still," I said. "Can't I just wear something a little less girlie?"

"I'm afraid the council is pretty strict about our rituals," she said. "Would you prefer another color?"

I shook my head. "No, the color is fine." The deep red fabric was the color of blood fresh from the vein, so that was something.

I heard a rustling behind me and turned to see Maisie standing before me in a dress almost identical in style to my own. Hers was a soft robin's egg blue with a golden rope crisscrossing her midsection. The sudden change surprised me, and I mentally lectured myself that I needed to get used to this, since I was going to be around mages all the time now.

"You're going to have to teach me how you do that."

Maisie adjusted the dress as she looked in the mirror. "Don't worry. You'll get started on your training soon enough." She smiled. "You ready?"

A quick knock sounded on the door and Adam stuck his head in. "The council's assembled," he said to Maisie. Then his gaze landed on me. He went still, only his eyes moving as he looked me up and down. "Um."

My cheeks heated, and I suddenly felt naked. I resisted the urge to cover myself and put my chin up instead. "What?"

His eyes lifted to mine and he cleared his throat. "Nothing. I just haven't ever seen you in a dress before."

"Doesn't she look great?" Maisie said.

A smile lifted the corner of Adam's lips. He nodded in response to Maisie but kept his eyes on mine. "Amazing."

I took a moment to look him up and down, too. He wore a shorter version of the chiton Maisie and I both wore. His was black with a golden thunderbolt embroidered over his heart. The chiton's design showed off his golden skin and well-muscled arms and legs. Never had a dress looked so utterly masculine, and I had a sudden urge to know what he was wearing underneath that skirt.

A tingle of sexual awareness had me shifting uncomfortably. But the question of Adam's undergarments made me realize something else—I wasn't wearing anything under my own chiton. "Hey, where are my weapons?"

Maisie shrugged. "They're with your other clothes."

"Mundane weapons aren't allowed at rituals," Adam said.

I sent him a pitying look. "You're funny." With hands on hips, I turned to Maisie. "Give them back."

Maisie raised her hands in a diplomatic gesture. "You're going to be surrounded by family, Sabina. No one is going to attack you."

"She's right, Red," Adam said quietly.

"Need I remind you that my own grandmother staked me less than a week ago? No offense, but I'm having trouble feeling safe among family right now."

Adam sighed deep from within his chest. "Honestly, Sabina? Even if you had a weapon, you wouldn't stand a chance. Most of the mages waiting in that room could disarm you with a passing thought."

"Oh, that makes me feel tons better. Thanks."

Maisie came forward and put a hand on my arm. "Sabina, I know this is difficult for you. But I swear on the grave of our father that no one will harm you here."

I opened my mouth to argue, but Adam caught my attention. With his eyes, he pleaded with me to drop it. I glanced at Maisie, who looked anxious. With a deep sigh, I nodded. I might not have known Maisie well enough to trust her yet, but I trusted Adam. "Fine, but I'll expect them back the minute this is done."

Maisie looked relieved and grabbed my hand. A tingle passed between our palms. Her expression went all serious. "I know you've sacrificed a lot to come here. But never doubt you made the right decision. This is where you belong."

That remained to be seen, but even I wasn't rude enough to rebuff Maisie's obvious sincerity. Not knowing what to say, I simply nodded.

A bright smile lifted her lips. "Good. Now that that's settled, you ready to go meet the Hekate Council?"

I let my breath out in a rush. I wasn't ready for any of this, but that never stopped me before. "Can't wait," I lied.

Getting to the council chambers required another elevator ride. When the doors opened in the basement of the building, I caught my breath. Instead of the stately meeting room I'd been expecting, the space looked like someone had dropped a hippie commune in the middle of the Senate. The place reeked of sandalwood and patchouli.

The elevator opened at the top of the room. Below, steps led down between row after row of coliseum seating. The seats were covered in colorful cushions, spread about like confetti. And standing among the rows were hundreds of mages dressed in chitons of every color imaginable.

At the bottom of the stairs, an open area that looked like the stage held a long table covered in colorful scarves. Behind it, five mages dressed in white chitons stood and watched our approach. It appeared that the white chitons were reserved only for members of the council, since I didn't see any among the crowd. I only recognized one of the members. After our disastrous mission at the Domi-nae's vineyards, Orpheus had arrived to help bring the bodies of the dead mages home. We'd only talked for a moment then, but he seemed nice enough.

After a moment of silence—the kind that usually follows a record scratching to a stop—the whispers and pointing began.

"That's her!"

"She's here!"

"Praise Hekate for bringing her home!"

Adam grabbed my hand and gave it a reassuring squeeze. Then he and Maisie exited the elevator, leaving me to walk out alone. The mages on either side of the steps watched in awe as I made my way down. Some even reached out to touch me as I passed.

I tried to ignore all this because, frankly, it was freaking me out. They were acting like I was some sort of royalty or something.

Orpheus came around the table and met us at the base of the steps. He took both my hands in his.

"Welcome, Sabina. As you can see, we're all thrilled you agreed to come."

I didn't mention that I hadn't had much choice. Instead, I forced a smile. "Thank you."

He then turned me toward the crowd and stepped in behind me. "May I present Sabina Kane, daughter of the hero Tristan Graecus and sister of Maisie Graecus, High Priestess of the Chaste Moon and the Oracle of New York."

Maisie came forward and raised her voice to be heard. "Welcome home, sister. After decades of being subjected to the evils of the Dominae, you may finally take your place among your true family."

Behind us, the audience broke out into another round of applause.

"The Hekate Council would like to thank you for assisting us in finding our loved ones who were taken by the Dominae," Maisie continued. "Without you, we might never have known their fate. You took a stand against our enemies despite great personal cost to yourself. With your support and knowledge, we will finally defeat our enemies."

Another furious round of clapping. I kept my eyes on Maisie. Her praise made me feel itchy.

"In light of all this and more, the ancient and venerable Hekate Council has created the Sacred Order of the Blood Moon to honor you."

My heart stopped. I'd never expected to be honored. I looked at Adam, who winked at me and smiled. I watched in shock as Orpheus came forward and handed some sort of necklace to Maisie. She turned to me and held the gold chain over my head.

"We, the ancient and benevolent Hekate Council, hereby dub thee Sabina Kane, High Priestess of the Blood Moon. May you use your exalted position to protect and serve the mage race."

She lowered the necklace around my neck. The gold chain felt cool against my skin. "Behold, all assembled, Sabina Kane is now under the protection of the Hekate Council. Any enemy of hers shall be enemy to us all."

I looked down. At the end of the chain, an amulet about the size of a silver dollar nestled between my breasts. A large moonstone sat in the center of a gold setting etched with characters that looked like hieroglyphs. I assumed they were actually Hekatian, the mage ceremonial language.

I met my sister's eyes, which glistened suspiciously. "What does it say?"

"It says: 'For she is the torchbearer, this daughter of Hekate; she will light the way.'"

My eyes stung, and I had trouble swallowing. "Thanks," I said, not trusting myself to say more.

Maisie wrapped me in a fierce hug. "Thank *you*, sister."

When the cheering and praises to Hekate finally petered out, Orpheus nodded to a nearby female mage with long silver hair. Wise eyes looked out from a youthful face bearing an impish smile. She wore a purple chiton and an amulet similar to the one I just received.

"Rhea Lazarus, High Priestess of the Elder Moon, will now commence with the cleansing rites," Orpheus said.

I paused. Was this the aunt Adam mentioned? I glanced at him for confirmation. But his eyes were on the female. The fond smile on his face gave me my answer.

Rhea winked back at her nephew before focusing on me. In her hands she held a bundle of dried herbs. She whispered something and the tip of the bundle sparked. Fragrant smoke rose from it and tickled my nose. She started chanting something I couldn't understand as she waved the smoldering bundle around my head. Then she moved in a counterclockwise circle around me.

I tried not to fidget during the process. The rest of the mages watched in silence. I guess they were used to having a weird old lady wave foul-smelling smoke in their faces.

When she finished her last lap, she snapped her fingers and a young female mage in a gray chiton came forward. She held a golden goblet out to me. "Drink."

I took the cup and looked inside. The liquid's lack of

color didn't give me any clues about its makeup. It could have been water or vodka or strychnine for all I knew.

I looked up to ask the girl what it was, but she vanished. And when I say vanish, I don't mean she'd walked away. *Poof*—she was gone. No one else seemed surprised by this.

I glanced at Adam. He nodded reassuringly. Since Rhea was his aunt, I figured I could trust her.

I raised the goblet to my nose and sniffed. The scent of lemons and something floral—roses maybe—shooed away any lingering doubts. I lifted the cup to my lips and took a large mouthful.

Turns out roses and lemon combined with salt and cayenne pepper tastes like burning. What's worse, the salty magma made my mouth swell and pucker like a monkey's ass.

I gasped and thrust the goblet at Adam, but Rhea's voice stopped him. "No. She must drink it all to complete the cleansing."

Adam's smile was apologetic as he backed away.

The expectant stares of the council and the crowd weighed down on me. Something told me I wasn't getting out of there unless I finished the foul drink. So, instead of being a baby, I decided to just get it over with.

"Bottoms up," I said. With a flick of the wrist, I tossed back the rest. My throat burned and my stomach roiled. When it was all gone, I gasped. "Nasty!"

Murmurs of disapproval echoed through the room. Next to me, Adam cleared his throat and shifted on his feet. I ignored all of this in favor of rubbing at my tongue with my palm, hoping to relieve some of the hellfire.

Adam nudged me. "Stop that."

"My uvula is on fire!" I whisper-yelled.

By then, the cayenne had started to wear off, but not the nausea. I swallowed against the hot spit pooling in my mouth. "I don't feel so good."

"You have to keep the potion down," said Rhea. "It must have time to work through your system."

Maisie was looking at me like I'd let her down. Like I'd failed some kind of test. "You'll be fine."

I glared at Adam with a look that clearly said, "What the hell did you get me into?"

He wouldn't meet my eyes. Ass.

Orpheus looked from Maisie to me. "Shall we continue?"

Maisie nodded resolutely. "Yes."

Casting one last anxious look in my direction, Orpheus cleared his throat. "Moving on. As you all know, the council is still considering a proposal to declare war on the Dominae."

Both cheers and boos met this announcement. Despite my discomfort, I forced myself to pay attention.

Orpheus slammed a gavel on the table. "In light of the divisive nature of this issue, we have delayed a vote until all parties can make their cases." A few in the crowd grumbled their impatience over the delay, but the members of the council all nodded. "High Priestess Maisie? Do you have anything to add?"

Maisie rose from her seat to Orpheus's right. Adam had said Maisie was the leader of the council, but from what I'd seen, Orpheus was in charge. I made a note to ask Adam about her role later.

"Thank you, Councilman Orpheus. I would like to report to the council that I had a troubling vision last night.

In it, Sabina was standing in the Sacred Grove at the Crossroads. Shadows closed in from all sides while drums beat in the distance."

A shiver passed down my spine, and I struggled not to shift under the curious glances coming my way. Worried murmurs spread through the room. Members of the council shot me speculative looks ranging from curious to downright antagonistic. Orpheus raised his hands for silence. "What is your interpretation of this vision?" he asked Maisie.

Maisie looked at me, her expression closed. "Obviously, the shadows represent our enemies and the drums are the drums of war. As for Sabina's role? That is harder to decipher. However, I believe it means she will be instrumental in whatever's coming."

A male mage in the audience jumped up. "The vision is a clear sign we must declare war now!"

"The vision is a warning against war!" A female this time.

Suddenly the room was filled with heated shouts for and against declaring war. I looked at Adam, whose jaw was tight. He'd told me the council was on the verge of declaring war before we left California. Either he'd exaggerated to get me to come with him, or things had gotten complicated after he left to come back for Vinca's funeral. I wasn't in favor of a war, but I was even less in favor of getting involved in politics, so I kept my mouth shut.

Orpheus banged the gavel like he was hammering a stubborn nail. "Silence! Fighting among ourselves will not solve this problem. You must allow the council you elected to debate the issue and figure out what is best for all magekind."

The audience quieted like a group of admonished schoolchildren.

A growl ripped through the room like an angry demon. I looked down and realized it came from my stomach.

"Are you okay?" Adam whispered.

The growl came again, this time even louder, drawing the eyes of the council. Lightning knifed through my midsection. I doubled over, clutching my stomach with both arms.

Cold sweat bloomed on my forehead, my chest. Searing pain tore through my intestines. I fell to my knees, groaning. Adam knelt next to me, his face a mask of worry. A circle formed around us. I opened my mouth to plead for help.

And projectile-vomited all over the feet of the ancient and venerable Hekate Council.

4

$\mathcal{A}$n hour later, I finally limped out of the bathroom to find Adam, Maisie, Orpheus, and Rhea waiting for me. Light-headed and covered in sweat, I felt about ten pounds lighter than when Adam carried me into Maisie's room.

I had no idea what the potion they gave me was called, but I had a few colorful name suggestions. I also wanted to kick Rhea's ass. But first, I needed to lie down.

"Feeling better?" Adam said, coming forward to help me.

"Well, let's see," I said, collapsing into a chair. "I think I threw up a kidney, but otherwise I'm fine."

Giguhl jumped into my lap and peered into my face.

"Eww." He waved a paw in front of his face. "Puke breath."

I swatted halfheartedly at the demon. I wasn't in the mood for his teasing. Especially since I'd rinsed with mouthwash before I left Maisie's bathroom.

Adam handed me a glass of water with a wink. I sent him a weak but grateful smile.

"Rhea, do you know what caused Sabina's . . . violent

reaction to the potion?" Maisie asked the silver-haired female.

Rhea shrugged. "There's no telling. If I had to guess, though, she had a lot of karmic smut to work off."

Maisie nodded as if this made perfect sense. "Well, she seems fine now. Hopefully, this will give her a clean slate going forward."

I really hate it when people talk about me like I'm not in the room. But I could hardly argue that I didn't have karmic smut. I'm not into New Agey bullshit, but I'd certainly committed my fair share of sins. And frankly, I kind of liked the idea of having a fresh start. I'd have preferred it not involve vomit, however.

"Sabina, I took the liberty of having rooms readied for you and Giguhl. I assumed you didn't have other accommodations lined up."

I shook my head. The thought of where I'd sleep hadn't even occurred to me. I guess on some level I'd figured I'd be staying with Adam, but it made sense Maisie would want me to stay with her. She certainly had plenty of room, whereas I had no idea where Adam lived or if he even wanted to put up with Giguhl and me as houseguests. "Sure, that'd be fine. Thanks."

"Excellent." Maisie smiled. "Your room is right next to mine, so we'll be able to catch up on the last fifty or so years of each other's lives."

I forced a chuckle. "Great."

"Wait," Giguhl said. "Does this mean I finally have my own room?"

"If it's okay with Sabina?" she said, glancing my way.

Giguhl looked at me hopefully. I shrugged and nodded. Sharing a room with Giguhl wasn't high on my list of priorities, especially once he morphed back into demon form.

"Will I have cable?" he asked.

Maisie smiled curiously at the demon. "Of course."

He pumped a paw in the air. "Yes!"

Back in L.A., Giguhl had discovered the home shopping channel. Back then, I'd tolerated the purchases because it kept him out of trouble. But now I had no job and was living off savings. "Don't get too excited there, demon. The home shopping channel is off-limits."

"Aww, c'mon!"

I glared at him. "I said no."

Giguhl crossed his arms. "Fine."

Maisie cleared her throat. I looked over, embarrassed. "Sorry, Giguhl has a small shopping addiction."

She nodded slowly. "Ah." She was obviously still confused but polite enough not to push the issue. "So now that the cleansing is done, we can get started on your magical training right away. Rhea, when do you want to do the vision quest?"

I looked at Adam, who wouldn't meet my eyes. "Wait a second," I said. "I thought Adam was going to continue teaching me magic."

Maisie and Orpheus exchanged a look. "Actually," Orpheus said, "there's been a change of plans. I've asked Adam to work on a special project for me, so he'll be unavailable to teach you."

"What kind of project? Surely he can fit in a few magic—"

Orpheus cut me off. "I'm afraid that's impossible."

"Why?" I knew I sounded argumentative, but part of the deal I'd cut with Adam before agreeing to come to

New York was that he'd teach me magic. I didn't like the idea that less than an hour into this, they were already reneging on the agreement.

Orpheus's jaw went tight; he obviously didn't like being challenged. "It's none of your damned bus—"

"Sir," Adam said suddenly. "If I may? I'd like to speak with Sabina alone."

Orpheus glared at Adam for the interruption but finally relented. "Fine."

Adam nodded at me. Frowning, I rose slowly and followed him into the hall. Before the door was even closed, I rounded on him. "What the hell's going on?"

Adam sighed. "The mission Orpheus gave me is in North Carolina. That's why I can't continue our lessons—I won't be here."

My stomach dipped. "What? Why?"

He leaned in, as if he wasn't supposed to be telling me this. "Queen Maeve is dragging her feet on committing to helping the council if we go to war. Orpheus needs me to go to the fae court and find out why."

I crossed my arms. "When?"

"Tonight."

"What!" Panic gripped my chest. Even though everyone I'd met so far was nice enough, the thought of being stuck here alone with a bunch of virtual strangers didn't appeal. "So you're just dumping me off and leaving me alone with a bunch of strangers?"

Adam ran a hand through his sandy hair. "Sabina, it's not like that. Believe me, I'd rather stay, but my first responsibility is to the council."

A dark suspicion rose in my mind. "Oh, I get it. Fine. See you around." I turned to go, but he grabbed my arm.

"What do you mean you get it?"

I shrugged. "You've been acting on orders this whole time. You were supposed to do whatever it took to get me here. So you promised me things knowing the council never intended to follow through. And now that I'm here, you're finally off the hook."

He glared at me for a moment. Then he threw back his head and laughed. Laughed!

"Nice. Have a good chuckle. Asshole." I turned to storm off, but he grabbed my arm and spun me around. I slammed into his chest, and before I could open my mouth to tell him to go to hell, his lips landed on mine.

Taken totally off guard, it didn't occur to me to fight unexpected intimacy. His lips were warm and insistent on mine. As the warmth of his lips registered, my brain switched off and my libido took over. I'd kissed Adam before—once. But that had been different. Then, I'd been reeling from the revelation I had a sister I never knew about, and Adam provided a welcome distraction to extreme emotional distress. Luckily the make-out session was interrupted before it could get too out of hand, and I decided it would never happen again. He was a mage, after all, and cross-racial mating was forbidden. I mean, look where it got my parents. But now, as Adam's tongue caressed mine, it was fairly apparent he hadn't gotten that memo.

He cupped my face with his warm palms. Unlike last time, there was no urgent groping or wild need. No, this kiss was almost tender, but no less dangerous for my equilibrium. I wrapped my arms around his shoulders and gave myself into the kiss. I was still angry with him for leaving, but I also knew this might be my last chance to touch him for Goddess knew how long.

Finally, slowly, he pulled back. When I opened my eyes, he was smiling down at me.

I cleared my throat. "Um."

"Now, are you going to stop being an idiot and tell me good-bye?"

I opened my mouth to protest being called an idiot, but he shook his head. "Don't start an argument. Not now. We can talk about all the reasons this is a bad idea when I get back, okay?"

I swallowed. He was so close. I could still taste him on my lips, and his sandalwood and hot-male scent made me feel a little drunk. "Bad idea?" For some reason, I was having trouble remembering why I'd thought that myself.

"We both have jobs to do, and right now neither of us can afford distractions." His voice deepened, and he leaned in so his lips were a fraction away from mine. "But please understand, if I could stay there's nothing I'd want more than to have you distract the shit out of me."

My stomach flip-flopped. I blew out a long, slow breath to ease the flutters there and farther south. "Wow, mancy, you sure know how to sweet-talk a girl."

His lips curled into a crooked smile. "I could recite sonnets if you'd prefer, but I figured you'd appreciate a more direct approach."

He leaned in again, but before he could deliver on the promise in his eyes, the door burst open. We stopped like two deer in headlights and turned to see Maisie framed in the doorway holding Giguhl. "Oh! I'm sorry!" Maisie exclaimed, her cheeks as red as mine felt.

"That's okay. Adam and I were just . . . talking." I stepped back. Adam frowned at me, clearly resenting the distance. But the truth was, I needed the space to clear my head. Adam was sex on a stick, no doubt about it. But he was leaving. And he was a mage. And, and, and. The list could go on.

"Don't stop on our account," Giguhl said. "It's about time you two got it over with."

Maisie covered her mouth, clearly amused.

"Giguhl," I said, a warning clear in my tone.

"Oh, please, Red—"

Right then, Orpheus and Rhea came to the door to see what the commotion was about. Oblivious to the new arrivals, Giguhl continued.

"— I was stuck in that godsforsaken car with you two for four days, remember? The pheromones were so thick I had to roll down the window."

I glared at the demon. If looks could kill, he would have dropped dead on the floor. Instead, he merely snuggled closer to Maisie and said, "I'm just sayin'."

My cheeks burned at Rhea and Maisie's knowing grins. Adam cleared his throat. "On that note, I should head out."

"Lazarus, be sure you report as soon as you arrive. I want hourly updates."

"Yes, sir." He turned to me. "Well, see you."

Hyperaware of our audience, I ignored the banked heat in his eyes and held out my hand. "See you."

He cocked his head and shot me a smirk. His warm hand closed around mine, and I swear I felt the touch all the way to my toes. "Try to stay out of trouble, okay?"

I opened my mouth to get the last word in, but he disappeared. I stood there with my hand extended like an idiot for a second. Then a cat snicker brought my attention back to the audience that had just observed one of the most awkward moments of my life. I lowered my hand and wiped it on the cloth of my dress.

"Well," I said lamely. "I guess that's that."

"Hmm, yes. I'd say so," Rhea said. I scanned her face for signs of judgment but found none. Overall, she seemed downright amused by the whole thing.

"If you'll excuse me," I said. "I think I'm going to take a walk to, ah, get some fresh air. Giguhl, you coming?"

The cat shook his head. "I'm good here. But if I could make a suggestion?"

I sighed, waiting for the punch line.

"You might want to consider a wardrobe change."

I looked down. Adam had me so flustered I'd forgotten I was still wearing the red chiton. "Maisie?"

"I'm on it." Static swirled around my body, replacing the dress with my old clothes. I patted my pockets, relieved to find my weapons back where they belonged.

"Thanks," I said. Having my own clothes—and weapons—improved my mood considerably.

"Where are you going?" Maisie asked.

"Just around the block to clear my head a little."

Giguhl snorted. "You might try a cold shower instead."

With a final glare at the demon cat, I turned on my heel and walked away. Over my shoulder I called, "Giguhl, change into demon form."

Poof. The hall filled with the acrid scent of brimstone.

Maisie gasped.

"Good gods," Orpheus said.

I smiled and kept walking. When Giguhl switched forms, he always ended up naked. I won't go into details, but a naked demon is a sight you don't want to behold more than once. I was about to turn the corner when Rhea finally spoke.

"Why is it forked?"

Thus far, the food in New York left a lot to be desired. Granted, I'd only been in the city about four hours, but back in California, none of my meals ever bit back.

"Ouch!" I reared back and checked to be sure my ear was still attached. My meal stared back with glittering eyes, black in the dim light. He had a few days' worth of scruff, and a diamond stud glinted from beneath greasy black hair.

"Fuck you, bitch." His attitude—and his blood—left a bitter taste in my mouth. Frustrated and too tired to deal with this shit, I pushed him away. Instead of running like a normal person, he had the nerve to pull a gun on me.

"Seriously?" I said. If I weren't so annoyed, I probably would have laughed. "I think you better hand over the gun before you hurt yourself—or I do it for you."

He pulled the trigger. The bullet ripped through the flesh just below my right collarbone. I might have been immune to the damage, but it fucking hurt.

"Godsdammit!" I yelled, pressing a hand to my chest.

"Gimme that thing." I jerked the gun out of his hands and threw it into a wooded area off the trail. His eyes widened and he stumbled back, mumbling prayers to the Virgin Mary.

"She can't help you now," I said menacingly. He tripped over his feet and ran off into the night. I briefly considered giving chase but decided it wasn't worth the effort.

Despite the empty trails this time of night, Central Park still hummed with energy. In the tree line, dark shadows shifted in my peripheral vision. A screech came from overhead. I looked up to see Stryx flying in tight circles over me.

"Go away," I grumbled. Ignoring the owl, I trudged on through the trails, hoping to find another meal. Not an hour ago I was puking out my spleen, and now my body had to heal the gunshot wound. That meant blood had gone from a want to being a need.

The chill October air held the promise of rain. Under that, the city scents of trash, exhaust, and humanity were muted and mixed with the smoky aroma of fallen leaves. I slowed my pace and took a deep lungful of air. Wincing, I pressed a hand against the chest wound. The hole was already closing, entombing the bullet lodged there—a morbid souvenir of my first visit to the Big Apple.

Needing a minute, I sat on a bench near the intersection of three trails. The famous "Imagine" mosaic memorializing John Lennon lay a few feet away. Someone had left an offering of red roses in the center of the circle. All around me, trees reached up toward the inky night sky, and just beyond, the spires of New York's cathedrals to the gods of commerce loomed.

What the fuck was I doing here? I settled back into the bench and allowed myself to wallow. Self-pity wasn't an emotion I indulged often. It was easier to avoid wallowing when I thought I was in control of my life. But now control was the last thing I had.

When I'd agreed to come to New York with Adam, I'd been pissed off and ready to leave everything behind. My need to make my grandmother pay for betraying me was stronger than my worries over leaving everything behind. I knew mages were different from vampires, but I figured I'd adjust. I was half mage after all—how hard could it be?

But now that I was here and had my first taste of mage life, I wasn't so sure I'd made the right decision. Maisie was nice enough, but I couldn't help distancing myself from her. I'd thought since we were twins we'd be more alike, but the reality was we couldn't be more different. Hell, even my minion liked her better than he liked me. Stupid fickle demon.

Plus, Adam's departure had thrown me for a loop. I'd expected him to stay and help me adjust to mage life, but now he was gone. It wasn't just that he wouldn't be continuing our magic lessons. I'd grown used to having him around over the last few weeks. I'd even started to think of us as a team. Not that I'd admit that out loud. Nor did I want to discuss that kiss. Gods! What the hell was that about? I guessed in that respect it was good he was gone. It gave me some space to clear my head. But eventually, when he returned, I'd have to figure out what to do there. I had a feeling where Adam was concerned, things could get very complicated very quickly. And more complications were the last thing I needed.

I'm not sure how long I sat there before the twig snapped behind me. Another. Someone or something wasn't worried about me knowing they were there. I stood slowly and started walking. They'd reveal themselves when they were ready—and I'd be ready for them.

"You picked the wrong woods tonight, Little Red Riding Hood." The voice came from behind.

I turned slowly, silently cursing myself for not bringing more weapons with me. Two males stood on the path. From the corner of my eye, I saw two others come from the tree line to stand behind me. Four-to-one odds. Not too bad, I thought.

"Can I help you?" I asked, keeping my tone conversational. Inside, my adrenaline kicked up a notch. A good fight would offer the perfect distraction from my troubles.

The males I could see were shaggy and lean, with mean, thuggish faces. They reminded me of a pack of young, hungry wolves. Not a strand of red hair in the pack, so they weren't vampires. No telltale sandalwood scent, so I knew they weren't mages. But they definitely weren't human.

The leader laughed. His flunkies chuckled while casting uncertain looks at him. He strolled forward, with the others getting his back. His laugh cut off as quickly as it started. "You're poaching on our turf."

"I'm sure I don't know what you mean." I crossed my arms, reaching inside my jacket for the knife hidden there.

"By decree of The Shade, this here's our official hunting ground."

"Who the fuck is The Shade?" I demanded.

He raised a shaggy eyebrow. "The Shade's the law. And the law says, anyone who poaches on our land deserves to be taught a lesson."

"And who the fuck are you?"

He put his arms out and snarled. "We're the Lone Wolves, bitch."

Freakin' great, I thought. Werewolves. Just what I needed. That certainly explained the eau de wet dog flying off the pack in nose-wrinkling waves. I'd never run into any weres in L.A., but I knew enough to recognize I'd just walked into a shitstorm. Again.

I shifted my weight onto my back foot. "The what?"

"Lone Wolves." He turned to show me the back of his raggedy jacket. Sure enough, a snarling wolf face stared back at me from the leather.

"Wait a second," I said. "Isn't it supposed to be 'Lone Wolf,' as in, you know, one? If there's more than one, then it kind of defeats the purpose of being 'lone,' doesn't it?"

The leader squinted hard, as if trying to follow my logic and getting lost. "Shut up, bitch. Hold her, boys."

Rough hands grabbed me from behind. I allowed them to do so. "Do you know who you're messing with?" I said calmly.

"Oh, this should be good," the leader said.

"My name is Sabina Kane." I said this a tad more dramatically than I'd intended.

The leader blinked. "Is that supposed to mean something to me?"

I opened my mouth to tell him—what? That I used to be an assassin on the Dominae's payroll? That I was, in fact, the granddaughter of the Alpha Dominae? What good would it do me now? Even if that information meant something to the weres, it wouldn't do me any favors. Hell, it might even convince them to turn me over to the Dominae. They'd probably put a hefty price on my head by now.

"No, I guess it shouldn't," I said instead. The reminder that my old life was gone hit me hard in the gut. Looked like I was the lone wolf now. But if these assholes thought

I was going to lower my neck in submission, they had a nasty surprise coming.

"Enough talk. We're gonna show you what we do to poachers." He nodded at the guys behind me, and their arms tightened on mine. The leader bared his teeth, which were sorely in need of a good brushing. He pulled back a fist while his buddy held me still.

This type of macho group always assumed a female would automatically submit under their awesome testosterone-drenched antics. Not this chick. I might not have had any silver on me to kill them with—*if* that even killed them—but I sure as hell had the ability to inflict some major pain.

I delivered a swift jab of my knee to his soft man bits. He yelped and fell down into the fetal position with his hands covering his groin. His friends seemed unnerved to see their leader whimpering on the ground. I took advantage of the distraction to free myself from the two holding my arms. Easy work given their haste to cover their own testicles.

I grabbed the knife from my coat and slashed the arm of the one to my right. He snarled and punched me in the gut. I spun and delivered an elbow to his nose. The cartilage gave with a satisfying crunch. Two down, two to go.

But those two were already running away. I took off after them. I couldn't risk word getting out to the Dominae that I was in New York. But I didn't know Central Park nearly as well as they did. They disappeared like rabbits into the brush. And when I got back to where I'd left the injured weres, they were gone, too. Frustrated and still hungry, I made my way back toward the park entrance.

I'd almost made it to my room. But just before I opened my door, Maisie's burst open as if she'd been waiting for my return. "Sabina! You're back."

She looked so eager standing there, like she was genuinely happy to see me. Unfortunately, after the night I'd had, I just wanted a shower and to sleep like the dead. Maybe I'd wake up and find out all this was just a dream. A really, really shitty dream.

But I couldn't very well just walk into my room and slam the door in Maisie's face. I turned around to face her. "Hey, Maisie."

Her eyes widened. "Oh, my gods, what happened to you?"

Judging from the hot spots of pain the weres had left on my face, I probably looked pretty rough. I opened my mouth to explain, but her eyes moved south and then widened. "Is that a bullet wound?"

My hand went to the splash of red on my tank top. "It looks worse than it is. The hole already closed." I pulled down the neck of the tank to show her the healed skin. She went pale at the amount of blood covering my skin and clothes. But she grabbed my arm and pulled me toward her room.

"I want you to sit down and tell me everything while I clean you up." She pushed me down into a chair and disappeared into the attached bathroom.

Sitting was a relief, but I didn't feel comfortable with her nursing my wounds. Especially since they'd heal on their own in no time. "Maisie, I'm fine. Really."

She reappeared from the bathroom carrying a washcloth and a couple of small brown bottles. "Nonsense. Now, tell me what happened."

She began dabbing the washcloth on my face. I sighed. I was too tired to argue with her, and if playing nursemaid made her feel better, then who was I to argue? "I just had a run-in with an unwilling blood donor is all. You know how it is."

She paused with the now-pink washcloth in midair. "You what?"

"I tried to feed from a guy and he shot me."

She lowered the washcloth. "Where did this happen?"

"In the park."

She closed her eyes. "Hekate help us."

I frowned. "What's wrong?"

She sighed deep and long. "Please tell me no one saw you feeding."

I looked down. "Um, well, that's the other thing. I kind of had a fight with some werewolves."

She dropped the rag and fell onto the edge of the bed. "This is bad."

"Don't worry, they only got in a couple of sucker

punches. I managed to kick most of their asses before they ran off."

She lowered her head into her hands and mumbled something I couldn't understand. Finally, she lifted her head and stood. "This is my fault."

"What, why?"

"I should have warned you. Maybe you're used to being able to feed anywhere and anytime you want, but things are different here. If The Shade finds out you poached on his lands without paying the blood tax, he'll be pissed. Plus, the weres are his allies, so they're well within their rights to demand compensation for injuring their people in their own territory."

"Oops," I said.

Maisie tilted her head. "Although if you didn't feed from humans, none of this would have happened."

"What's that supposed to mean?"

"Why you find it necessary to attack innocent humans is beyond me."

"Gee, Maisie, do you think maybe it's because I'm a *vampire*?"

She glared at me. "*Half*-vampire."

"Whatever. Surely it's not a surprise I needed blood."

"I need blood, too, but I've never bitten anyone. How was I to know you handled it any differently?"

I paused. "Wait, what? You've never bitten anyone? How is that possible?"

Maisie crossed her arms. "Believe it or not, there are plenty of ways to satisfy your need for blood without harming anyone."

I raised an eyebrow. "Yeah, but where's the fun in that?"

The look she sent me was similar to the ones Giguhl often saw from me. "This isn't a joke, Sabina. I need you to promise me you won't feed from another human while you're under the council's protection."

"Well, technically, I didn't feed from a human tonight. He shot me before I could get a good mouthful." She pinned me with another look. I sighed. "If you think I'm giving up blood while I'm here, you're crazy."

She crossed her arms. "I'm not asking you to give up blood. I'm asking you to not attack people. And if the morality of the issue doesn't sway you, then consider this: The last thing anyone needs right now is a feud to break out among the dark races in the city because you couldn't control your bloodlust."

I sighed again. There was nothing I hated more than politics. But I certainly didn't want to cause trouble for Maisie or the council. "Fine, I'll keep my fangs in check. But you're going to have to clue me in on another way to get blood."

She sent me a relieved smile. "That's not a problem. When I was young, Ameritat anticipated that I'd have issues needing blood. So she opened a blood bank in the city."

My eyes widened. "You have an entire blood bank at your disposal?"

"Well, technically its main purpose is to give back to the community. But yes, it also lets me meet my need for blood without harming anyone."

"Not to argue or anything, but isn't that kind of hypocritical? After all, those humans donate blood to help heal other humans, not to make sure you have fast food."

"Not at all. Blood has a limited shelf life. Refrigerated blood can only last forty-two days before it has to be destroyed. I have a deal with the bank that I get the blood a few days before the expiration date. Plus, sometimes donated blood doesn't pass safety screenings. Since I'm immune to human illness, that fresher blood comes to me, too."

"Let me get this straight," I said with a grimace. "You only drink old or diseased blood? That's disgusting."

"It's not so bad. Sure, the anticoagulant they add gives it an odd aftertaste, but you get used to that."

I put a finger in my mouth and made a gagging noise.

She shrugged. "You got a better option?"

"Synthetic blood?" I hated the stuff myself. Besides being weaker than human blood, the flavor was about as appealing as drinking piss. But I figured the human-friendly product might appeal to someone of Maisie's obvious moral standards.

She shuddered. "Are you kidding? That stuff tastes like shit. Might as well drink water as weak as it is."

A shocked laughed escaped my lips.

Maisie cocked her head. "What?"

"You surprise me, is all. I figured you'd be all self-righteous about it."

"Sabina, I might not like killing humans, but that doesn't mean I'm a saint. My body craves blood just like yours. But I believe in the mage stance that humans are to be respected, so I do what I have to do to refrain from harming them. Bagged blood is a decent compromise between violence and self-denial."

I smiled at my sister. As much as I resented her security and the obvious love all mages had for her, I couldn't help but like her. She was practical and, dare I say it, kind of cool. "Okay, fine. I'll drink the bagged stuff while I'm here."

She nodded, but her expression became pensive.

"What's wrong?" I asked.

She waved and let out a short laugh. "It's just the way you said it made it sound like you're just visiting. I'd kind of hoped you'd embrace mage life and stay for a while."

I shifted on my seat, uncomfortable with the turn of conversation. "Maisie, look, I've only been here a few hours. Let's just see how it goes, okay?"

She waved her hand and laughed. "Of course. You're totally right. I'm just excited to have you here after all these years. I don't know about you, but I have a sudden urge to sing 'We Are Family.'"

Here's the thing. Maisie had known about my existence for years. I'd found out about her only a little over week ago. So, while she'd had plenty of time to get used to the idea of having a twin, I didn't have that luxury. Besides, given my experience with family so far, I was a tad reluctant to jump right into performing a Sister Sledge duet.

I forced a smile. "How about we skip the singing and bond over a pint of blood instead?"

"Sounds perfect." She walked to a small fridge set in a wet bar along the wall. "Name your poison."

I rose from the chair with a groan. "Anything's fine."

Her head popped up. "Hmm, you know, I've got a couple pints of AB neg I've been saving for a special occasion that'll be perfect."

I perked up. AB negative, due to its rareness, was like the Cadillac of bloods. Given the vomiting, bullet wound, and fight I'd endured that night, Maisie's idea was akin to offering a fat girl cake. "Hell, yeah."

She heated up two bags and poured them into pint glasses. The scent wafted to me, making my fangs throb and my mouth water. Finally, she handed me one and raised her own glass. "To family."

I clinked my glass against hers. Not having had the best track record with family—given my own grandmother tried to kill me a week earlier—I amended my response to something I felt more comfortable with.

"To new beginnings."

I'd just taken the first sip when she spoke. "So, you and Adam, huh?"

I spewed blood like an arterial wound. Maisie pounded me on the back when I started choking.

"Oh, I'm sorry!"

I wiped blood from my chin with the tissue she offered. "Thanks," I said, my voice hoarse. "Went down the wrong pipe."

She sent me a knowing look. "Should I take it from your response that Adam is off-limits as a bonding topic?"

I licked my lips. "It's not off-limits. There's just nothing to talk about."

"Sabina, no offense, but when I opened that door you two looked like you were trying to swallow each other whole. I'd say that qualifies as something to talk about."

I cringed at her entirely accurate summary of the kiss. "Look, it's not a big deal. I think it was curiosity more than anything."

"Curiosity? Like you were wondering what his tonsils tasted like?"

I shot her a baleful glance. "No. More like, we've been spending a lot of time together and we're both healthy adults. It's only natural to wonder." This was bullshit, of course. I'd already indulged that curiosity back in California, and I could hardly claim I'd forgotten the taste of him after that time. I hadn't. Not that I'd ever admit that out loud.

"Hmm," Maisie said. "So you're not planning on pursuing anything with him when he gets back?"

I shook my head. "Definitely not. Don't get me wrong, Adam's great." She nodded her agreement on that count. "But we'd never work out."

She frowned now. "Why not?"

I opened my mouth to share my long list of reasons but stopped myself. Maisie might be my sister, but I wasn't about to have a heart-to-heart about Adam with her. Or anyone, for that matter. To discuss it would imply it was a big deal. And it wasn't. Adam was hardly the first male I'd been attracted to in my fifty-four years. I'm not some giggly schoolgirl who thinks a kiss means happily ever after. Chicks like me don't get happily-ever-afters. I might be able to handle happy-for-a-night-or-two. But the idea of having even that with a mage—just like dear old Dad— brought up all sorts of Freudian issues I wasn't too keen on exploring.

"Hold on," I said, turning the tables. "Shouldn't you be upset about that kiss? I mean, what about the whole ban on fraternizing between the races?"

Maisie raised her eyebrows. "First, who am I to judge when you and I are the result of such an affair? And second"—she shrugged—"you're half mage, so I don't think the laws apply in this case."

"Look," I said with a sigh. "I've had a long night. The last thing I want to do right now is talk about a stupid kiss that didn't mean anything."

Maisie drew back. "Okay, I'll drop it for now. But I should warn you: Adam is one of my best friends. I don't want to see him get hurt."

I choked on a laugh. "Maisie, my to-do list is fairly long, but I can assure you hurting Adam isn't on it. He's my friend, too, and I respect the hell out of him. That's exactly why what happened earlier won't be happening again."

She narrowed her eyes, looking like she wanted to say something else about it. But her expression betrayed the exact moment she thought better of it. "Understood."

Frustrated, I drained the last of my blood, grimacing at the chemical aftertaste. "The sun's coming up soon. I'd better hit the sack."

She nodded, toying absently with her own glass. "Good idea. You'll need a good night's sleep for tomorrow night."

I set down my glass, glad for the change of subject. "What's tomorrow night?"

"We're heading up to the council's estate near Sleepy Hollow for your vision quest."

I frowned. Images of drugged-out shamans flittered through my head. "What exactly does that entail?"

She shrugged. "It's pretty straightforward. You'll drink a special tea that will bring on visions. Afterward, we'll interpret the symbols to figure out your magical path."

I rubbed my forehead. All this talk of paths and symbols and other woo-woo stuff made my head hurt. "Can I ask you something?"

She smiled. "Of course."

"Have you considered the possibility that I don't have any special magical skills?"

Maisie crossed her arms and smiled ruefully. "Of course

not. Sabina, you have a demon familiar. I'd say that's a pretty clear sign you've got some magic in you."

I shook my head. "Yeah, but isn't that pretty standard stuff?"

"The summoning is common, yes. But most mages can only control a demon long enough to carry out a specific spell. Very few can control one for long periods. The fact you can do so without really thinking about it is quite remarkable."

I rolled my eyes. If anyone had bothered to ask me, which they obviously hadn't, I'd tell them I didn't control Giguhl at all. Sure, I could command him to change to and from demon form, but otherwise I spent most of my time doing damage control or arguing with him. Call me crazy, but if I really controlled Giguhl, shouldn't he be more, you know, submissive?

"Look," Maisie continued. "Go to bed. Tomorrow we'll have some answers and can formulate a plan. Until then, there's no need to worry."

I nodded. "Okay, I'll see you tomorrow night." I moved toward the door.

"Oh, Sabina? You might not want to eat anything between now and the vision quest."

I paused with a hand on the doorknob. Considering I'd spent a good portion of my night worshipping the porcelain goddess, Maisie's words didn't comfort me about the "relative painlessness" of the vision quest. "Why?"

She paused as if choosing her words carefully. "You're better off with an empty stomach. Trust me."

It was clear she wasn't just talking about blood. It's a myth that vampires are undead. The old movies that claimed we never ate food were wrong. Truth is, we're

born just like humans. We get hungry and thirsty, and satisfy those needs with real food. The only difference is we
also need blood to satisfy a more urgent hunger. The food
didn't sustain us by itself, but we definitely enjoyed a good
burger as much as any mortal did.

As I made my way back to my room, I realized that
Maisie didn't know me at all if she thought I could trust
anyone that easily.

7

"I received this today while you were sleeping." Orpheus tossed a letter on the table.

His office was on the first floor, where all the administrative offices for the council were located. He stood behind his massive oak desk, looking more like an angry politician than an ancient mage. He'd summoned Maisie and me to his office right as we headed toward the courtyard to leave for the Crossroads.

At first I was relieved at the delay. After Maisie's warning about having an empty stomach, I was not looking forward to putting myself through another potentially nauseating rite. But when I opened the letter and was hit with legalese so thick it made my eyes ache, my relief was short-lived.

Maisie was reading over my shoulder. I gladly handed the paper to her. She read it for a moment, her eyes widening with each line.

"What is it?" I asked.

"This," she said with a grim expression, "is the fallout

from your little fight in Central Park last night. The Shade is demanding a duel."

I frowned. "What the hell?"

"You injured werewolves under the protection of The Shade," Orpheus said. "He's demanding you fight the leader of the pack to pay for your crime."

"Can someone please tell me who The Shade is?" I asked. The werewolves had invoked that name like they'd been speaking about some mysterious force of nature. I just wanted to know why I should give a damn he was pissed at me.

"He's a vampire," Maisie said. "Runs the Black Light District. The Hekate Council trusts him to keep the peace between the nonmage dark races in the city. You're lucky it's just a duel. He's not known for taking infractions lightly."

"Wait, you don't seriously think I'm going to do this."

Two solemn gazes met my incredulous one. "Sabina, you broke the rules," Orpheus said. "Poaching on were territory is forbidden. But even if that could be overlooked, you injured two weres under The Shade's protection. The Alpha of their pack is totally within rights to challenge you."

"But I didn't know I was poaching!" I said. "And they came after me. Why am I being punished for defending myself?"

"Ignorance doesn't excuse your actions," Orpheus said. "Dark-race relations are sensitive enough as-is with this war brewing. If I override The Shade, it will send the wrong message to both the weres and vamps in the city. You will report to The Shade's bar for the fight tomorrow night."

"And if I refuse?"

Orpheus stared at me hard. "Then, Maisie's sister or not, I will personally deliver you to The Shade."

Rhea waited in the courtyard with Giguhl and the young female who'd assisted her during the cleansing ritual. Memory of the noxious potion they'd had me drink made bile rise in my throat.

"This is my assistant, Damara," Rhea said. "I hope you don't mind if she assists me in administering the vision quest."

I forced a smile at the girl. "Not at all. Hi, Damara."

The assistant ignored my outstretched hand. Instead, she asked Rhea, "Shall we get going?"

I shrugged off her dismissal. She was young and, judging from her slouched posture and all-black ensemble, was probably in the throes of some sort of teen-rebellion phase.

"Shotgun!" Giguhl called. He'd insisted on joining us on this little expedition. I'd considered refusing but figured he'd get in less trouble if I kept him close.

I grabbed his arm before he could leap for the car. "You're in the back. We'll let Rhea or Maisie sit up front."

"I'm fine with the back," Maisie said. "Giguhl can sit between us."

And that's how I ended up crammed in the backseat with my demon and my sister. It could have been worse, though, I mused. At least Giguhl had the bitch seat.

We'd been on the road for forty-five minutes already. New York's concrete and steel had given way to trees and open sky. I tilted my head and looked at the moon. A shadow passed over the pale crescent. Wings. Looked like Stryx had arrived just in time for the festivities.

"Sabina?" Maisie said, peering around Giguhl's huge green head, "I'm sorry if Orpheus was abrupt earlier."

I shifted in the seat to look at her. "What's his deal, anyway? I thought you were the leader of the council."

"Technically I am. But I'm really only a figurehead. In ancient times, a spiritual class ruled mages, but over time, we transitioned to a democracy. So the council is elected, but my position passes on through our bloodline. My role is more spiritual and diplomatic. Orpheus really runs things. It's kind of like the Queen of England and the prime minister."

"Gotcha," I said. "That explains why he's so worried about relations between all the races, then."

"Yes, exactly. I'm sorry you have to fight the duel, but I'm afraid there's no way around it."

"Duel?" Giguhl said, perking up.

"I'll tell you later." Orpheus's heavy-handedness had annoyed me, but the truth was, I kind of looked forward to the duel now. All this magic stuff made me feel like I was in over my head. But fighting? Now, that was something I felt comfortable doing.

"Why is the estate way out here?" I asked to change the subject.

Rhea turned in her seat to look at me. "The Hekate Council prefers the security for our sacred rituals. It's harder to control the environment in the city. We also enjoy the space the estate afford us, and of course there's the Sacred Grove. There's a ley line running under the spot."

"Ley line?" Giguhl asked. I was glad he asked instead

of me. The term sounded familiar, but the fact I couldn't remember what it was served as yet another reminder of my utter ignorance when it came to magical stuff.

"They're like rivers of concentrated magical energy running through the earth," Maisie said. "They add power to all our rituals and spells."

"Anyway," Rhea continued. "The other reason we like it out here is a lot of mages live in Sleepy Hollow. The chaotic energy of the city is too much for many of our kind. The local humans think these mages are just humans with pagan beliefs, and everyone gets along. It's nice."

Soon, the headlights glared off a set of large gates in the middle of the road. The two sides met to form an iron Hekate's Wheel similar to the one at the Prytania Place, only bigger. Underneath the symbol, letters spelled out the name of the estate.

"Crossroads?" I read aloud.

"Hekate is the goddess of the crossroads," Maisie explained. "Among other things."

The area tingled with magical wards. I also noted several mundane security measures like the ones Adam pointed out the night before at Prytania Place.

"This reminds me of the Adamantine Gate in Irkalla," Giguhl said, looking around. "The only thing it's missing is that bitch Cerberus."

I looked over my shoulder. "Wait, the three-headed dog is female?"

"Duh, yeah. She's got a serious case of eternal PMS, too."

"Good to know."

A long dirt road cut through heavy woods for another mile before the house appeared like an apparition through the leaves. The building was a collection of stone towers, balconies, and elaborate geometric designs done in terra-cotta and ochre. My eyes moved restlessly over the facade, trying to digest the colorful mosaic of architectural styles—Moorish, Victorian, Gothic, with a dash of the Prairie School here and there. I'd never seen anything like it, and I certainly hadn't expected such an odd headquarters for the Hekate Council. Back in California, the Dominae's compound was a stately Mediterranean style mansion. But this reminded me of something out of *Ali Baba and the Forty Thieves* or the Brothers Grimm.

Damara pulled the car to a stop in front of the steps leading to a wide archway. I got out and took stock. The house was imposing up close, like the fairy-tale fortress of an eccentric wizard.

Rhea clapped her hands and rubbed them together. "Allrighty, then. Who's ready for a vision quest?"

8

The nausea hit almost immediately. I curled up into the fetal position on a pile of dead leaves. Cold sweat blossomed on my back and forehead.

"Easy. Don't fight it. It will pass soon," Rhea said, mopping my face with a cool, damp cloth.

Hunching over, I retched as my stomach emptied on the roots of an ancient oak. Between heaves, I cursed Rhea in colorful language. She just rubbed my back and said nothing.

When no bile was left to toss, I fell onto my back, my eyes clenched tight.

My stomach gurgled. "If I shit my pants, I'm gonna kill you."

I rolled onto my side. My head swam like another bout of cookie tossing was imminent. I lay very still and breathed through my nose until it passed.

Freakin' Maisie with her "It's relatively painless." When the world was done spinning, I was going to kick her understatement-making ass.

"I hate everyone right now."

Rhea chuckled softly. "I know. It will pass soon and the visions will begin."

I swallowed and nodded. Given the experience so far, I wasn't looking forward to the vision portion. Rhea assured me the visions would give us clues about my magical path. From the looks of things so far, the path would be covered in puke.

Earlier, when Rhea led me into the oak grove, torches burned around the perimeter of the clearing, casting orange light and shadows on Rhea's face. My steps faltered when I saw the stone altar at the center. Rhea urged me forward with a hand at my back.

Energy thrummed through me as I approached. With each step, the intensity grew. I glanced back at Maisie, who nodded encouragingly. Giguhl gave me a thumbs-up and then joined Damara near the entrance of the grove. I took a deep breath and steeled my resolve.

Part of me wondered why I continued to put myself through these weird—and nauseating—mage rituals. But the truth was, I was willing to do just about anything that would infuriate my grandmother. She hated mages more than just about anything in the world. Nothing would piss her off more than finding out I'd gone to the dark side, so to speak. Maybe it wasn't rational, but I also liked the idea of being able to zap the shit out of her the next time we met. And if going through this crazy vision-quest thingy helped me learn those skills, I'd do it.

Given the solemn atmosphere, I was surprised to see Rhea pull a red thermos from a backpack at her feet. Without much pomp or circumstance, she poured the tea into the little plastic cup. "Bottoms up."

I took an experimental sniff. "It smells like ass."

Rhea nodded. "Yep. Drink up now." She placed a hand under the cup to guide it to my lips.

What the hell? Might as well get this over with. The first sip nearly made me gag. When she'd first mentioned tea, I'd been expecting something like Earl Grey or Lemon Zinger. Instead, the liquid tasted oily and bitter—like evil.

"What the hell is in this?"

"Ayahuasca."

"Aja-what-a?"

She repeated it slowly. "It means 'spirit root.' It's only found in the Amazon. Shamans there use it to induce visions and gain insight. The brew contains other ingredients, but if I told you I'd have to kill you," she joked lamely.

I couldn't help but wonder if the tea would kill me before I'd had a chance to make her tell me.

"Now," she continued, "chug-a-lug."

"You've got to be kidding. I'll puke."

She muttered something under her breath that sounded like "If you only knew." Louder, she said, "Stop being a baby. The faster you drink it, the less you'll notice the taste."

I looked at her skeptically. Then I shrugged and gulped down the rest of the vile potion. Gasping for breath, I tossed down the cup and glared at Rhea.

"See? Not so bad, was—"

She probably continued her thought, but I was suddenly too busy being doubled over as the first tidal wave of nausea hit.

Thirty minutes of torture had passed, but now things seemed to be calming down. Before, even a slight breeze made me turn green, but now I could actually open my eyes without wishing for the sweet release of death.

"Better?" Rhea asked, leaning over me.

Not trusting myself to speak, I nodded slowly, staring up at the shadowed leaves above. A crisp breeze swooped through the clearing. Leaves danced on the wind like autumn's confetti.

"Odd," I said. As the leaves swirled and dipped, they left colorful light tracers in their wake.

"What is it?"

"Those leaves." I lifted a heavy hand to point, but it dropped back to the ground.

"What about them?"

"Pretty." My body felt heavy, as if I'd become rooted in the soil. The ley line buzzed in my ears, calling to me.

Rhea patted my shoulder. "Just relax now and let the visions come."

I barely heard her. My thoughts scattered and rolled like mercury. Leaves swirled above me like neon streamers. At first, they undulated hypnotically. Gained speed and switched direction. Shooting toward me like arrow-tipped ribbons.

Orange and purple became blue and red. The ribbons braided together in a double helix. My DNA lit up the night.

The braid rises above me. Up, up, up.

Split apart, flying. Blue jay and cardinal soar together. Honeyed song. No words, but I understand. Laughter.

They sing upon the branch. My song. The song of my sister. Movement, morphing. Serpent appears, slithering toward the pair. Must warn them. Move. Fly! The snake opens its maw and waits. Blue and red fly into the dark cave.

Ruby eyes sparkle against black scales. Frozen. Mouth

opens. A flash of bloody iron fangs. The skeleton clock is ticking. Ticking. Ticking.

Wind whips up like the serpent's tail. Scales scald my skin. Forked tongue licks away tears. No. NO. NO!

Iron fangs flashing, piercing, sucking. Blood first, then body. Sliding down forever.

Solid gives way to void. Water dripping. Cold, clammy fear. Black everywhere. Shadow upon shadow. Souls whisper from beyond, "We will obey."

The midnight dogs emerge from the gloomy crossroads. Eyes of fire beckon, command me to follow.

Into the cavern. Deeper. Blood drips from stalactites into the pool. Dark whispers. Darker laughter. A black swan glides across the mirrored surface. Faces reflected. Ones I knew. Ones I loved. Ones I killed.

She rises from the water. Dry white robes flutter in an unfelt breeze. She is lit from the inside. Untouchable. Ethereal.

Fall to my knees. Forgive me.

Sobbing now. So sorry. Kissing her hem.

Butterfly lips on my skin. Gone, she's gone. Again.

The skeleton clock is ticking, ticking, ticking. Time to go.

A male appears. His face is hidden in shadows. Unknown yet known. Dead yet alive. He takes my hand. Together, we fly.

I am the breeze on my face. I am the serpent's tail. I am the end and the beginning.

I am the night.

I am the night.

I am the night.

9

The room was silent when I finished talking. I was relieved Damara had taken Giguhl for a tour of the grounds to give us some privacy. It was bad enough telling Maisie and Rhea about my freaky visions. What was worse, the stoic expressions on their faces when I finished told me I wouldn't like their interpretation.

Maisie cleared her throat. "You're certain that's everything?"

I nodded. "I think so. Why?"

Maisie and Rhea shared a look. "The symbols you recounted confirm a vision Maisie had several months ago."

"Is that a good thing or a bad thing?" I was leaning toward bad, since the darkness of the vision still clung to me like a shadow. The females were silent, as if weighing how much to tell me. "Will someone please just tell me what they mean?"

Rhea smiled serenely. "Sabina, what do you know about the *Praescarium Lilitu*?"

"The book of prophecies?" I crossed my arms. "Adam

told me in California you guys believe some of the prophecies Lilith outlined in the book are coming true, whatever
that means."

"He's right, they are coming true," Maisie said. "And
your vision quest confirms it."

"Wait." I waved an arm. "How do you know? Adam
told me the Caste of Nod is rumored to have the only copy
of the *Praescarium Lilitu.*"

The Caste of Nod was supposedly a mysterious cabal
of dark races. From what I could tell, no one really knew
what exactly they did besides protect the book. However,
their name had been invoked for centuries to scare kids—
the dark-race version of the Boogey Man.

"It's true we don't have access to the sacred text, but
over the centuries, parts of the prophecies have been
leaked. Maisie's visions over the last several months cor-
roborate what we've been told about them."

"So what does all this have to do with me?" All this
talk of secret sects and prophecies made my skin feel too
tight.

"The images you shared just now confirm you're a
Chthonic mage."

Rhea looked at me like she'd just made some huge revelation, but I had no freakin' clue what a Chthonic mage
was. "And?"

"A Chthonic is a type of mage who manipulates dark
energy to manifest magic," Maisie whispered helpfully.

"Dark energy? You mean like black magic?"

"The concepts of white and black magic are constructs
of superstitious mortals," Rhea said. "In truth, there is
no absolute good or absolute evil. Chthonics tap into ancient, primordial energy of the earth. We're talking the

heavy stuff here: death, fertility, the underworld, the dark feminine."

"Chthonic powers are very rare," Maisie added, "and the fact you have them is a big deal. Lilith and Hekate are both Chthonic goddesses, and your powers are heavily connected to their energy."

The two females looked at me expectantly, their eyes glowing with excitement I didn't feel. "That's funny. I don't feel Chthonic."

Maisie frowned, clearly not amused. "That's where Rhea comes in. She's going to train you to harness all that energy. And once you do, you'll be a formidable mage."

I sighed. "Look, I get that you guys think this is a big deal, but I have trouble buying it. If I'm so powerful, why haven't I ever been able to do magic?"

Maisie blinked. "We've discussed this. You have done magic. The mere fact you can not only summon a demon, but keep one as your minion, is proof."

I rubbed my chest absently. "Okay I'll give you that, but how does all this tie in to the Lilith prophecy?"

Maisie held a hand toward the door. "I need to show you something."

Smudges of dread appeared in my stomach. Some part of me understood the import of all this, but my mind had switched into skeptic mode out of self-defense.

She led me through the house and upstairs to a round room set in a tower. Rhea followed silently and stopped just inside the doorway. The indigo ceiling had been painted with stars to look like the night sky. On the floor, a circle of blood marked this room as a place of magic. And in the center, a large table sat like an altar. Except instead of being an actual altar, the surface was covered in tubes of oil paint, rags, and canvases. The scent of turpentine hung heavily, but I found it a nice reprieve from the constant onslaught of sandalwood I'd been exposed to since I'd arrived in New York.

"What is this room?"

"I call it the Star Chamber. I use it as my studio when I'm here. Being so close to the ley line tends to make my visions come more often than when I'm in the city."

She walked across the room, to where a sheet covered an easel. "This painting is the one I did after I had the vision of you a few months ago." She lifted the sheet slowly, revealing swirls of color inch by inch. Finally, the entire painting was revealed and I caught my breath.

The central figure, a female with black and red hair streaming behind her, soared with her face upturned toward some light source—maybe a moon—just off the edge of the canvas. In her right hand she held a golden lotus and in her left, something that looked like an egg. Her body glowed against a dark background of swirling blacks, blues, and purple. Far below, a flower garden spread out like scattered jewels. The entire thing had a dark, dreamy quality. But beyond that, I felt this odd sense of déjà vu, as if I'd seen this image before.

"Pretty," I murmured, moving closer. Now I could see faces in the churning colors of the night sky. "What does it mean?"

Maisie nodded. "The vision came to me right after the mages started disappearing. It was a dark time, and I'd been praying to Hekate for guidance. I'd promised our grandmother I wouldn't look for you until after she passed. She'd been the one to enter into the agreement with the Dominae after we were born to keep our existences a secret from each other, so it made sense. She passed a year ago, and then mages started disappearing and the council came to me, hoping I could help them locate those missing." She motioned to the painting. "When this came to me, I knew it was time to find you, and that somehow you'd be instrumental in helping us find those who went missing. So I asked Adam to go to California."

I looked at the female in the painting again. Even though her face was obscured, I had to admit the hair was a dead giveaway for her identity. Or was it? "But how did you know this was me? After all, it could just as easily be you."

Maisie shook her head. "Look closely. She has the eight-pointed star on her right shoulder."

I squinted and leaned in. Sure enough, a tiny star lay exactly where mine was in real life. "Wait, I met the faery who was the midwife at our birth. She said you have the same birthmark."

"I do." Maisie turned her left shoulder and pulled down the fabric of her shirt. "But mine is on the opposite side."

"That's weird." Seeing my birthmark on Maisie's shoulder made me feel disoriented. For so many years I'd hid the mark, since my grandmother believed it was a reminder of my shameful beginnings. And here was a person who shared the same mark but felt no shame whatsoever about it.

"Do you think it means something that our marks are mirror images?" I asked.

Maisie smiled. "Sabina, I'm an oracle. I believe everything involving symbols is significant. But I have no idea what it means. I'm sure it will reveal itself in time, though. But even if the birthmark wasn't a clue, there are others.

For example, the fact it's clearly night could speak to the fact you live like a vampire, active only at night. Plus, I don't just read the symbols. I also have to trust my visceral instincts, and in this case, I know it's you because it *feels* like you."

Clearly, I was out of my depth with all this talk of symbols and prophecies and feelings, but I nodded anyway. "So you said this told you to look for me to help find the mages, but there's obviously more to it, right?"

"Yes, the timing of the vision was what told me you'd be involved in finding the mages. But the image itself told me you had a far larger role to play. The golden lotus is a major symbol for Lilith. And the scene itself re-creates the flight of Lilith from the Garden of Eden after she was spurned by Adam."

I cocked my head. Now that she mentioned it, I realized that's why the image felt so familiar. Every vampire is taught the dark-race version of the creation story. Lilith was the first wife in Eden, created from dust just like Adam. They were supposed to be equals, but when she demanded Adam lay beneath her during sex, he balked. Tired of his heavy-handed ways, she invoked the forbidden name of God and flew from the garden.

"I remember the story," I said. "But I don't get what it has to do with me."

Rhea came forward then. "Remember what we said about the Chosen uniting the dark races? The prophecy as we know it predicts Lilith's return. Call me crazy, but I think a vision where you're literally re-creating Lilith's emancipation from Eden is a pretty clear sign *you're* this new Lilith."

I had no response to that bombshell. I was literally

speechless. Not because I felt overwhelmed with honor or anything. But because the idea was so freakin' ridiculous my mind exploded.

Maisie watched me closely, allowing me to process her revelation. Rhea, however, misinterpreted my silence as awe. "I know it's a lot to take in, but with the war looming we don't have time to waste. We need to get your training started immediately so you'll be prepared."

I waved my hands in the air and shook my head, as if trying to shake off the crazy. "Hold on just a damned minute. Prepared for what?"

"Haven't you been listening?" Rhea said. "Your destiny is to unite all the dark races. In order to do that, you have to learn to harness your magic."

"And by unite the dark races, you mean what exactly?"

"Overcome centuries of hostility among the races, bring us all together peacefully, and lead us."

A bark of laughter escaped my lips. "Riiight. I'll get right on that."

"Sarcasm is the weak mind's crutch, Sabina," Rhea said. "You can do better than that."

I crossed my arms. "How about this: You're both insane! I'm not a leader."

"Not yet, but you will be," Rhea countered.

"Look, lady, I get that you believe all this woo-woo bullshit." I motioned wide to indicate the painting, the prophecy, the vision quest, everything they'd told me. The females frowned at me. "But I'm a realist. I don't believe in destiny. I don't believe in prophecies. And I sure as hell don't believe in being some foretold Chosen."

"Why not?" Maisie said.

"Because I believe in free will. Choice. And I *choose* not to be the Chosen."

"It doesn't work that way, Sabina," Rhea said. "The universe has a plan for you. You can insulate yourself from the truth by believing in the illusion of choice. But one way or the other, your choices will eventually take you exactly where the universe wants you to go."

Seeing we weren't ever going to agree on the issue of fate, I decided to try another tactic. "What if you're wrong about all this?"

Maisie and Rhea frowned. "What do you mean?"

I pointed to the painting. "You admitted you have to interpret the symbols in your dreams, which means there's a chance you'll misinterpret them. So I repeat, what if you're wrong?"

"There's always a margin of error. But in this case, the evidence is quite strong I'm correct. In addition to the proof I've mentioned, there's something else. You've survived being staked by apple wood not once, but twice. That's pretty remarkable, given no other vampire could survive such an attack. Neither could a mage without immediate intervention, by the way. So that begs the question, why are you immune? One could argue it's because you have a special purpose that requires super-preternatural powers."

I rolled my eyes. "Or one could argue that the mixing of my blood gave me the immunity. Have you ever been staked?"

She shook her head and frowned.

"Right, so how do you know you're not also immune?"

"If it's all right with you, I think I'll skip trying it out just to see."

I smiled tightly. "And you still haven't answered my question. What if you're wrong?"

Maisie crossed her arms. "If I'm wrong, then the universe will offer another sign to help us correct course."

"Oh, that's convenient. Look, I'm sorry if this offends you, but what you call evidence, I call delusions. You want to prove something to me? Don't offer up dream analysis and drug-induced hallucinations. Show me hard evidence. Show me facts. But don't expect me to go all in on this Chosen thing based on faith alone."

Rhea smiled. "Ah."

I frowned at her knowing expression. "What?"

"Oh, nothing. It just makes sense now. You've lived your entire life following orders. The Dominae trained you to be a machine, trusting only their authority and ignoring your own instincts. But then you found out they lied to you, and you were forced to wake up. I'd imagine something like that makes it hard to trust anything or anyone—including yourself."

My jaw tightened. "Don't psychoanalyze me, mancy."

She laughed. "It's not psychoanalysis. It's facts. Isn't that what you wanted? The Dominae betrayed you, and you did something about that. But now you're struggling. You're used to taking orders and using your fists to deal with problems. And now we're asking you to believe that there's more to you than being a death machine. We're asking you to rely on your instincts and to tap into powers you were raised to hide. It's only natural you'd be scared."

I leaned toward Rhea, towering over her. She met my menacing stare with a serene smile. Her lack of intimidation pissed me off even more. "I'm not scared."

Her eyes narrowed. "Prove it."

"I don't have to prove anything to either of you."

"Then prove it to yourself. Prove that the Dominae didn't break you. Prove that there's more to you than fists and that chip on your shoulder."

I realized then the fists she referred to were clenched and ready to strike. I forced myself to relax, releasing the knots in my shoulders and allowing the blood back into my fingers. My anger was blinding me to Rhea's strategy, and I'd allowed her to poke at the recent, tender wounds I hid behind layers of swagger. "I see what you're doing, mage."

"I fully expect you do. You're a smart girl." She smiled. "I'll tell you what, you don't want to believe in the prophecy, that's cool. Time will tell whether it's true or not. Instead, why not focus on the other benefit of learning how to use your magic?"

I narrowed my eyes. "What's that?"

"You're already physically strong, no doubt about it. But think about the added advantage being able to use magic would give you in a fight."

I paused, thinking it over. I'd been trained to be a killing machine when it came to vampires. But fighting magic users? The playing field suddenly changed to favor mages. That's how the race had survived so long despite the vampires' hatred of them. During the last war, called the War of Blood, the mages were winning before they sued for peace and the Black Covenant was drawn up. Luckily for the vampire race, the mages weren't as bloodthirsty as their dark-race rivals. If it had been the vampires in the lead, the world would be a very different place today—a mage-free one.

And since vampires were now my enemy, too, knowing how to use magic would definitely work in my favor.

"And as I recall, your grandmother isn't dead yet," Rhea continued as I thought it over. "Chances are good you'll face her again at some point. Think about how shocked she'll be to learn you have a few new tricks up your sleeve."

I cursed under my breath. The old woman was wily. I knew she was manipulating me, but damned if the image she painted didn't appeal to my ego. I'm not proud to admit that I would love to see the look on my grandmother's face when I used magic against her. She'd fucking flip her gourd. After all, she was the one who tried to do everything in her power to keep me from exploring my mage side. Becoming a kickass mage would piss her off bigtime. I felt a smile spread on my lips.

"Just so we're clear, I still don't buy that I'm destined to lead the dark races."

"Fair enough," Rhea said. Behind her, Maisie's worried expression turned into a wide smile. However, Rhea wasn't done. "But I reserve the right to say 'I told you so' when it happens."

I rolled my eyes. "And I reserve the right to laugh in your face when it doesn't."

She smiled. "It's a deal."

10

*H*old up, they think you're a what?" Giguhl's claws held up his face as he lay on his stomach. He kicked his hooves behind him like a sixteen-year-old at a slumber party.

I nudged him with my hip to sit down. It was my bed, after all. "K-thon-ic," I enunciated. "I guess it's some kind of dark magic involving death and sex and stuff."

His shaggy eyebrows raised. "Awesome!"

I shot him a look. "You think so?"

"Hell, yes. Think about it, Sabina. You're gonna be so kickass once you know how to do that stuff."

"I thought I was already kickass," I said with a raised eyebrow.

"Well, yeah, but now you'll have wicked mage skills to back up your vampire ones."

I shrugged. "I guess so."

"Wait, why aren't you more excited about all this?"

I plucked a string on the comforter. "There's something else."

He rolled his goat eyes. "Isn't there always with you?"

This from a Mischief demon. I ignored his dig and explained about the prophecy.

Giguhl's face remained expressionless during the explanation. Although, once I got to the part about the Caste of Nod, he sat up straighter. "Oooh. I've heard of them."

"Really? Where'd you hear about them?"

"Duh, we're not totally cut off in Irkalla. We hear things about you earth dwellers from the demons who are summoned here for nefarious purposes."

For some reason, I figured demons didn't pay much attention to dark-races politics on earth. A lot of times when people used the term *dark races,* they included the demons. Technically, though, demons were their own species, since they existed before Lilith was even created. So while the vampires, mages, and faeries squabbled like angry siblings over who was in Lilith's favor, demons pretty much stayed out of it. It was complicated, though, because Lilith became Queen of Irkalla when she married Asmodeus, and then went on to have her own demon offspring, which meant some demons were related to the rest of the dark races and some weren't. Frankly, the whole dark-race-genealogy thing made my head hurt.

"Okay, so what did you hear?"

He leaned in with the posture of a conspirator. "Word is the caste gets together every year for a huge orgy somewhere near San Francisco."

I huffed out a breath. "No offense, G, but that's not exactly the kind of intel I was looking for."

"Well, excuse me, oh, Chosen One."

I glared at him. "Don't call me that."

His lips curled up wickedly. "Would you prefer 'New Lilith'?"

I swatted his arm. "I'd prefer it if you'd be serious for a second. I don't know what to do here."

He frowned. "Why do you have to do anything about it? You said yourself you don't believe in fate. So do whatever you think is right. If Maisie's right and you do have a destiny, then it sounds like your choices will lead you where you need to go anyway."

My mouth fell open. I wasn't used to receiving practical advice from Giguhl. But the weird thing? He was totally right. I didn't have to make any decisions tonight. As far as I was concerned, Maisie's prophecy didn't change my original plan. I'd just go through the magic training and use it to suit my own purposes. "When'd you become so insightful?"

He smiled wickedly. "Lady, I piss insight."

As much as I'd bitched about having to do this stupid were-wolf duel, the truth was I was looking forward to it. After Rhea and Maisie's revelations the night before, I needed to work out some tension. Rhea kept harping about how I needed to rely on my physicality less and my intuition more, but I'd found a good fight is the best form of stress relief around.

Speaking of Rhea, Maisie had appointed the old mage as my chaperone. She explained that as the leader of the mage race, it wasn't safe or proper for her to enter the Black Light District.

"What exactly is a Black Light District?" I asked.

"It's where the rougher elements of the city's dark races go to indulge a variety of vices—strip clubs, brothels, the usual," Rhea explained. "The Shade works out of a bar there called Vein."

I'd argued that I didn't need a chaperone at all but had been overruled. Luckily, no one saw a problem with me taking Giguhl for moral support.

"That's fine, but how are you going to get him there?" Maisie asked.

"What do you mean?"

"Sabina, you can't wander through the city with a demon. And if he's in cat form, you're going to have problems using public transportation."

"Oh," I said. "I hadn't thought of that."

Rhea piped up. "I have an idea." She performed a little mojo and a duffel bag of sorts appeared in her hands.

Giguhl eyed the bag with suspicion. "I know you don't think I'm getting in that thing."

I shot Giguhl a look. "Don't be a baby. It's just to get from here to the bar. I'm sure you can switch back to demon form once we get there." I glanced at Rhea for confirmation. She nodded.

"I don't know, Red. It's embarrassing," he said.

"Look, I don't have time to argue right now. Either you're coming in the carrier or you're not coming at all."

The demon crossed his arms, looking just like a pouty toddler. "Fine."

Getting into the bar was its own headache. After we took a cab to Hell's Kitchen, Rhea led us to a hole-in-the-wall Chinese takeout joint. She led us into what appeared from the outside to be a walk-in freezer. We walked into the cold room, past shelves filled with slabs of meat. After she closed the door in, Rhea moved to the back and pulled on a meat hook. The sound of metal scratching against concrete made me flinch. The false wall opened to reveal a set of stairs. At the bottom, a short hallway took us to a door marked "Private."

"This is it. Go ahead and let him change back now."

I put the duffel down next to the door and unzipped it. "Okay, G. Time to switch back."

After the transformation, Giguhl took the clothes I'd brought along. "That bag constitutes demon abuse," he complained as he changed.

I nodded impatiently, keeping my eyes averted. He looked ridiculous in the gray sweats and red *Demons Are Horny* T-shirt, but I'd be damned if I was walking in a club with a nude demon.

Once he was done, Rhea opened the door. A mage bouncer sat on a stool just inside. He nodded at Rhea like he knew her and waved us in.

Even though Rhea had told me Vein was dark-races only, it surprised me to see all the races mixing so casually. Back in L.A., you'd never see mages sitting cheek to fang with vamps without fights breaking out. Not to mention you never saw werewolves in California. Nymphs and other faeries were common in L.A., but they mainly had their own hangouts.

Back in California, vamps were at the top of the food chain, and the Dominae ran everything with iron fists. That's not to say mages or faeries didn't exist there, but they tended to avoid interactions with us. Occasionally a brave mage would wander into a vamp bar, but it rarely ended well. But here I got the impression the races not only tolerated each other, but that they even hung out. Odd.

"Looks like we're not in Kansas anymore, Toto," I whispered to Giguhl.

"No shit," the demon replied.

"You're supposed to bring demons in through the back entrance for the fights." The bartender was a vamp with a thick neck and greasy copper hair. The name "Earl" was embroidered into his black shirt. He eyed Giguhl, as if he expected him to tear down the place any minute. Meanwhile, his gray dishrag made lazy circles on the bar.

"That won't be an issue," Rhea said reasonably. "I'm here to see—"

"Look, lady, I don't have time for this. Demons aren't allowed in the main bar. If you wanna stay, you're gonna have to take him to the basement."

Rhea slammed a hand on the bar, impeding the rag's progress across the sticky surface. "I have an appointment." Thus far I'd only seen her in her earth-mother guise, but I enjoyed this tough side to Rhea. She wore it well.

The bartender stopped wiping and glared at Rhea. "I don't give a rat's ass if you're meeting the Queen of the Fae, lady. Take the demon outside before I do it for you."

Giguhl snorted behind me. "I'd like to see you try, fang boy." He'd lowered his voice a couple of octaves for effect. I tried not to roll my eyes at his posturing. Although, truth be told, I would enjoy watching Earl try to move Giguhl. But only if I had popcorn and a good seat from which to watch the fireworks.

Rhea leaned over the bar and grabbed the bartender's collar. "I don't think you're using your ears. I have an appointment with The Shade."

Tension crackled, and patrons swiveled their eager gazes to the standoff at the bar. I think I even heard a pin drop somewhere back near the pool tables.

Just then, a phone on the bar back rang. The shrill sound

cut through the electric silence like a knife. Unlike most normal phones, this one had no buttons—just a single red light, which flashed maniacally with each ring.

"That would be your boss," Rhea said quietly. She jerked his head toward the phone and released the bartender. "Answer it."

Earl scowled but hurried over and picked up the receiver. As he whispered into the mouthpiece he looked across the bar and up at a large mirror in an ornate frame. It hung near the balcony on the second floor. Obviously, someone was keeping an eye on things. I sensed a presence behind the mirrored surface. I couldn't see anyone, but I could feel eyes on me. I ignored the hairs prickling on the back of my neck and focused on having Rhea's back in case this all went south.

The bartender hung up and came back over, looking sheepish. "I apologize for the misunderstanding. The Shade said you should go down to the locker rooms behind the fight pit to get ready for the duel. It will begin in half an hour."

Giguhl leaned in and whispered in my ear. "Remind me not to cross Rhea."

I nodded and looked at Rhea. The aggression she'd displayed a few minutes ago had evaporated. She flashed an easy smile to the bartender. "Thanks."

The bartender looked at the mirror, hesitating. "He also asked me to tell you the demon isn't allowed in the fight area. He'll have to stay here."

"Now, wait just a—" I began. Rhea grabbed my arm for silence.

"That will be fine," she said. "Please make sure he's taken care of while we're gone."

"Rhea, what are you doing?"

She put her mouth to my ear. "We're not in a position to make demands here, Sabina. They don't want you to sic him on anyone if you lose."

I glanced at Giguhl. He shrugged. "It's fine with me. Just don't get yourself killed, okay?"

"Thanks for the vote of confidence."

"I'm here to help."

"Behave yourself while I'm gone, please."

He tried to look innocent. "Who, me?"

Other than the altercation in Central Park with the Lone Wolves, I'd never fought a werewolf. Rhea, however, knew a thing or two and used the few minutes before the fight to give me some pointers. She led me to a small room, which looked like a locker room of sorts.

She held up a square package and a bottle of glue. "Silverleaf for your fangs."

I frowned. "My fangs?"

She nodded. "Some vamps use silver caps against weres, but the leaf is better. When you break the skin, it flakes off and gets into their bloodstream."

"Will it kill him?"

"No, it takes a major dose of silver directly to the heart to kill a were. But this will hurt like hell and slow him down."

"Is all this really necessary?"

She shot me a look. "The full moon is a week or so away, so he won't be in full were form, but even so he'll be incredibly strong. Plus, he's pissed you harmed members of his pack. You'll need every advantage you can get."

Sighing, I took the supplies from her. I wiped a finger across my teeth to dry them. Then I brushed some of the adhesive on both fangs. The fumes made my eyes water. Rhea helped me press the thin sheets of silver on the enamel. "Keep your mouth open for a sec so the glue can dry."

While I stood there with my mouth open, she busied herself covering my chest, arms, and neck with more of the leaf. By the time he was done, I felt like the Tin Man. I finally closed my mouth. The glue tasted like ass, and the silverleaf had flaked off on my tongue. I choked as a few flecks tickled the back of my throat.

"It's best if you can bite a vein, but just breaking the skin will help."

I looked at myself in the mirror. With my new blinged-out fangs and metallic skin, I hardly recognized myself.

"I thought you were all about nonaggression," I said.

She shrugged. "Normally, I am. But sometimes aggression is warranted, especially when it's in self-defense. If you didn't fight the Alpha tonight, his pack would hunt you down. At least this way, you have a fighting chance."

I nodded at her practical approach. "What else do I need to know?"

"The fight is to the surrender. Since he's the leader of his pack, surrender will mean he's dishonored and they'll kill him anyway. So for him it's a fight to the death. He'll be out for blood from the word go."

"That's comforting. What happens if I kill him?"

She frowned. "All his property will pass to you. But I would recommend you avoid killing him at all costs. This is about settling a debt, not murder."

I ignored that. I'd do what I had to do to win, no matter what the consequences. "Are weapons allowed?"

She shook her head. "No, that'd be too easy. This is hand-to-hand all the way."

I nodded, digesting that. Hand-to-hand I could definitely handle.

"I don't think I have to remind you to be careful."

I shot her a look. "It's not like I want to be injured, Rhea."

"I know. It's just your sister would be devastated if something happens. As would I. If this wasn't such a complicated situation, Maisie never would have allowed you to fight."

My eyes narrowed. "Don't worry. I'll make sure to survive so your plans for me won't get screwed up."

"Sabina, I'm not talking about the prophecy." Rhea sent me a sad look. "Is it really so hard to believe someone would be worried about you just because we care?"

Yeah, it was actually, but I didn't want to argue with her. Instead, I took a deep breath. "Let's do this."

11

Rhea led me to a dim room. A fight pit sat in the center with a couple of bare bulbs offering the only illumination. I'd expected an eager crowd of weres shouting for my blood. Instead, two lone males stood under the light. I found the lack of witnesses and the silence more intimidating than I would have an unruly crowd.

The one on the right nodded slightly as we approached. "Sabina Kane."

The scent of wet dog and apple juice drifted to my nose. His hair was wet with the stuff and his hand was sticky with it. I certainly wasn't going to clue him in that the forbidden fruit had no effect on me.

I nodded back. "And you are?"

"Michael Romulus." He offered a hand to shake. I looked at it a second, wondering if it was a trick. But his eyes held steady, almost a dare. I gripped his rough palm with just enough pressure to let him know I meant business. He met my gaze levelly and squeezed back just enough to let me know he didn't give a shit if I was female—he meant business, too.

Funny, his calm confidence and rangy frame didn't scream Alpha male. He was wearing khakis, for chrissakes. If anything, his companion looked more the part with his bulging biceps and hairy knuckles. But I knew better than to underestimate Michael. Sometimes the smaller packages held the nastiest surprises. Besides, I might not know much about werewolves, but I knew one didn't rise to Alpha of a pack without some serious fighting skills.

I pulled my hand from his and wiped it on my jeans. "And him?" I jerked my head in the direction of his companion.

"This is Rex. My second in command. He'll act as my witness."

I nodded at the hulk. "This is Rhea Lazarus."

The three exchanged polite nods.

"We've met," Michael said.

I glanced at Rhea. I guess it shouldn't have surprised me that she knew the were, but I found it odd she hadn't mentioned it earlier. On the other hand, I guess it explained why she knew enough about them to help me prepare for the fight.

Michael nodded at Rex, who pulled a sheet of paper from his pocket. "Whereas Sabina Kane—hereafter known as the accused—is charged with poaching on territory reserved for the exclusive use of the Lone Wolf pack and all its affiliates, led by one Michael Romulus—hereby known as the plaintiff—and whereas the accused also resisted vacating the territory when asked by representatives of the plaintiff, and whereas—"

I interrupted. "Jeez, what are you? A lawyer?"

Michael frowned. "Yes."

I rolled my eyes. "Look, I got it. We don't need a bunch of legal mumbo jumbo. I poached—unknowingly, I might add—and I hurt two of your guys, in self-defense, by the way. So now I have to fight you."

Michael nodded. "Our seconds will not interfere, and no weapons may be used. The fight is to the surrender. Do you agree to those terms?"

"I think we both know surrender isn't an option."

He inclined his head to acknowledge the truth of my statement. "Shall we?"

I turned and walked back to the edge of the pit. Rhea put her hands on my shoulders. "He's going to fight dirty."

Over Rhea's shoulder, I watched Michael speaking quietly to his companion. "And you think I won't?"

Rhea looked me in the eyes. "Don't get cocky out there. That apple cologne he's wearing might not hurt you, but he's strong enough to rip off your head if you're not careful."

I jerked a nod. "Got it." A shadow moved behind a two-way mirror set high in the wall. It could have been a trick of light, but I doubted it. Someone was watching us. The Shade?

"Let us begin." Romulus's commanding voice sounded unnaturally loud in the dark room.

Rhea squeezed my shoulder and backed away. Across the ring, Romulus's second did the same. My opponent walked calmly into the center of the pit. He raised one hand and beckoned me with a curl of his fingers.

The corner of my mouth curled up. Anticipation thrummed through me. The delicious tension was kind of like the few moments leading to orgasm. My body yearned to fight. For the last few days I'd felt off-kilter, a stranger in a strange, magical land. But this filthy fight pit, with its bloodstain varnish on the floor and the lingering scent of sweat and violence, felt like a home away from home.

I blocked everything out but Romulus. Zeroed in on his eyes. My breath deepened. Long, deep inhales followed by slow, emptying exhales. I reached down deep for the tight ball of rage I kept hidden for special occasions. It bloomed like a black rose inside me, releasing the bitterness I'd accumulated over the last month. I called up an image of my grandmother and transposed it on Michael's face. Oh, yeah, I had plenty of wrath that needed venting on someone. Might as well be the werepuppy.

Something must have changed on my face, because Romulus's eyes widened and he took a hesitant step back.

My vision blurred around the edges as I flew toward my prey. If he'd been mortal, he wouldn't have seen me coming. But Romulus was a predator, too. He spun away before I could sink my bared fangs into his flesh. He grabbed my arm and jerked me around, wrenching my shoulder. He swung a fist around and clocked me on the side of my face. Pain bloomed on my cheek, the sting of skin splitting open.

I kicked back and caught him in the ribs. I spat a mouthful of red on the concrete. He crouched low, growling and baring his teeth. He leapt off his haunches and barreled into my midsection. I slammed into the wall. Air escaped my mouth in a whoosh. I looked up to see him barreling toward me. I spun out and caught him in the stomach with a sidekick. He came up with a wicked backhand. I ran at him and wrapped my hands around him, propelling him back. He dug in, fighting the momentum. I clawed at his back, tearing his shirt and scoring my silver-caked nails across his flesh.

He yelped and tore himself away. Tendrils of smoke lifted from the wounds. He looked up at me with feral eyes. We circled each other. Playtime was over. Time to end this.

Rhea and Rex didn't make a sound. No words of encouragement or warning. Tension hung over the pit like a bubble filled to bursting.

I flashed my fangs at Michael. "You ready to surrender yet?"

He laughed humorlessly. "I'm just toying with my food."

"Eat this." My fist crunched against his mouth, his teeth scraping my knuckles. For a guy who hated silver, his bones sure felt like metal. I followed the punch with a downward kick to his knee. True fact, it only takes twenty pounds of pressure to break a knee. I'm not sure if Romulus knew this before, but he sure as hell knew it now. He fell to the ground, gripping the broken joint.

From the corner of my eye, I saw Rex make like he was about to step in. "Don't even think about it." The menace in Rhea's voice was unmistakable.

I stood over Michael. "How about now?"

He looked up at me. His eyes glowed with hatred. Before I saw it coming, he grabbed my leg and pulled it out from under me. I fell flat on my back, the concrete jarring my spine and knocking the air from my lungs. Romulus's weight slammed into me, and he went to work on my face. Rivulets of blood blurred my vision, but the pain was clear as crystal and just as sharp. I bucked my hips and struggled to break free, but the hits kept coming. He finally stopped tenderizing my face and moved to my ribs. I felt one give way and puncture a lung. I wheezed for air through blood bubbles clogging my throat. Shit was getting serious, and I needed to do something before the pain overwhelmed me. Grabbing one of his flailing arms, I snapped with my fangs, not caring where they landed as long as they got him *somewhere*.

Finally, I got a hold of his forearm. I bit down as hard as I could, feeling flesh give way. Romulus jerked above me with a howl. He ripped the arm from my mouth, leaving a tag of skin behind. I spat it out, along with a mouthful of blood. With a trembling hand, I swiped the red from my eyes. No time for licking my wounds. The bite might have hurt him, but I was in worse shape.

I struggled to my knees, wobbling slightly. Romulus kneeled nearby, his arm close to his body. Blood smeared the front of his khakis and shirt. Some of it was mine, obviously. But I'd managed to bite a good-sized chunk out of his arm. We both panted like wounded animals, watching each other. His arm smoked and sizzled, and I think I saw a flash of bone as he released the useless arm to hang limply at his side.

A cough rattled in my chest, causing a spark of pain in my side. But I wasn't done. Not by a long shot. Surrender was never an option. Unlike Romulus, no one would kill me if I gave up. But I'd have to live for eternity knowing I'd surrendered.

I dragged myself off the ground and shambled toward him. He sighed and took a defensive position, raising his one good arm to form a fist. We fell into each other like two boxers at the end of a brutal round. Holding each other up with our stubbornness, jabbing at ribs and kidneys and anything else we could reach. He collapsed to his knees, taking me with him.

But still we punched. My head fell to his shoulder while my hands slapped at him. Opening my mouth seemed to take every ounce of strength remaining. My fangs broke the skin and sunk into his jugular. His body went stiff and then sagged. I tried to swallow blood to regain some strength, but the wound started bubbling and smoking. The few drops I got tasted like acid. With a final burst of strength, Romulus shoved me back. We both fell in a heap on the floor.

The air rattled painfully from my lungs. My face felt like someone had taken a mallet to it. And the thought of trying to move made my muscles cramp in protest. Michael's own raspy breath sounded from nearby. He obviously wasn't faring much better.

I swallowed. "You s'render?" I slurred.

"N'er."

Footsteps approached from both sides. Shadows fell over us.

The world tilted as hands locked behind my back, pulling me upright. I groaned in protest, but Rhea held on. I glanced sideways through swollen eyes to see Romulus receiving the same treatment from Rex.

"Boss, you okay?" Rex asked. Obviously, Romulus's second wasn't the brightest bulb in the box.

"I think it's pretty clear they can't continue," Rhea said.

"But no one surrendered," Rex said.

"It's a draw, then."

"No way, mancy. They're gonna have to just rest for a second and get back at it."

"You're joking," said Rhea. "Look at them. They're done."

"What the fuck am I supposed to tell the pack?" Rex said.

A new voice entered the discussion. "You'll tell them The Shade stopped the fight. If they have a problem with that, you send them to me."

I turned my head toward the new arrival. I couldn't make out more than an outline. But I knew that voice. And before I passed out, I managed to mutter a name I hadn't said in thirty years. "Slade?"

12

Rhea's face hovered over me when my eyes blinked open. My ribs throbbed like someone had taken a crowbar to them. It hurt so bad I could do little more than take shallow, wheezing breaths. In addition, my face felt like one large bruise. I moved my jaw to ask where I was but flinched as lightning speared through my skull.

Rhea helped me sit up. "Drink."

I expected a potion of some sort. Something to quicken the healing and perk me up. Instead, the ferric scent of blood teased my nostrils and its rich taste coated my tongue. I swallowed greedily. Now I didn't mind the chemical aftertaste or coldness of the bagged blood.

"More," I whispered. My body was jacked up after the fight, and it would take a lot more than one cup of blood to heal the damage.

Rhea calmly set down the cup and looked me in the eyes. "That's all you're getting."

I narrowed my swollen eyes. "Why?"

"Look, Sabina, we both know I could give you more

blood or even a potion to make the pain you're in noth-ing but an unpleasant memory." She shifted on the seat, which made my broken ribs scream in pain. I hissed as cold sweat broke out on my chest. "But if I did that, you wouldn't learn your lesson."

"What?" I panted.

"You've earned these wounds. The choices you've made have led you to this moment. If I remove those con-sequences, you'll never learn to moderate your behavior in the future."

I wasn't sure if it was from the excessive pain or the torture of listening to Rhea's lecture, but bile rose in my throat. "You're a real bitch, you know that?"

Rhea smiled and patted my arm. "Yes, dear."

"Can I have some water at least?" I snapped. "Or is thirst part of my penance?"

"Of course you can have water," she said with a patient smile. "Giguhl? Would you please get Sabina a glass of water?"

For the first time, I realized Giguhl had been sitting in a chair across the room this whole time. His arms were crossed, and his posture told me he was in full sulk about something. When Rhea asked him to get me water, he rolled his eyes and sighed. "Fine."

"What's wrong with him?" I asked.

Rhea shook her head. "We'll discuss it later."

While I waited for my surly demon to bring me a drink, I took stock of my surroundings. A familiar scent lingered in the air, but I couldn't place it yet. We were in an office I didn't recognize. A glass-and-steel desk sat about five yards away. I lay on a black leather couch next to a coffee table matching the desk.

Giguhl handed me the glass and trudged back to his chair without a word. I took a long drink, swishing the water in my mouth first to wash away the silver flakes.

"Where did the weres go?" I asked Rhea, since apparently Giguhl wasn't speaking to anyone.

"Rex took Romulus back to the pack. He'll recover. Not sure he'll be too happy with the outcome when he does, though."

Mention of the outcome reminded me of the latecomer to the fight. *That* was where the familiar scent came from.

"Slade." The word came out sounding like an expletive. As far as I was concerned, the name ranked right up there with *asshole*. "Where is he?" I tried to sit up. The blood was helping a little with the pain, but I was still in a world of hurt.

Rhea, however, had other plans. "You need to rest." She pushed me back gently. "He'll be back soon. I take it you know him?"

I relaxed back into the cushions and nodded. My wounds might be healing, but I was shaky as hell. "He used to work for the Dominae in L.A."

"An old friend, then?"

I narrowed my eyes. "More like frenemy."

"In that case," said Rhea, "I suppose asking you to be civil during our meeting is a waste of breath."

"You could say that."

The door opened then. Slade strolled in like he owned the place, which I guess he did. Giguhl perked up.

"Hey, Slade!" he said with more enthusiasm than necessary.

Slade nodded at Rhea and Giguhl as if they'd all already gotten acquainted while I was out, but his eyes were on me.

I jerked up, ignoring the stitch in my side. I didn't want to face him lying down. Rhea tried to help me up, but I waved her away.

Slade slowed and a smile crept across his face. "Sabina Ka—"

He was interrupted—by my fist.

"Sabina, no!" Giguhl yelled.

I heard a loud curse and movement at my back. The scent of sandalwood filled my nostrils. "Stop!" Rhea grabbed my arms and held me back, surprisingly strong for a mage.

Slade smiled through blood streaking his lips and chin. "Nice to see you're still feisty as ever."

A growl came from somewhere deep inside me. "Feisty? Try furious, asshole."

I didn't like surprises. Although, truth be told, Slade wasn't a surprise, exactly. He was more like a bombshell.

"Come, now, Sabina. I'm not your enemy."

"Could have fooled me."

"Sabina." Rhea's quiet tone held a hefty dose of reprimand.

Then I got a load of the smug smile on Slade's face. The first thing I learned in assassin school was never to let emotions get the best of you. Hell, Slade himself had reinforced that lesson when we worked together. Allowing an enemy to make you lose your temper was like giving them a weapon to use against your most vulnerable spot. I took a deep breath and willed my muscles to loosen, my jaw to relax, my heart rate to slow.

Rhea felt the change and loosened her grip. Stayed

close in case she needed to step in again. However, Giguhl looked like a child witnessing Mommy and Daddy fight for the first time. That really burned my ass. Giguhl was my demon, but he obviously had a man crush on Slade. What the hell had happened while I was out?

Slade didn't seem impressed by my demon. Instead he went with a patronizing, "Good girl."

Now he was just trying to taunt me. I let the condescending tone slide off my back. "You owe me ten grand. With interest and adjusted for inflation."

He laughed. "Still funny, too."

I clenched my jaw, knowing he was trying to goad me into losing my temper again.

"Sabina, The Shade deserves our thanks. He agreed to let the fight stand as a draw. Your debt has been paid."

"Stop calling him that ridiculous name. His name is Slade."

"Let's not bicker over trivialities. Sabina, I don't go by that name anymore. Here"—he motioned with his hands—"I'm The Shade. But since you're an old friend you can call me Slade."

"Don't do me any favors, asshole. We're not friends."

Slade laughed. "Surely you're not still mad."

"Mad about what?" Giguhl prompted. "Does someone want to clue us in here?"

"No," I snapped.

"Sure," Slade said at the same time. "Sabina and I used to work together."

Giguhl shot me a look. "*Worked* together, huh?"

His emphasis on the word made it clear the demon wasn't buying it. Good instincts, that Giguhl.

"Among other things," Slade said with a smile. I gritted my teeth, not wanting to get into this in front of Rhea.

I met Giguhl's interested gaze. "We *worked* together on a case. But *Slade* here took credit for the kill and ran off with the payday."

I felt Slade's stare and glanced over. What I hadn't mentioned was Slade and I had slept together—once—before he screwed me in a different way. The heat in his eyes now told me I wasn't the only one remembering the more carnal aspects of our past dealings.

"You know why I left, Sabina," he said quietly.

I shook my head. "I don't want to talk about it. It's ancient history."

"If you say so." His sardonic look made me want to punch him again. But I was already embarrassed about my earlier lack of control. No reason to give him more proof I was anything but over what happened last time I saw him.

A brief, awkward silence followed. Rhea had gone silent, preferring to observe the fireworks rather than get involved. On the other hand, Giguhl was obviously itching to find out all about the subtext zinging through the conversation. Too damned bad. Meanwhile, Slade looked like the cat that swallowed the canary. I just wanted to shove that canary up his ass.

"So," he said. "The fight went well. Don't worry about Romulus. The fight was fair. He can save face with the pack by claiming I stopped the fight."

He sat in his leather executive chair and motioned us to take the chairs opposite. I sat and took stock of the changes in Slade. Thirty years ago, he'd been an assassin with a chip on his shoulder. Looking at him now, though, it was clear the years had smoothed out the rough edges and buffed them to a shine. I'd bet money the charcoal pinstripe number was designer. His hair was darker, too, just a shade darker than the light auburn of his younger days. His posture was that of a man accustomed to calling the shots. But his devilish sense of humor lurked under the powerful veneer. Okay, fine, he was still hot. Also still an asshole, I quickly reminded myself.

Giguhl cleared his throat and nudged me. I realized then Slade had been staring at me, too, and the room had gone silent. "What?" I asked him.

"Damn, it's good to see you," he said. "When the Lone Wolves told me who kicked their asses in the park, I thought they were joking. But the description they gave me couldn't have been anyone else."

That statement told me he knew why I'd left Los Angeles, but not exactly why I'd come to New York. Something told me to keep my sister out of this discussion.

"Well, I wish I could say the same—about seeing you again, I mean."

The corner of Slade's mouth lifted. "That's the past talking. We're not so different now, you and me."

"What the hell is that supposed to mean?"

"I defected from the Dominae. You betrayed them."

I shook my head. "That's different."

"Is it?" he asked with a lifted brow.

"So I can tell the Hekate Council Sabina's debt has been paid?" Rhea interrupted.

Slade sighed and grimaced. "Not exactly. There is still the issue of the unpaid blood tax."

"Blood tax? What the hell is that?" I asked, scooting to the edge of my seat in case I needed to sock him again.

"All vampires must pay a blood tax if they want to feed in my city."

Rhea elbowed me to keep quiet. "Not to split hairs here, but this is the Hekate Council's city. And considering who Sabina's sister is, I'm sure you can make an exception in her case."

Slade's eyes swiveled to me. "Sister?"

I cursed under my breath. Time to change the subject before he realized the sister in question was a high priestess of the council and the oracle of New York. A guy like Slade? He'd find some way to use that bit of intel in his favor. "It's a long story. And Rhea's right. I shouldn't have to pay the blood tax."

"And why is that?"

"A. The only time I tried to feed I was a victim of *suckus interuptus*."

"How so?"

"The guy shot me," I admitted.

Slade threw back his head and laughed. "Priceless!"

My cheeks flamed, but I forged ahead. "B. The Hekate Council has requested I forego feeding from humans for the time being. So there's no reason for me to pay your tax."

"You have already bitten a human in my territory, therefore you owe me a retroactive payment of two grand."

"What?" I yelled. "That's highway robbery!"

"Come now, Sabina. Surely two grand is spare change for someone with an assassin's salary."

I gritted my teeth. "As you already pointed out, I don't work for the Dominae anymore."

Slade nodded, seeming unimpressed with my predicament. Knowing Slade, he knew every last detail of what had happened. And I'm sure he loved the irony. I'd been pissed at him not just for taking my money, but also for abandoning the Dominae. And now here I'd committed the worse crime against them—betrayal.

"Anyway," I continued, "Seeing as how I'm out of a job for the time being, I'm finding it hard to justify paying that much money for feeding rights I have no intention of using."

"Then I'm afraid we've reached an impasse," Slade said. "Unless . . ."

I rolled my eyes at his baiting. Rhea cleared her throat—a warning to hear Slade out. "Unless what?" I sighed, not bothering to hide the impatience in my tone.

Slade rubbed his lower lip, thinking. "How about a compromise? You let your demon here compete in my Demon Fight Club, and I'll forgive the tax."

Giguhl stiffened next to me. I glared at him to keep quiet. "What the hell is Demon Fight Club?"

He leaned back in the chair, looking pleased with himself. "It's exactly what it sounds like. Two demons meet in the ring and duke it out. The customers love it, and I love the money they bring in."

Giguhl shifted next to me. I glanced at him. He was trying to look casual, but his posture told me he was interested. However, I wasn't thrilled about the idea of spending any more time with Slade than necessary. "I don't know—"

"I think it sounds fu—" I shot Giguhl a glare, cutting him off.

"I need to think about it," I said to both Slade and Giguhl.

Slade nodded. "Think about it, but let me know ASAP.

If you say no, you'll be paying interest for every day you made me wait."

"I said no, Giguhl."

"C'mon, Sabina." The cat hadn't shut up since we left Vein. He stuck his little bald head up through the open zipper of the bag. The partition between us and the cabbie afforded enough privacy that I felt comfortable allowing it. But if the cat didn't stop his bitching soon, I was going to change my mind.

"I said we'd discuss it. Later." I turned and watched the New York streets zoom by. Rhea had been quiet since we left the bar.

"You're just being stubborn." He crossed his arms, clearly telling me he thought I was a jerk for not liking his new buddy.

I sighed and looked at him. "It's not that. It's the principle of the matter. I shouldn't have to pay Slade a dime."

Rhea sighed. "Sabina, I hate to break it to you, but Slade is well within his rights to demand compensation. And I think Orpheus will agree when I tell him what happened."

I cursed under my breath. "I guess it's a good thing Orpheus isn't my leader, then, isn't it?"

Rhea tilted her head. "Quit fooling yourself, Sabina. You can't expect the council to offer you protection and training without them expecting you to follow their rules."

"Maybe I'll leave, then."

Giguhl laughed. "Whatev. You're just being pissed because Slade screwed you over a long time ago."

He was hitting a little too close to home, so I ignored

that and shot back. "Did you ever think the reason I don't want you to fight is I don't think you'll last five minutes in the ring?"

He put a paw over his heart. "That hurts, Sabina."

"If I might add something here," Rhea chimed in. "If Slade's willing to accept Giguhl's participation in the fights as payment, and the demon's willing, then refusing the compromise might send Slade the wrong message."

"What do you mean?" I asked.

She shrugged. "Given that you two have a history, perhaps he'll see your refusal as a sign he can still get the best of you."

I sighed. Gods, I hated being backed into a corner. But damned if she wasn't right.

"Please," Giguhl said. He sent me his wide-eyed kitty look.

I looked from the cat's pleading expression to Rhea's challenging one. I was outnumbered and outmaneuvered. Again.

"Gods! Fine. But if you get hurt, it's your own damned fault."

"Aw, Sabina. Does that mean you won't kiss my boo-boos?"

Rhea chuckled and I felt a smile crack on my own lips. "You're a real pain in the ass, you know that?" I said without heat.

"That's why you love me." There was a beat of silence, and then: "So you and Slade, huh?"

I shifted in my seat. Talking about Slade was bad enough, but doing so in front of Adam's aunt made me feel self-conscious. "Not much to tell. We knew each other."

"Knew each other? Like in the biblical sense?" Giguhl asked.

"Obviously," Rhea chimed in. "Most women don't deliver an uppercut to old platonic friends."

I let that comment pass. "It's not a big deal. Water under the bridge. Ancient history. I barely even remember him."

"Mmm-hmm."

"Shut it, Mr. Giggles."

"I'm just sayin'. I saw the way he looked at you."

I chanced a glance at Rhea. She met my eyes over Giguhl's head and nodded. "Agreed."

I looked from the mage to the demon. "You're both crazy."

"Crazy nothin'. You'll see." With that, Giguhl ducked back inside the bag for a nap.

I spent the rest of the ride avoiding Rhea's knowing gaze.

13

"You ready to learn about the wonderful world of magic?" Rhea said in an overly chipper voice. She'd asked me to meet her in the foyer of Maisie's apartment at the butt-crack of dusk. It was now six in the evening, and I was dragging.

What's worse, Rhea insisted I bring Giguhl with me. As a result, I had to listen to his steady stream of complaints as she led us through the building to the area they used as a school. I was ready to send him back to bed when Rhea opened the door on the top floor of the building.

"This is the gymnasium," she said, waving us inside. The room smelled of old sweat and vinyl from the blue mats covering half the floor. "It's not used very often, so we'll have plenty of privacy for your lessons."

Damara was waiting for us. She'd accessorized her standard black ensemble with a scowl. Guess I wasn't the only one who'd woken up on the wrong side of the bed.

"Is everything in place?" Rhea asked.

Damara nodded. "Yeah."

Rhea didn't seem fazed by the younger mage's bad attitude. "Okay, then. Sabina, I thought we'd start tonight by testing the skills Adam taught you and work up from there. Did you bring your grimoire?"

I held up the leather-bound journal Adam had given me in California. He explained then I was supposed to fill the book with all the magical tips and spells I learned.

Rhea held out a hand for the book and I gave it over. "Let's see here." She started flipping through the pages. Seeing page after blank page, she looked up. "Where are all your spells?"

I leaned in and flipped to the last page. "This is the only one I have." I pointed to instructions for summoning Giguhl. Adam had written them in the back of the book before giving it to me. Looking now at his bold, masculine script, I felt a little ache in my chest. Since he'd left, I'd worked very hard to keep my mind on less complicated subjects, like prophecies and turf wars with werewolves. Yes, getting involved with Adam would be a colossal mistake. But try telling that to my libido.

If Rhea noticed my woolgathering, she gave no indication. Instead, she read through the spell and nodded. "Hmm. It's a bit clunky. I can teach you how to summon the demon using an abbreviated spell without all the ceremony."

Glad for the distraction from thoughts of Adam, I looked up. "Oh yeah?"

She nodded. "Adam's specialty isn't demon summoning. He's an energy manipulator. This spell is textbook stuff, but with your latent talents and some training, you'll be able to do this in your sleep. But for now, why don't we run through this the way he taught you?"

Beside me, Giguhl raised a claw. "Question. How can she summon me when I'm already here?"

I looked at the demon, thankful he was paying attention. I felt, like, totally disconnected from what was going on. Like I was watching myself through frosted glass.

"That's easy," Rhea replied to Giguhl. "She's going to summon a different demon."

That got my attention. "But I've never summoned another demon." Suddenly my hands were damp. The reality of the situation hit me smack in the face. Rhea wasn't easing me into this magic stuff; she was determined to throw me in the deep end. If I didn't want to sink, I had to get my head in the game.

"Don't worry. The process is the same, you just have to change the demon seal you trace during the incantation."

"Wait, what?"

Rhea sighed. "Every demon has a unique sigil. This is Giguhl's." She opened the book again and pointed to the symbol Adam drew in the journal. The design was pretty simple—a circle with a zigzag in the center. "Anyway, a demon's unique seal is similar to a telephone number. When you trace it, you call the demon directly."

"Oh." I looked at Giguhl for confirmation. He nodded, looking bored.

Rhea turned to her assistant. "Please get the salt so Sabina can cast a circle." The young mage turned and walked to a table under the windows, muttering to herself the entire way. While Damara grabbed a box of sea salt, Rhea snapped her fingers. A book appeared in her hand.

"Anyway," she continued, "the trick is knowing the right sigil. The stronger the demon, the more complex and secret the design." She flipped through the pages as she spoke. "Now we just have to figure out who you should summon."

As she searched for a likely candidate, I wiped my damp palms on my jeans. Here's the thing. While I felt comfortable with Giguhl now, the truth was our first meeting hadn't gone well. Adam had summoned the demon to test me. And by test, I mean Giguhl staked me. I'd survived, but it was touch and go there for a few minutes.

"What if the demon I summon tries to kill me?" I knew I could survive a staking, but demons had other means of killing I had no idea how to defend against.

Rhea looked at me over the pages of the book. "That's what the circle's for. It binds the demon." She looked at Giguhl. "You're what? A seventh-level Mischief?"

Giguhl's chest puffed out with indignation. "Fifth level."

Rhea pursed her lips. "Hmm." She finally stopped on a page and nodded. "Okay, let's see how strong you are. The demon you're going to summon is named Furfur."

I laughed, suddenly relieved. "Furfur?" A demon with such a silly name couldn't be so bad, I thought. Until I got a look at Giguhl's face.

"Um, do you think that's a good idea?" he said to Rhea, sounding uncharacteristically serious.

Rhea simply smiled. "It'll be fine. I think. And if not, we're all here to help."

That didn't sound good at all. "Wait. Why is Giguhl worried?"

Rhea opened her mouth to speak, but Giguhl beat her to it. "Furfur is a Count of Irkalla who rules twenty-six legions."

Rhea waved a hand, shooing away Giguhl's concern.

"We'll have to take a couple extra precautions, but it's nothing you can't handle. Trust me."

Call me crazy, but trust didn't come so easily these days. "I don't know, Rhea."

"Look, all you have to do is cast a triangle inside the circle for extra protection."

It's not that I was scared, exactly. Surely Rhea wouldn't have me summon a demon I couldn't handle, or at least not one she couldn't handle if shit went down. I looked at her now, and the challenge in her eyes and the smirk on her lips all but dared me to back down. To hell with that.

"Okay, fine. I'll do it."

Her smile widened. "Thatta girl."

For the next few minutes she walked me through casting a circle in salt on the floor, followed by a smaller triangle inside. Then she made me trace Furfur's sigil over and over on the page until I had it memorized. Unlike Giguhl's, Furfur's design was a irregular collection of shapes in an asymmetrical pattern. Once I felt I had a good grasp on how to draw it, Rhea stepped back and closed the book.

"Now picture the sigil in your mind when you evoke the demon. And whatever you do, don't cross that line." She pointed to the border of the circle. "Good luck."

Rhea joined Giguhl and Damara several feet away. Giguhl sent me a halfhearted thumbs-up while Damara yawned and looked at her watch.

I swallowed and stepped up to the circle. A trickle of sweat rolled down my back and I rubbed my hands on my jeans. "Here goes nothing," I muttered. I took a deep breath and exhaled it slowly. Closing my eyes, I focused on clearing my mind. Furfur's sigil lit up in my mind, neon against a black background. I raised my right hand and let it hang there for a second. Then, releasing my breath, I traced the complex design in the air.

"Idimmu Alka!"

My stomach dipped. A split second later thunder boomed through the room. I jerked and my eyes flew open. In the center of the triangle, a roiling black cloud appeared. Instead of the brimstone odor that always accompanied Giguhl's appearance, the room filled with the sharp scent of ozone.

I didn't dare take my eyes from the cloud. My breath caught, as wind wiped through the circle, blowing away the cloud.

I'd never imagined what a half-man, half-stag would look like. Never occurred to me. But as I stood there looking at Furfur, I realized he was exactly that. Shrewd eyes stared out from a man's face, and his upper body was covered with muscled bare flesh. But the antlers jutting from the sides of his head were so big I wondered how he held them up with his human neck. Four powerful flanks covered in fawn-colored fur made up the lower half of his body.

I stared in shock for a few moments, unsure what exactly I was supposed to do now.

"Well?" His voice was hoarse, like he'd smoked a dozen packs a day for a millennium.

"Um." I wanted to look over my shoulder for guidance, but even I knew better than to turn my back on a demon. "Hi."

A bolt of electricity zapped through the circle, crackling off the invisible barrier between us. I flinched and took a step back. He didn't move. "I don't have time for games. What is your bidding, mage?"

"Rhea?" I called over my shoulder.

"Yes?"

"Little help here?"

"You're doing great," she said.

"Ask him a question about your future," Giguhl said. "Furfur is required to tell the truth when bound by a triangle." I heard a scuffle behind me. Then, "Ow, hey!"

"We're conducting a lesson here, demon," Rhea scolded. "If you're going to give her the answers, you can leave."

"Sorry," Giguhl muttered.

This exchange made Furfur narrow his gaze at a spot behind me, which I assumed meant he'd finally noticed the audience. I figured having a Count of Irkalla pissed at him wouldn't do Giguhl any favors, so I waved my hands. "Hey, Bambi. Over here."

More lightning crackled through the circle, but Furfur transferred his attention toward me. "That's better," I said.

I rubbed my hands together. If this demon had to tell the truth about my future, then this was too good an opportunity to pass up. And I knew exactly what I was going to ask. "Okay, here's my question. Do I have a destiny?"

Furfur tilted his head and pursed his lips. As soon as I'd asked the question, I regretted it. What if he told me Maisie was right about the prophecy? Was I ready to handle that kind of pressure? Finally, after what felt like forever, Furfur smiled. "The answer to your question is . . ." He paused for dramatic effect. I held my breath. Not a sound could be heard in the room. "Yes."

I blew out my breath. Shit, leave it to me to ask a vague yes-or-no question. "No, what I meant is, what is my destiny?"

Furfur shook his head. "You have used up your question."

I frowned at the frustrating demon. "Rhea? Is he telling the truth?"

"Yep. You only get one."

I heard Giguhl mutter, "Smooth move."

"Shit," I said. "Fine. You can go now."

Nothing happened.

"Ahem." This from Rhea.

"Godsdammit," I said. I was so flustered by my mistake, I'd forgotten demons have to be sent back to Irkalla by their summoner. "*Idummu bara nadzu.*"

Another burst of thunder, another black cloud, and then Furfur disappeared.

"Well, that was lame," Giguhl said.

I turned and speared my demon with a glare. "You might have mentioned the one-question rule."

"How was I supposed to know you'd ask a stupid one?"

"Children," Rhea said, stepping between us. "Let's not focus on the negative. Sabina successfully summoned a Count of Irkalla without incident. I'd say this lesson was a success."

Success, my ass, I thought. Sure, I'd managed to summon and send away a demon, but I'd also embarrassed myself. Not knowing the protocol and unwritten rules frustrated me. Magic was a new world to me, and I felt like a stranger in a strange land. I didn't like it at all. My rational side told me experience would teach me these things, and experience was gained by making and learning from mistakes. But the impatient, inner-critic side—far stronger than the rational most days—was already busy with the

beatdown. How could I be so stupid? I spent years learning to be an assassin. I'd paid my dues and prided myself
on my skills. I wasn't some wet-behind-the-ears mage. I
was an ass-kicking vampire with five decades behind me.
I should have known better than to make a mistake like
that. The fact I had very little experience with magic didn't
matter. I expected myself to do better. And the prospect of
making more mistakes as the training continued made me
feel like a balloon filled to bursting.

"Sabina?" Rhea said. "What's going on in that head of
yours? You look like you're ready to kick someone's ass."

Yeah, I thought. My own.

I shrugged. "I was just going back over what happened.
Next time, I'd appreciate a little warning about what to
expect."

Rhea smiled. "How will you learn if I spoon-feed you
everything? Learning is done best by doing."

"But I screwed up."

She tilted her head. "No, you didn't. Screwing up would
have been getting us all killed. No, you learned something.
That's never a mistake."

"But you could have just told me—"

She waved a hand. "Sabina, let's clear one thing up
from the beginning. I'm not here to hold your hand and
ease you into mage life. This here's a magical boot camp.
You're going to make mistakes. Get used to that right now.
But I guarantee you'll never make the same mistake twice.
So quit beating yourself up for not knowing everything. I
don't expect it, and neither should you."

I nodded, but inside, every fiber of my being argued
she was wrong. Fifty-three years of being told I had to be
faster, smarter, and better than the average vampire didn't

go away overnight. My grandmother had drilled the quest for perfection into me from infancy. The granddaughter of the Alpha Dominae could never settle for average. Add my mixed blood to that equation and I had even less leeway. If I wanted respect and acceptance, I had to prove myself.

But Rhea was right about one thing; I wouldn't make the same mistake twice.

"I think that's enough for one evening," Rhea said. "Tomorrow night we'll get started on harnessing your Chthonic powers. Good work."

I nodded and headed for the door. Giguhl joined me in the hall. "Giguhl, I want you to give me a crash course in demons."

His eyebrows raised in surprise. "Really?"

I nodded. "If I'm going to be summoning them, I better start learning more about how you guys tick, right?"

Giguhl nodded absently. "Sabina, you do understand you're not going to learn everything about demons over-night, right? I don't even know everything, and I've been one for half a millennia."

I slapped him on the back. "I guess we better get started, then."

14

We ran into Maisie on the way back down to our rooms. Giguhl was busy chattering away about the complex structure of demon government as we walked back. Maisie exited the council chamber with a worried frown on her face and didn't notice us at first.

"Hey, Maisie," I called in greeting. She startled but quickly erased the frown lines from between her eyes.

"How'd training go?" She was smiling now but still seemed distracted.

I sighed. "Rhea certainly has some interesting teaching methods."

Maisie caught the sarcasm and frowned. "But you're making progress, right?" Her urgent tone told me she was worried about my answer. I tried to figure out her angle. Obviously, Maisie believed there was a direct link between my magic training and her prophecy that I was the Chosen. Of course she'd want me to learn quickly. Especially if the council was getting closer to a vote on the war.

"I guess so," I said, wanting to be positive but not overstate things. I didn't like the idea of Maisie or anyone else pinning hopes on me.

Maisie relaxed a fraction. "I want to hear all about it, but I'm on my way to a meeting with a diplomat from Queen Maeve's court."

I perked up. The mention of the Queen of the Fae made me think of Adam.

I wanted to stop her and ask if she'd had any word from him. I told myself this was mere curiosity over how his mission was going, but I knew better. I missed him. As a friend, of course. We'd spent so much time together over the last several weeks, I'd grown used to having him around. That was all. But after the way Maisie had given me the third degree about Adam the other night, I didn't want to encourage her.

"Is everything okay?" I asked instead.

Maisie shrugged. "As good as can be expected with the council at each other's throats. Now I have to go talk to the fae delegate and explain to them why we're no closer to a vote. The queen won't be pleased." She glanced at her watch. "I really need to get going. Let's chat later about your training, okay?"

I nodded absently as she hurried down the hall. As much as I didn't want to get involved with politics, I was concerned about the outcome of the council's vote. Despite Maisie's prophecy, I still believed there had to be another solution. Maisie, however, didn't have that luxury of waiting and seeing what happened. I might bitch and moan about having to learn magic and deal with Maisie and Rhea's theories about the prophecy, but I didn't have a fraction of the pressure Maisie was facing. The council relied on her visions to make decisions, and they relied on her diplomatic skills to keep their allies happy. Judging from the tense set of her shoulders as she walked away, those pressures weighed heavily.

"Hey, Maisie?" I called after her.

She stopped and turned, looking harried. "Yeah?"

"Good luck."

Her face brightened with surprise. "Thanks." She waved and hurried off.

I turned to find Giguhl watching me with an assessing look.

"What?"

"Nothing," he said, but obviously he was reading into the exchange I'd just had with my sister.

I was just fine with him holding his tongue. With that one little "good luck," it felt like the tide shifted. I could feel the pull of the vortex, sucking me further into mage life. Every day I got more and more involved, whether I liked it or not. But I preferred to fool myself for a little longer. At least until I understood the situation a bit more. Soon enough, the day would come when the mages would force my hand and demand I openly declare my support.

"Anyway." I changed the subject. "You were talking about the bureaucracy in Irkalla?"

He smiled knowingly but went with the non sequitur. "Oh, yeah, demons love the red tape. If they could, they'd make you wait for fifty forms in triplicate just for permission to take a crap."

He continued to dissect demon social structure as we made our way back to Maisie's apartment. I only half listened. In the back of my mind, I considered what would happen if the council voted for war. And as hard as I tried, I couldn't imagine anything positive about that outcome.

*   *   *

The next night I pushed my way through the crowd gathered in Vein's underbelly. My elbows put me at the receiving end of some insults and shoves, but I forged ahead.

Giguhl stood on one side of the pit where I'd fought Michael Romulus a few nights earlier. His scaly green chest glistened under the single lightbulb hanging from the concrete ceiling. The light illuminated the determination in his goat eyes.

I glanced to my left and saw his opponent, a smaller demon with a bat's face and a barbarian's body. As I watched, he spread his arms wide and emitted a high-pitched screech. I cringed and covered my ears, but everyone else went wild.

Giguhl spat in the corner, seeming unaffected by the other demon's showboating. It was a macho side of Giguhl I'd never seen before. As far as I could tell, the fight was just about to begin.

"Oh, hell, no!" I yelled over the noise. I started pushing my way to the right, trying to reach my demon. I'd agreed to this, and even made the call to Slade to set it up, but now, watching the wild crowd and the murder in the bat demon's eyes, I changed my mind.

"Giguhl!" I had to yell to be heard over those who felt the need to scream advice at my demon. "Giguhl!"

His head turned and he saw me. A huge smile spread over his face. "Sabina!"

I grabbed his green biceps and pulled him toward me. "I've changed my mind."

"What do you mean?"

"I don't think you should fight."

Giguhl snorted and gave me a friendly nudge. "Sabina, get real. I'm gonna kick his ass."

"No, you're not."

His eyes narrowed. "Why not?"

I paused, trying to figure that out for myself. "Because," I said finally.

Giguhl laughed. "Ah, you're worried about me."

"Am not," I muttered.

Slade made his way through the crowd to my side. I'd managed to avoid him since we got to the bar, but now he butted in. "What's going on?"

"He's not allowed to fight," I said.

Slade frowned and shook his head. "Once a challenge has been issued, the fight must proceed. It's the third rule of Demon Fight Club."

"Fuck the rules. He's my demon, and I revoke permission to fight."

"This is so embarrassing," Giguhl said. "Stop acting like my mother."

"What if you get hurt?"

"Sabina, I'm a five-hundred-year-old, grown-ass demon. The neighborhood I come from in Irkalla makes prison look like preschool. You think I can't defeat a freaking Defiler demon?"

My cheeks flamed under the weight of two male stares. Of course Giguhl could hold his own. To question his ability to fight was an insult. I sighed. "Fine, but you better kick his ass. I'm not playing nursemaid if you get hurt."

Giguhl smiled like the Cheshire cat. "Just sit back and watch the master at work."

Confident the fight would go on, Slade walked to the

center of the pit and held his hands up for silence. The crowd obeyed immediately.

"It is time to review the rules of Demon Fight Club. Rule number one?"

Everyone yelled, "You do not talk about Demon Fight Club!"

My mouth fell open. Was Slade for real with this shit?

"Two!"

I rolled my eyes. "Let me guess . . ."

The crowd shouted, "You do NOT talk about Demon Fight Club!"

"Excellent!" Slade nodded approvingly without a trace of irony. "Now for the rest. Number three: Once a challenge has been issued, the fight must proceed." He paused to shoot me a look. My jaw clenched as I glared at him, but the unoriginal bastard wasn't done. "Four: Only two demons to a fight. Five: No weapons, magical or mundane."

I glanced at Giguhl. That rule must explain the brass collar around his neck. Brass dulls magic, so if a demon tried to use a spell against an opponent they'd be shit out of luck.

"Six: Once a fight begins," Slade continued, "it must continue until someone begs for mercy."

He paused again. The tension in the room grew, and I knew I wasn't going to like rule number seven.

"And rule number seven is?" he said finally.

"No mercy!" The crowd really let loose then. All around, money exchanged hands as mages, vamps, and fae placed bets on the outcome. Looked like the crowd was favoring Bat Face in three-to-one odds.

Out of nowhere, the bell rang. My heart skipped a beat, and I grabbed Giguhl by the biceps.

"Giguhl, it's not too late to back out."

He looked down at me. "You heard the rules, Sabina. Now watch and learn."

With that, he jogged to the center of the ring to meet his foe. He bobbed and weaved as he went, like a demonic Rocky Balboa. I just prayed the Defiler demon's dirty appearance wasn't an indication of his fighting style.

The Defiler demon came out of the corner like an angry bull, heading straight for Giguhl's midsection. Surprisingly agile given his size, Giguhl jumped out of the way. The Defiler's momentum carried him right past and straight into the crowd, toppling a few mancies in the process. Giguhl threw his arms in the air and jogged in place, much to the crowd's delight. He ate up their attention, which, unfortunately, distracted him from his opponent.

"Giguhl, watch out!" I yelled. He didn't turn around in time to get out of the Defiler's way and ended up being knocked back twenty feet. The crowd finally caught on to the danger of being so close to the action. Everyone backed up a few steps, widening the circle.

The impact didn't faze Giguhl. He jumped up with a cocky smile. The Defiler responded with a lightning-fast volley of punches and kicks. The force of the attack knocked Giguhl to the ground. This time he rose more slowly. A stream of black blood dripped from his mouth.

"Fuck." I started to move in, regretting my decision to allow Giguhl to go through with this. Then I realized he'd never forgive me if I interfered. Demons and their fragile egos. So, I clenched my fists and settled for yelling advice to my demon.

"Go for the 'nads!"

"The eyes! The eyes!"

"No! You've got to keep your hands up!"

I felt someone's eyes on me. Looking around, I found Slade standing on the other side of the ring staring at me. He held my gaze for a moment, but the sickening sound of fist meeting flesh brought my attention back to the action.

Giguhl's lip swelled to the size of a roll of quarters and blood oozed down his chin. The Defiler came at him with another furious round of punches to Giguhl's midsection. The noise from the crowd was deafening, but I could have sworn I heard a couple of ribs crack.

I stepped forward, ready to put an end to the slaughter, but stopped when a terrified shriek ripped through the arena. The hair on my neck bristled at the bone-chilling sound. Somehow, Giguhl suddenly had the Defiler face-down on the ground. One black claw held the beast's face to the floor, and the other pulled one of its arms back so far the joint popped out of its socket.

"Yes!" I yelled.

Giguhl dropped the arm, which plopped to the ground like a piece of meat. Changing tactics, he pulled the Defiler's face off the ground by its oily black hair. With his other claw, Giguhl swiped at the demon's face, leaving streaks of blood pouring onto the concrete.

Despite my relief over Giguhl gaining the upper hand, I felt unsettled. I'm certainly no stranger to violence, but his savagery surprised even me. Over the bloody scene on the floor, Slade caught my eye again. His amused smile made me feel nauseous. I wanted Giguhl to win, but I couldn't reconcile this bloodthirsty fighter with the demon who would curl up next to me in cat form.

"Mercy!" The single word caused everyone in the room to gasp. It had come from the Defiler, who was now missing a nose. One of his eyes had rolled across the floor and landed near Slade's feet. He kicked it aside as he came into the ring.

He lifted Giguhl's arm in the air. "The winner is Giguhl!"

The crowd went wild again, chanting his name. "Gi-guhl, Gi-guhl!"

Slade waved his hands for silence. The room went silent except for the pitiful whimpers of the Defiler.

"Rule number seven?"

"No mercy!"

"So shall it be!" Slade slapped Giguhl on the back and gestured to a mage standing off to the right. The mage was a short, balding male with greasy black hair. He scowled and trudged into the ring to stand over the demon.

The Defiler begged for mercy, but the mage refused to look down at his demon. Instead, he performed a complex series of glyphs in the air before chanting the words to send the demon back to Irkalla. The Defiler disappeared, leaving a pool of black blood on the concrete.

Giguhl glanced at me with a huge smile. I tried to smile back, but the whole thing didn't sit well with me.

Looked like my little demon was all grown up.

15

*W*hile Giguhl cleaned up after the fight, I sipped on a Bloody Magdalene in the bar. Earl had gone light on the vodka, which was fine with me because I needed the blood more.

I wasn't sure where Slade got his blood, but it wasn't the blood-bank crap Maisie insisted I drink. Knowing Slade, he probably had some black-market source that supplied him with fresher blood than Maisie's supply. But even Slade's stuff had the chemical tang of anticoagulant. I still craved blood straight from the vein, but after the fight with Romulus, I figured Maisie's rules about not feeding from humans might end up saving me some trouble.

In one corner of the bar, a nymph sat on a male vampire's lap. Her makeup had been applied with a trowel, and her hair had been teased into a big blond rat's nest. Her legs were encased in ripped fishnet stockings, and I could see the garter peeking out from under her fuchsia pleather skirt. She giggled at something the vamp said, but the emotion didn't reach her eyes.

As I watched like a voyeur, the male ran a pale hand up her thigh and squeezed. He wore a large gold ring on his middle finger with a red stone in the center. The faery grimaced at his groping hands, but the smile was back in place by the time he looked at her again.

Memories of another nymph weighed heavily. We'd buried Vinca less than two weeks ago. But before I'd come into her life and gotten her killed at the vineyard, she'd served time in the faery porn industry. Watching the nymph on the vampire's lap now, I wondered if Vinca had ever worn that hopeless expression. The idea made my fists clench. I wanted to go over and rip the nymph from the male's lap. I wanted to shake her and tell her there had to be a better way to make a living. I wanted to warn her to get the fuck out of the city before it ate her alive.

Yet even as I willed myself to rise, I saw the male lift the top of the ring. From it, he withdrew a small green pill. The faery's glossy pink lips spread in a genuine smile—the first spark of genuine happiness I'd seen on her face. The male lifted the pill to her lips, and her tongue darted out to take it. She swallowed it greedily.

As the two proceeded to tongue-joust, I turned away. Who was I kidding? I wasn't anyone's savior. I certainly didn't have any room to preach to others about how to live their lives.

I finished the drink and motioned Earl to bring me another. I saw Giguhl come out of the back room and head toward me. As he passed, several patrons stopped him to shake his hand. Two nymphs, dressed in the same hooker couture as the one I'd been watching, hung from his biceps like gaudy ornaments. A high, feminine laugh caught my attention. It was the other nymph. She didn't notice my stare. She was too busy leading the vampire to a back room by his dick.

"What up, player?" Giguhl said, coming to a stop in front of me. The nymphettes didn't give us so much as a sideways glance. Giguhl preened under their adoration.

"Hey, G. You ready to head out?" I said.

His scraggly black eyebrows lowered in a frown. "But Tansy and Cinnamon invited me to a little party."

I shooed the nymphs away, ignoring their whines, and pulled Giguhl away for a little sidebar. "G, you know those nymphs are prostitutes, right?"

He paused for a second, and I worried I'd just crushed his special dream of a ménage à fae. My worry was short-lived, though, because the next thing I knew he threw back his horned head and howled with laughter. "Of course I know that! Why do you think I'm so excited?"

"You don't mind paying for sex?"

He cocked his head to the side. "Sabina, I'm a demon. And the last time I checked, there wasn't any hot demon-ess ass available on this side. So, I'm making do with what's available. Plus, my room at Maisie's has access to the Temptation channel."

I frowned. "The Temptation channel?"

He nodded eagerly. "I can't believe I ever wasted time with home shopping when I could have been watching porn twenty-four/seven."

I pinched the bridge of my nose and prayed for patience.

"Anyhoo, Tansy and Cinnamon are all in to try some new maneuvers I learned from *Lawrence of the Labia*."

I opened and closed my mouth a couple of times like a

confused carp. I had absolutely no idea how to respond. So I just nodded and said, "Make it quick."

"Yes!" Giguhl pumped a claw into the air. He turned to go, but I grabbed his arm.

"Wait, how are you going to pay for it?"

Giguhl dug a wad of bills from his pocket. "Slade gave me my cut after the fight."

I gritted my teeth at Slade's presumption. Something told me he usually paid a demon's keeper directly instead of the demon. The fact he'd gone straight to Giguhl told me he was trying to buy Giguhl's affections, as it were. "Fine. Just don't spend it all in one place."

As my demon skipped off with two fae hookers, I plopped back down on the stool and ordered another round. Looked like I was in for a long night.

It didn't take long for Slade to appear, ready to give me shit. He wore another expensive suit and a calculating expression. He sat on the stool next to mine without asking if I minded. I did, of course, but it was better to feign disinterest with a guy like Slade. The minute they knew they got under your skin, they had the upper hand.

"That demon of yours is going to make both of us a lot of money."

But at what cost?

Something triumphant shone behind Slade's blue eyes. But was he celebrating Giguhl's contributions to his bank account, or the fact he'd maneuvered me back into his life?

"Don't get any ideas," I said, facing him. "My debt is paid. He's not fighting anymore."

"Hmm," he said. "Giguhl seemed to think otherwise when I spoke to him a few minutes ago."

I shrugged. "Doesn't matter," I bluffed. "He does what I say."

He pursed his lips and signaled Earl for a drink. "Listen, Sabina, I know I screwed you over in L.A. And I'm truly sorry. But you have to understand, I had no choice. I'd already decided that would be my last job before the Dominae told me you were going to work with me. I was burned out. Totally fried. I had to leave."

"Regardless, you screwed me over. You could have just taken your half of the payday and skipped town. No harm, no foul. But you didn't do that. You took it all."

"I needed it all. I'd already set up buying this bar, and I needed the entire amount to start over. I'm sorry you got screwed, but I didn't have a choice."

I turned a glare on him. "We all have choices, Slade. And all choices have consequences. In this case, the consequence was me hating you. Deal with it."

He sighed and nodded. "Fair enough. But if you want my opinion, this has nothing to do with the money. Not really."

I lifted an eyebrow. "This should be good."

He leaned in close, like he was going to whisper a secret. "I saw the hope in your eyes when I left you that evening."

"Right, the hope I'd be ten grand richer."

He shook his head. "Don't fool yourself. I know the look of a female who has expectations beyond one night, and, sweetheart, you had it."

I choked out a laugh. "Don't flatter yourself, asshole. The sex was fine, but I wasn't looking for a relationship."

"Bullshit."

I shrugged. "I'll admit I liked the idea of us maybe teaming up on more assignments."

He shot me a dubious look.

"Okay, fine, maybe a partnership with benefits. But I wasn't looking for love, Slade. Give me some credit."

He still looked unconvinced but let it go. "Regardless, I think you need to get over it. That was thirty years ago. We've both changed. You're not your grandmother's naive little soldier anymore. Admit it, you understand now why I had to get out."

I sighed. "Look, I might understand, but I still don't trust you."

The side of his mouth curled into a smile. "I don't suspect you trust anyone."

I inclined my head. "Touché."

"I also suspect you could use a friend outside the mage race right about now."

I frowned. "What's that supposed to mean?"

"I can't imagine growing up in the Alpha Dominae's household fostered a love of all things mage. Especially given your mixed blood. One might imagine your grandmother drilled those lessons in extra good to make sure they stuck."

I neither confirmed nor denied these suspicions, but he was dead-on. "Go on."

"I'm just saying. Maybe it would help to have someone not in the mage fold to talk to. Someone familiar. Someone who's been in a similar situation."

I held up a hand. "Wait a second. You're not seriously suggesting we become friends."

He looked me dead in the eyes. "That's exactly what I'm suggesting."

"Ha! Please recall a few minutes ago when I told you I don't trust you. Isn't trust the foundation of all friendship?"

He tilted his head. "You don't believe that any more than I do. You can't ever truly know or trust anyone, can you? Look where that got you with the Dominae. You trusted them your whole life, and look what happened. At least with me, you know what you're getting into. I'm a son-of-a-bitch, no doubt about it. But I also know this town, and I understand the politics among the races. I could be a very good friend to have."

I narrowed my eyes at him. There was a catch, of course. "What's in it for you?"

He took a sip from the scotch Earl set in front of him. "You said yourself you thought we could be partners. Maybe we should explore that option."

"What kind of partners?"

He shrugged and set down his tumbler. "I need someone I can trust with some sensitive jobs. Light stuff, nothing you couldn't handle."

"Ah," I said. "Why me? Guy like you probably has dozens of flunkies begging to do your dirty work."

"No one with the kind of training you've had. Plus, you're new in town. No loyalties or history with any of my competitors."

I sighed and nodded. Before I teamed up with Slade on my first official assassination, the Dominae had used me as an Enforcer. Shaking down vamps who hadn't paid their tithes. Roughing up those who needed a message to get back into line. So I knew exactly the kind of work he was talking about. Probably, he also wouldn't mind putting my assassin skills to work every now and then to knock off a competitor or two.

I didn't trust Slade. We'd established that. But I had to admit to myself his offer was tempting. After all, my savings would run out eventually, and I currently had no source of income. Padding my nest egg with some side work intrigued me. But working for Slade didn't. Besides that, I found myself cringing at the idea of making a living as an Enforcer again. One of the appeals of coming to New York was getting a fresh start. If I agreed to Slade's offer, I'd be right back where I started thirty years ago.

"Look, Slade, I understand there might be certain benefits to the partnership you're offering. But I'm gonna pass."

His eyes narrowed. "Gonna pass on working for me, or on being friends in general?"

I stopped and thought about it. Making an enemy of Slade wouldn't do me any favors. I had to play this the right way. "Working for you. I'm fine right now. That might change at some point, but for now I don't need the work. As for being friends, well, I'm willing to work on not wanting to kick your ass every time I see you."

Slade laughed. "Beggars can't be choosers, I guess."

I shrugged and took a sip of my drink. A small smile hovered on my lips. Though I wasn't ready for Slade to be my BFF—far from it—it was kind of nice hanging out with a vampire again. Especially one who wasn't loyal to the Dominae.

"So I guess it would be too much to ask for the benefits you mentioned earlier, huh?" His expression was serious, but the devilish light in his eye hinted he was trying to provoke me.

"You would be correct. But I'm sure one of your nymphs wouldn't mind helping you out."

Slade set his elbows on the table. His posture was relaxed, as if he was enjoying our banter as much as I was starting to. "I prefer my bedmates a little less fragile. But then, you already knew that."

A flash of Slade slamming into me against a wall pushed its way into my mind. I blinked away the image. Definitely not a healthy train of thought.

"Oh, I don't know," I said. "In my experience, nymphs are stronger than they look." I was referring, of course, to Vinca. Another unhealthy train of thought, but a damned sight better than thinking about fucking Slade again.

At that moment, a door to the back rooms opened and Giguhl stumbled out looking dazed, with a blue satin demi-bra hanging around his neck. The stupid grin on his face indicated the nymphs he'd disappeared with weren't too fragile, either.

"On that note," I said, "I better get my demon home. He's had a big night."

Slade nodded. "Sabina?"

I stopped. "Yeah?"

"I'm glad you don't want to kick my ass anymore."

I allowed the smile to show this time. "Just make sure it stays that way."

He saluted me with his scotch. "Yes, ma'am."

16

Our first stop after leaving Vein was to grab some cash for the cab ride home. I finally found one on Forty-second Street near the flashing lights of Times Square. But when I entered my pass code into the ATM, the thing started beeping manically.

"What's wrong?" Giguhl asked, his voice muffled by the carrier and the cacophony of Times Square at night. He'd been so spent from his quality time with Tansy and Cinnamon that he didn't even argue about switching back to cat from for the trip home.

I slammed a palm on the machine. "It ate my card!"

"Uh-oh."

I'd have chosen a more colorful response. As it was, I shocked several passersby with a string of invectives against the Dominae. They'd obviously found my secret accounts. Freakin' great. Now I couldn't get to any of my money.

"What are you going to do?"

I turned my back on the traitorous machine. "I have no

clue." A passing tourist shot me an odd look for speaking to my handbag, so I ducked my head and kept walking.

My boots struck an angry percussion on the sidewalk. A chilly wind whipped down the street, bringing with it the sour scent of sewer. On the street, cabs honked like angry geese. And on the sidewalk, people bustled past like determined arrows headed for a target.

Freaking New York, I thought. Los Angeles had smog and traffic, too. But it also had a temperate climate, beaches, and adequate parking.

Giguhl shifted in the bag. "Sabina?"

"Yeah," I said.

"Where are we going?"

"I have no idea." Pressure built in my head, my lungs. I wondered if this was what the proverbial fish out of water felt like.

The scent hit me just as I crossed in front of an alley. Smoky, spicy, and sweet. I stopped in my tracks and inhaled deeply. I looked to my left and saw a neon sign down the alley advertising The Happy Hookah Lounge. The scent of smoke and blood summoned me into the darkness like a bent finger.

Smoking blood was a popular activity in certain circles of the vamp community. My own grandmother liked to lace her tobacco with a little opium for an additional high. The scent had followed me for most of my life, clinging to my clothes and hair when I came home from vamp bars.

After walking around the swirling vortex of motion that was New York, the reminder of home was bittersweet. As tempting as it was to indulge in a little emotional wound prodding, I continued on past the alley. Pretending I belonged among vampires didn't cut it anymore. I'd never belonged among them, and trying to do so now might end up putting me in the path of more of the Dominae's assassins.

Besides, I'd had enough of a walk down memory lane tonight to last me for a while. Talking to Slade was . . . interesting. I still didn't trust him. But I was willing to admit that my old grudge didn't hold as much water now. Slade might have screwed me over and pulled a disappearing act on the Dominae, but I betrayed them. It didn't matter that they betrayed me first. Now I understood how my blind loyalty to the Dominae had guided my decisions. And now, after all these years, Slade and I were on the same side again. Funny how life works sometimes. So funny I would have cried if I'd been the crying type.

A cab zoomed past, reminding me I should probably head back to Maisie's place.

"Hey, G?"

"What?"

I grimaced. The goddess save me from surly feline demons. "How much money you have left from the fight?"

Silence.

"Giguhl?"

I swear I heard a sigh come from the carrier. I lifted the bag up to look into one of the mesh side panels. A pair of guilty cat eyes stared back. "Well?"

He scooted back from the panel. "Five bucks."

"What?" I shouted. "You won a grand!"

"Those nymphs bewitched me! They made me do naughty things, Sabina. Naughty, expensive things."

I cursed. "Well, how are we supposed to get home now?" Ever since I'd arrived in the city, I'd relied on cabs to get around. Consequently, I hadn't really paid attention to little details like street names. But I knew enough to guess five bucks wouldn't get us very far.

"How about the subway?" Giguhl said in a small voice. I glared into the carrier. He cringed back. "I'm just sayin'."

With a disgusted sigh, I swung the bag down roughly. A thump and a "Hey" followed the move, but I ignored it. Instead, I looked around for another solution. Sure enough, not twenty feet from where I stood, a descending staircase led into the bowels of Manhattan. What was worse, I spotted Stryx sitting on a lamppost nearby. He screeched my name and blinked his red eyes as if in challenge.

"Awesome." I took off toward the sign like an inmate headed toward death row. It's not that the subway scared me. Being a vampire with secret mage skills and an assassin to boot tended to make one immune to trivial worries like muggings or sex offenders. But for some reason, the idea of sitting in an enclosed tube, barreling through underground tunnels, freaked my shit.

I reached the bottom of the stairs and figured out how to pay for a card that would allow me access to the tunnels. Once through the turnstile, though, I entered a labyrinth. At any moment I expected a freakin' minotaur to jump out at me. Instead, I just got jostled by impatient mortals who understood the mysterious caverns.

A map covered in multicolored lines hung on the wall. It looked like there was a subway stop right near Prytania Place, so I was in luck. Two trains went that way, so I mentally flipped a coin and chose the C train.

I followed the signs to the track for the C and found myself standing on an empty platform. After the constant barrage of humans and the scent of their blood teasing me, I appreciated the break.

"Looks like we're early for the train," I said to Giguhl.

"Are you sure this is right? Shouldn't there be more people?"

I plopped down on a bench. "The map said the C will take us almost to Maisie's front door."

"Since no one's around, will you let me out of my prison?"

I looked around and shrugged. "Okay, but just for a minute."

I unzipped the bag. I'd barely finished when Giguhl's little bald head appeared. "Freedom!" He took a deep breath. "Eww, it smells like ass down here."

I picked him up out of the bag so he could sit on my lap. "Stay."

His ears twitched, and he cocked his head to look at me. "I'm not a dog, you know."

I laughed. "Sorry. When you're the cat it's hard to remember you're really a badass demon."

He sniffed, making his little nose twitch. "Damned straight, sister. I kicked that Defiler's ass tonight."

"Yes, you did. Where'd you learn to fight like that? I wouldn't think a Mischief demon would have wicked street-fighting skills."

He plopped his butt down on my lap. "It's precisely because I'm a Mischief that I needed to learn how to fight. Irkalla's got this stupid caste system, and we're low on the totem pole. It was either learn to fight or become some Lust demon's butt boy, you know?"

"In a weird way, yeah, I kind of do." Granted, I'd never had one of my classmates try to sodomize me, but I understood having to defend myself from bullies. Growing up a mixed-blood among vampires wasn't exactly a cakewalk.

Despite my own status as the granddaughter of the Alpha Dominae, my classmates found plenty of opportunity to remind me I'd never be accepted.

"Sabina?" Giguhl said. "Are you sure this is the right train? Seems like one should have come by now."

"Hmm, you might be right." I rose, ready to put Giguhl back in his bag so I could go find the A train platform. Right then, a screech echoed through the tunnel. The hair on the back of my neck prickled. The sound hadn't come from an inbound train. Instead, it sounded suspiciously similar to Stryx. I stilled, looking around for the owl, but the tunnels were now eerily quiet. Surely I'd been hearing things. What would an owl be doing down in the subway?

Shrugging off the feeling, I reached for the bag. Giguhl didn't protest and ducked back inside. I left the top open, figuring he'd feel less confined that way.

I'd almost made it to the stairs back up to the entrance when a burst of magical energy hit me from behind. It shoved me forward, tripping on the first step. Out of instinct, I dropped the bag and swiveled, grabbing the gun from my waistband as I went.

The demon leaned against a concrete column next to the tracks. His posture was casual, but his appearance sent cold sweat down my back.

He was about the same size as Giguhl, but that was as far as the similarities went. This guy had black leathery wings, with red thorns at the tips. Ram's horns jutted from his forehead and curled back over his massive head. A red leather kilt wrapped around his black hips. Scaly black skin covered the intimidating bulk of his torso and arms.

I aimed the gun between his glowing red eyes. "Identify yourself."

He chuckled, a low, mocking sound. "You won't live long enough for it to matter."

I cocked my head to the side. "Humor me."

"I am Eurynome." He raised a black claw and a zing of energy sent the gun flying from my grip and into his. Eurynome caught and crushed the metal in one claw. My stomach twisted with fear. Vampires or mages I could handle. But demons were almost impossible to kill. And I knew enough about demon summoning to know I couldn't banish him without a circle.

"Uh, Giguhl?"

"What?" Giguhl hissed from behind the trash can where he'd taken cover.

"Demon form! Now!"

The trash can he was behind flew across the platform, and a puff of smoke signaled his change from cat into demon.

Eurynome's red eyes moved from me to Giguhl. I smiled. "Say hello to my little demon friend. Get him, Giguhl!"

Giguhl growled and launched at the other demon. He barely made it three steps before Eurynome launched a bolt of demon magic that sent Giguhl's body flying into a column. He bounced off the concrete, leaving it cracked, and flopped to the ground. I ran over and knelt next to him. He groaned and opened his eyes. The horizontal pupils dilated and expanded as he shook off the daze. My smugness melted away in favor of fear. If Giguhl couldn't touch Eurynome, what chance did I have?

As I tried to help Giguhl up, Eurynome threw back his head and laughed. The sound shook the walls around us. "Stupid girl," Eurynome sneered. "Did you really think a pitiful Mischief demon could defeat the Duke of Death?"

I looked at Giguhl and mouthed, "Duke of Death?"

For the first time since I'd known him, I saw real fear in Giguhl's eyes. He nodded. "He's right, Sabina. There's no way I can beat him. He's too strong."

I clenched my teeth and took a deep breath. No way was I going down like this—killed on a subway platform by a demon wearing a kilt. "Bullshit. We can do this together."

Giguhl shook his head sadly. "There's no way."

"Listen to your minion, Chosen. Accept your fate."

"Like hell." I narrowed my eyes and crouched low, ready to fight for our lives. The familiar surge of adrenaline coursed through me. I might die tonight, but I'd die doing something I loved. Before I could take two steps, Eurynome hit me with a ball of something that short-circuited my brain and left every nerve ending on fire. I collapsed into a heap on the ground, totally helpless.

"Sabina, no!" Giguhl's voice sounded far away, like he was speaking through a tin can attached to a string. I tried to open my eyes, but I didn't have the power. I felt like millions of fire ants swarmed over my skin. They burrowed into my brain, my stomach, my throat.

Vaguely, I heard the sounds of a struggle. An enraged roar broke through the haze. Through the pain, I felt the air shift. A blast of heat and energy washed over my sensitive skin. I curled up against the onslaught of sensation. I raised my hands to block out what sounded like two freight trains colliding nearby.

Lost in my own agony, I didn't notice when the tunnel went silent. I groaned as the world shifted. A rhythmic rocking motion followed. The movement intensified the pain, but I was helpless to stop it. A panicked voice yelled at me to hold on.

So this is death.

"Sabina?" That voice. Vaguely familiar, yet echoed as if the owner spoke through a tunnel.

"Wake up."

Can't. I'm dead.

"Open your eyes, dammit!" A sting on my cheek.

I swatted at the annoying prickle of pain. I didn't want to feel anything anymore. I prayed for numbness to wrap me in its ambivalent arms.

"Get her some blood."

Mmmm, yes. Blood.

"Stick it under her nose."

Pour it in my mouth.

The ferric scent of blood tickled my nose. My gums throbbed. My fangs pricked my tongue, followed by the coppery taste of my own blood.

"She's coming around."

My face scrunched against light coming through my eyelids. For a moment, I saw the pink spiderweb veins there. Someone wrenched my lid open. I jerked away, hissing at the unholy bright light.

"C'mon, open up for me."

Fingers dug into my jaw, forcing my mouth open. Then my throat filled with a pool of blood. Choking, I fought against my captor. "Swallow!"

The mass of liquid forged a painful path down my throat. Once it cleared my airway, I jerked up, coughing and sputtering. My eyes flew open. At first all I saw was a wall of white light. I blinked against the pain. Then, slowly, I could make out shadowed figures leaning over me.

Consciousness was a blessing and a curse. Blessing because I knew I was alive. Curse because I wished I were dead. My skin sizzled with pain, like I'd bathed in acid. Someone screamed. Me? Must have been, because my throat suddenly burned along with the rest of me.

"Is there anything you can do to stop it?" A male voice. Orpheus?

"No," the first voice said. "The spell he used was meant to paralyze her. It won't kill her, but right about now she probably wishes it would."

"Can you ease her pain?" Despite my pain and confusion, I recognized this voice was Maisie's. Something clicked in my fevered brain, and I tried to speak, to beg Maisie for help, but no words came out.

"The best thing I can do for her right now is knock her out again," the first female said—Rhea. "The blood we just gave her will help her body fight off the spell, but it will work faster if she's not also fighting the pain. When she wakes up, I can give her something to regain her strength, but until then we have to just wait for it to run its course."

Maisie sighed. "Okay."

I tried to struggle. Not because I didn't want an end to the pain, but because there was one voice I hadn't heard. Where was Giguhl?

But my struggles were useless. My body had become my prison. A new, intense pinch of pain came from somewhere near my elbow. Blessed unconsciousness descended.

"You're one lucky lady," Rhea said cheerfully.

I glared at her, feeling anything but. My extremities still prickled like they'd fallen asleep. My skin was sensitive even to the slightest breeze. I was so weak I couldn't lift my arms, and my head hurt so bad even the slightest light made my eyes feel like they would explode.

Rhea sat on the edge of the bed. Her smooth, cool hands picked up my wrist to check my pulse. She kept her eyes on her watch for a moment and then set my hand down again with a nod. "You'll be up and around in no time." She gave my arm a little pat.

I gritted my teeth together. My fangs were throbbing. "I need blood."

Rhea patiently smiled, as if she was used to dealing with surly patients. "We're having some delivered."

"Not the bagged shit. I need fresh."

"Not possible. Even if we'd allow it, you're too weak to subdue anyone long enough to bite them. Besides, bagged blood is just as nutritious as the fresh stuff."

I wanted to yell, but I didn't have the energy for a losing battle. As much as I hated the taste of Maisie's bagged blood, it was more important that I regain my energy fast. But since I had to wait for even that, I figured I'd get some answers.

"Where's Giguhl?"

"He's resting. The fight with Eurynome took a lot out of him."

I digested this. Relief he was alive flooded me, followed by awe. Somehow, Giguhl had managed to defeat Eurynome and carried my body out of harm's way despite his own injuries. I owed that demon my life. "Is he wounded?"

"Yes. But not gravely. He just needs rest."

"He killed Eurynome." Not a question. I figured that was the only way Giguhl could have gotten us out of there in one piece.

Rhea shook her head. "No. He threw him in front of a train and hauled ass before Eurynome could untangle himself from the wreckage."

A prickle of fear skittered down my back. "He's still on the loose?"

"I don't think so. Whoever summoned him probably sent him back to Irkalla after he failed."

I swallowed and asked the question I'd been avoiding. "A mage sent him?"

Rhea paused, her expression grave. "Yes. Only a powerful mage could summon a demon of that magnitude and control him outside a circle."

I tamped down the emotions this revelation brought up—anger, frustration, fear. "Any idea who?" I tried to keep my tone casual, but it broke on the last word.

Rhea sat down again, her demeanor reassuring. "Not yet. But Maisie and Orpheus have the Guards investigating. We'll find whoever did this, and they will be punished."

We both knew her words were hollow. Any mage powerful enough to pull off something like this would also be smart enough to cover their tracks. But they sounded nice.

"Do you have any idea why a mage would be out to get you?" Rhea asked evenly.

I snorted. "I could ask you the same question. I have a long list of enemies, but I didn't think I'd been here long enough to actively recruit any mages to it."

Rhea opened her mouth to respond, but Maisie ducked her head inside the door with Damara behind her carrying a cooler.

"You're awake. How are you feeling?" Maisie asked, rushing to my side.

"Shitty, but I'll live."

Maisie smiled, but worry hovered behind her eyes. "Thank the goddess for that."

"Sabina and I were just discussing the whys of the situation," Rhea said.

Maisie grimaced. "Sabina, don't worry about all that right now. You need to focus on getting better."

I knew she was just worried, but her don't-worry-your-little-head demeanor bugged me. "Maisie, I'm fine."

She shot me a look that implied otherwise.

I frowned at her. "Fine, I'm a little weak. Once I get some blood in me I'll be good as new." I shot a significant glance at the cooler in Damara's hands. The girl stood so quietly I'd almost forgotten about her, but I hadn't forgotten about the blood.

"Regardless, you have to believe we're doing everything in our power to find out who's responsible." As she spoke, Maisie motioned Damara forward. The girl handed Maisie two pints of blood. I watched her movements eagerly even as I steeled myself to argue with Maisie.

"Thanks, Damara," I said. The girl nodded curtly as she set down the cooler.

"Damara, will you please go check on Giguhl?" Rhea said.

The girl hesitated. "Are you sure you don't need my help here? I could clean up this mess." She motioned to medical supplies and potion bottles littering the room.

Rhea shook her head. "I have it under control. Make sure Giguhl has plenty of ice, please." I'm not sure if Damara understood why Rhea wanted her to go, but I did. No doubt my discussion with Maisie was about to get pretty heated, and the fewer witnesses to that, the better.

The girl paused, looking like she wanted to argue more, but under Rhea's decisive gaze she finally nodded.

"Tell Giguhl I'll be in to check on him soon," I said as she made her way to the door. She didn't look at me as she jerked her head in the affirmative and left.

Once she was gone, I turned back to Maisie. "No offense, Maisie, but someone sent that demon to kill *me*. In case you've forgotten, killing is my game. And I'll be damned if I'm going to sit on the sidelines."

Maisie paused in the process of pouring a pint into a glass. She looked at me for a few moments. I stayed silent as she weighed her options. I'd stated my case, and arguing further would lessen its impact. Maisie might not have known me as well as she'd like, but she knew my background. The mage who sent Eurynome after me fucked up big-time. If they'd been smart, they'd have sent someone who didn't hesitate to kill. Someone who didn't play games with their victims. You want to kill an assassin? You get the job done. The fact I'd escaped death meant only one thing: I wouldn't rest until the mage who tried to

kill me was killed. And if that mage was as good as Rhea
claimed, they had to know that. Which meant Eurynome's
attack wouldn't be an isolated incident.

Finally, Maisie sighed and stuck a straw into the glass.
I grabbed it and pulled out the straw. Then I tipped back
the glass. I was ravenous. So hungry the cold, tinny taste
barely registered. While I'd drained the glass, Maisie
started talking.

"Sabina, I know you're angry. I know you want revenge.
But the situation is complicated. You have to understand.
We have laws and protocol we have to follow. Besides at-
tempting to murder the sister of the council's leader, this
mage is also responsible for the death of dozens of humans
who died on the train that crashed into Eurynome. We
managed to cover up the incident so the mortal authorities
didn't catch on to the supernatural aspects of the wreck.
But the council wants to bring this mage to justice. You
can't just run out and start shooting my people. We'll in-
vestigate, track down the responsible party, and then make
sure justice is served. And we'll do so without more inno-
cents getting caught in the cross-fire."

I lowered the glass and heaved a big sigh. Goddess save
me from the mage moral code. For them, everything had
the gray tinge of moral relativism. But I'd grown up in a
world of black-and-white. An eye for an eye, a bullet for
a bullet. Plus, back in L.A., a few dead mortals wouldn't
have warranted a discussion. To vampires, that was no different than flies lying dead on sticky paper.

But here was the rub: I had zero clue who was after
me. I didn't even know more than a handful of mages, and
those not very well. I needed the council's resources, but to
use them, I had to play by the council's rules.

Maisie held out a hand for the empty glass, ready to re-fill it. Frustrated, I shook my head and grabbed the bag of blood from her hand. My fangs ripped into the bag's silicone walls. I squeezed with my hand, forcing the blood to spray into my mouth. The cold liquid filled my gut, making it feel slushy, but soon enough my cells would go to work. They'd work as hard as my brain was trying to find a way to get around the council.

"If I might make a suggestion?" Rhea said quietly.

Maisie and I turned to her. She came forward, looking thoughtful. "Let the Guards do their job." I opened my mouth to argue, but she held up a hand. "In the meantime, use this. Harness all that restless anger and need for action and channel it into your magic lessons."

I tossed the empty bag on the table with a huff. "If I'm going to work off my restless anger, as you call it, I'd be better off entering Slade's fight club. At least then I'd be able to punch something."

Rhea cocked an eyebrow. "Child, you haven't even begun to know the physicality of harnessing serious magic. Summoning demons? Child's play compared to what you'll be able to do once you tap into your Chthonic powers."

I narrowed my gaze and watched Rhea. She looked convinced of what she was saying. If she was right, I might be able to fight fire with fire the next time the mysterious mage came after me. I had to admit the idea appealed.

"Okay, fine." I looked at Maisie. "But I want updates. You get any leads, I want to know about it."

Maisie nodded.

Rhea wasn't done, however. "I should warn you that if we're going to ramp up your training, I'll expect long hours and total commitment. We don't have time to waste with you arguing about my methods."

Already the blood was working its own magic. My skin no longer crawled. My headache eased and my stomach settled. I itched to get out of the bed and move. And now Rhea had offered me a focus for all the energy building in my muscles. I was almost praying she'd put me through the wringer to keep my mind occupied while the council waded through its own red tape. My lips curled into a smile.

"Sounds good." I turned to Maisie. "You got any more blood in that thing?"

An hour later, I felt almost good as new. Four pints of blood and having a goal did wonders for my energy. I knocked on Giguhl's door softly. I needed to thank him for saving my life, but part of me hoped he was asleep. Gratitude wasn't a familiar emotion for me. Generally, I avoided asking for or needing help as much as possible. Back in L.A. this approach wasn't difficult, since most vampires wouldn't help a mixed-blood anyway. But ever since my life got turned upside down, I'd found myself in a position to need help again and again. Not that I'd admit it out loud. In fact, up until tonight's near-death experience, I'd managed to brush off the help Adam or anyone else had given me as unwanted or unneeded after the fact.

"Yeah?" Giguhl's voice sounded through the door, weaker than it should have been.

I cracked open the door and peeked inside. "You up for company?"

A lump in the bed shifted, accompanied by the sound

of sheets sliding together and a soft gasp. "As long as you aren't going to yell at me."

I frowned and moved farther into the room. "Why would I do that?"

As I got closer, my eyes adjusted to the darkened room. Giguhl rested against a mound of pillows with the covers pulled up to his chin. The bed was too short for his seven-foot frame, so his hooves jutted from the bottom of the covers and hung off the end of the bed. He looked pitiful. He shrugged and wouldn't meet my eyes.

"It's my fault you got hurt."

My eyebrows shot together and my eyes narrowed. "No, it's not. Why would you think something dumb like that?"

He relaxed a fraction, presumably because I hadn't started shouting. His eyes moved in my direction, but he still wouldn't meet my gaze directly. "You told me to fight Eurynome, and I failed."

I couldn't believe he was blaming himself for that. "Giguhl, you saved us. When it happened doesn't matter. And as your master or whatever, I forbid you to blame yourself. Especially when you're the one who's still injured."

He finally looked at me then. The gratitude I saw there made me want to squirm. I hadn't done anything except state the facts. I changed the subject. "So what's hurt exactly?"

Giguhl cringed. "It's embarrassing."

"More embarrassing than getting shot in the ass?"

He nodded gravely.

"I promise I won't make fun of you."

He looked unsure. "Swear it."

I rolled my eyes and made a cross-my-heart gesture.

"Okay, see, it's like this: Eurynome is a big dude, right? Probably as heavy as the train that crashed into him."

I nodded. He was exaggerating, of course, but I got his drift. "Sure."

I swear I saw a faint spot of pink appear on his cheeks. "Well, it seems during our fight, Eurynome hit me with a spell to weaken my healing ability and lower my resistance to injury."

I rotated my hand in the air. The suspense was killing me.

Giguhl inhaled and closed his eyes. Then, on the exhalation, he rushed ahead. "When I threw him, well . . . I pulled my nut sack."

I stared at him in shocked silence. A laugh bubbled up in my throat. I didn't speak, knowing it would escape if I tried. I swallowed and focused on keeping my features schooled into a sympathetic expression.

Faced with silence, Giguhl forged ahead. "Rhea said the official name is a scrotal hernia."

A snort escaped. Giguhl's head shot up and his eyes narrowed. I held my breath, but my lips trembled from the effort.

"You said you wouldn't laugh!" Giguhl crossed his arms and glared.

I shook my head and tried to look innocent.

His voice took on a serious, paternal tone. "Testicle injuries are no laughing matter, Sabina."

That did it. Laughter exploded from me, so forceful I doubled over with it.

"Hey!"

I didn't respond. I was too busy holding my sides. On

some level, I understood it wasn't nice to laugh at his injury since he got it trying to save me. But I couldn't help it.

"You're an ass," he declared finally. He crossed his arms indignantly, but his wince ruined the effect.

Realizing he was actually in pain, I struggled to get a hold of myself. I wiped the tears from my eyes and took a deep breath. "Sorry."

He nodded regally, obviously still offended.

Now I really felt bad. I was so used to Giguhl never taking anything seriously it was easy to forget he had feelings. "What can I do to make it up to you? Do you need an ice pack or something?"

"Nah. Damara brought me ice earlier." He pursed his black lips and narrowed his eyes, seeing an opportunity. "But there is one thing that might make me feel better."

I tilted my head. "What?"

"You could agree to let me fight at Vein on a regular basis."

My mouth fell open. "You've got to be joking! How are you going to fight with your . . . issue?" I nodded vaguely toward his crotch.

He shrugged. "Rhea said I should be back in fighting shape in the next day or so."

I leaned back, crossing my arms. "I don't know, G."

He rushed ahead. "I know you don't like Slade, but he's not so bad."

I held up a hand. "It's not about Slade." I paused to judge whether this statement was true, and decided it was. Slade and I had come to an understanding of sorts.

"Then what?"

I shifted uneasily in my chair. Truth was, seeing Giguhl lying in bed injured brought out my protective instincts.

I might have laughed at the specific type of injury, but I didn't like that he was in pain. The impression I got was he'd barely been able to beat Eurynome. If that train hadn't come, or a dozen other what-ifs, Giguhl might be dead. Sure, he defeated the Defiler demon. But what if the next one was stronger?

"I'm not sure how to say this without injuring your manhood," I began. Giguhl cringed. "But I don't want you to fight because I don't want you to get hurt."

He opened his mouth to argue, but I held up a hand. "Let me finish. Have you thought about what would happen if you lost? When you beat the Defiler, his handler sent him back to Irkalla, right?"

"Yeah, but that's different. Those handlers summon demons specifically for the fights. When they lose, the handlers have no use for them anymore, so they're sent back."

I narrowed my eyes. "If that's all, why does the last rule state no mercy?"

"Don't know. My best guess is they're sent to the Pit of Despair for punishment." Seeing my narrowed eyes at that little tidbit, he rushed ahead. "But I'm your minion, so that would never happen."

I grimaced. "Still, I don't like it."

Giguhl rubbed his chin for a moment. "Would you like to have an income?"

I frowned. "What?"

He sat up a little straighter. "Think about it. I can fight, and you can manage me. We'll be like Rocky and that old dude."

I rolled my eyes. "The old dude wasn't his manager, Giguhl. He was his coach."

"Same difference. Admit it, it makes sense." I started to shake my head, but he forged ahead. "I get to have some fun, and you get your money problem solved."

I had to admit to myself that this plan appealed far more than cracking skulls for Slade. Granted, in this scenario Slade was still in the equation, but only indirectly. The truth was, I'd need an income sooner or later. I couldn't live with Maisie forever doing nothing more productive than taking magic lessons. Eventually, I'd need to get my own place in the city or move on to somewhere else. Both of those options required money.

The other issue here was more complex. If Giguhl wanted to fight and knew the risks, who was I to tell him no? The minion subject was one I avoided dissecting too closely. Giguhl seemed to believe he was my minion or familiar or whatever, which was why he was asking permission. Granted, I usually bossed him around when he needed it. But this fight-club thing had nothing to do with me. Not really. And when it came down to it, I considered Giguhl more a sidekick than a minion. And sidekicks had free will. So as much as I hated it, I couldn't stop him. "Okay, you have my blessing. But I refuse to take half of your winnings. You're the one fighting, so you should keep most of the money. You can pay me a cut. Say, twenty percent?"

I could see he wanted to argue, but he'd just won a battle and didn't want to push it. "Sounds like a deal to me." He stretched out a claw to shake on it but stopped short as a grimace spread across his face. Taking pity on him, I rose and leaned across the bed to complete the formality.

"Thanks," he said.

I held his gaze for a moment, my hand clasped in his claw. "I should be the one thanking you."

The corner of his mouth curled up into a smile. "We'll call it even."

I snorted. He'd saved my life and gotten himself injured in the process. I'd just given him permission to potentially get his ass kicked. Hardly a fair trade. But I could tell from the look in his eyes he didn't want me to wax poetic about his bravery and personal sacrifice. But he did want something. "What is it?" I asked, willing to do almost anything he asked.

"I need the bedpan and some help."

Almost anything—except help him use a bedpan.

I ran to the door. "Rhea!"

18

The room was pitch-black. Not just because the lights were out, but also because of the blindfold Rhea slipped over my head.

Needless to say, I'm not a fan of blindfolds. The last time I'd worn one, I'd ended up allowing a sociopath vampire-slash-demon named Clovis Trakiya to feed from me. I felt more comfortable wearing a blindfold in front of Rhea—at least she couldn't vein-fuck me. But as a mage, she could fuck me up in other ways if she wanted.

I took a deep breath and reminded myself Rhea was trying to help me. Sure, she was a pain in the ass, but she had to be to deal with teaching me, I guess.

So I went with it, figuring she knew what she was doing. Besides, my hands were free, so I could defend myself if need be. Or so I thought.

Something hard slammed into my head. Pain crashed through my skull.

"Ow! What the hell?" I said, ripping off the scarf. The metal orb about the size of a golf ball rolled across the floor away from me. I swung around to glare at Rhea. She stood next to a table with a stack of more balls.

"No questions, remember? I can't teach you how to kill demons, but I can teach you how to defend yourself enough to get away."

"And using me as target practice is the way to do it?" I rubbed my forehead. A small goose egg throbbed hotly on the spot. "Can I at least do this without the blindfold?"

"The blindfold is necessary because you have a bad habit of using your fists to solve your problems. Fists won't help in a demon fight. For that you have to use your instincts and your magical weapons. So we're going to try this until you learn how to anticipate an attack and fend it off using only your magic."

"You're insane if you think I'm going to stand here and let you throw ball bearings at my cranium all night."

She ignored that and continued as if I hadn't spoken. "Now, the first rule of this exercise is, you're not allowed to fight with your limbs. I've left your hands unbound. But the first time you try to block or catch a ball, I'll bind you. Got it?"

"You expect me not to defend myself?" I said through gritted teeth.

"Don't be pissy. I expect you to use your magical weapons instead. And don't start bitching about not knowing how to use them. That's the point of this lesson. You're not going to tap into those skills unless you're forced to."

This was sounding better and better. "And if I refuse?"

She paused. "Then the next time someone sends a demon after you, you better pray Giguhl's there to save your ass again."

I cringed. The fact I couldn't defeat Eurynome on my

own still bothered me. I wasn't used to relying on others to save me. I sighed. "So how do I tap into this power?"

She smiled. "You'll figure it out on your own soon enough. Trying to figure it out will actually delay it. Your powers are instinct-based. Stop thinking so much and *feel*."

I cursed. "So now not only can I not use my fists, but I also can't use my mind?"

"Nope. It's not the mage way."

"If that's the mage way, it's amazing your race has lasted this long."

"Or perhaps it's not so amazing. Vampires are so one-dimensional. Every decision is driven by the predatory instinct. They're totally driven by the id."

I shot her a get-real look. "Now you're quoting Freud?"

She raised an eyebrow. "You don't like Freud? Then how do you feel about Jung? When mages tap into their magic, they're connecting with the collective unconscious, the energy, that connects all things."

"So you're saying that in order to tap into that energy I have to be weak and stupid?"

Rhea slammed her magic staff on the ground. "Enough!"

My mouth fell open at her outburst.

"You think you're fooling anyone with your tough act? You think I don't see that you use sarcasm and anger like armor?" She leaned in. "You're not fooling me at all. When I look at you, I see a wounded child. You want to be angry? Fine. I would be, too. But be angry at the ones who hurt you. Be angry at yourself for your self-deception. But for fuck's sake, stop being a martyr about it and stop taking that shit out on me for trying to help you."

My blood ran hot and cold through my veins. My jaw clenched so hard I felt like my teeth would shatter. "I don't recall asking for your help."

Rhea crossed her arms. "Not in so many words, no. But let me ask you this: Why did you come here?"

"That's funny, I've been asking myself that same question."

"Maybe, just maybe, on some level you understand that if you're ever going to be whole you have to get in touch with the side of yourself you've suppressed for the last fifty-odd years."

I threw up my hands. "Jesus, what is it with you? I came here because I wanted to meet my sister." It was a lie, and we both knew it. I came here looking for vengeance.

She pursed her lips and raised her eyebrows. "Bullshit. We both know you came here because you want to stick it to Lavinia Kane. Well, listen up—you'll never defeat her without magic. You'll never be good at magic until you face your own demons. And I'm here to help you. I know it's scary, but you can't grow unless you face that fear head-on."

My head jerked up. "I'm not afraid."

Rhea snorted. "All anger is motivated by fear. And you've got it in spades. You can either continue to delude yourself, or you can grab it by the throat and use it." She moved closer and put a kind hand on my shoulder. "You have so much promise inside you. Let me help you find it."

This whole conversation made my stomach cramp. But Rhea was issuing a challenge. To back down now would be to admit the fear was winning. Because Rhea was right. I was terrified. Terrified of trying. Terrified of failing. But more than that, I was terrified my grandmother had been right—that I was just the unfortunate by-product of a terrible mistake made by my parents. Nothing special. A godsdamned waste of space.

The rage came from nowhere. Angry tears stabbed my corneas, clamoring for release. I took a deep breath, trying to corral them back into the dark box where I normally kept them hidden. Still, they pushed and prodded, hovering at the edges of my lower lids.

My grandmother's words came back to me then. The words she'd spoken when she found out I was immune to the apple stake she'd slammed into my chest. The words that encapsulated everything she'd felt and thought of me all these years but had never spoken until that moment.

You're an abomination!

The dam broke. A tidal wave of pent-up anger overcame me, and suddenly I was drowning in it. I needed to punch something. My veins filled with lava. My fists clenched into rocks. My chest filled to bursting with a scream I'd been holding back for five decades. I choked on it, refusing to let Rhea watch me implode.

Rhea saw the change, of course. But she didn't back away or cower. Surprising, since I was so angry my eyes were practically glowing. "How you feeling?" she asked.

It was hard to speak. My jaw ached from clamping my teeth together. "Like I want to kill someone." Not just anyone. Lavinia Kane. I wanted to wound her. I wanted to maim her. I wanted to watch her bleed. But most of all, I wanted her to know some of the pain she'd imposed on me my whole life.

Rhea nodded. "Okay, good. Now I want you to embrace that anger."

The muscles shook. My fingers itched to strangle something—or someone. "I need to punch something. Hard."

"Close your eyes."

My head jerked side to side. Surrendering to these emotions would make me insane. I knew it.

"Sabina, listen to me. Close your eyes. Good. Now take a deep breath."

Air rasped into my lungs, scraping my windpipe raw.

"Now I want you to visualize collecting your anger into a glowing ball in the center of yourself."

I did as instructed, desperate for something to help alleviate the intensity. Imagining the anger as red neon filling my body, I concentrated on pulling it up through my legs and arms and spine. I collected it into a swirling mass in my diaphragm. I placed a hand over the spot and felt intense heat boiling under the skin.

"Now, when you feel something coming at you, I want you to imagine shooting it down with that mass of energy you've gathered. But whatever you do, do not open your eyes."

A metal ball hit me in the arm before I could formulate a reply.

My eyes flew open. "Godsdammit!"

"I warned you," she said. A band of cloth suddenly stretched across my eyes. I tried to rip it off, but it wouldn't budge. Fucking mages.

Slam. This one hit my chest.

"Fuck!"

"Focus!" Rhea shouted.

Bam! My shoulder.

I took a step, intent on finding Rhea and throttling her, blindfold or no. But something weird happened. My ears picked out something whistling through the air. Without thinking, I stepped to the right, and the ball whizzed past me. A split second later, glass shattered somewhere behind me.

"You'll be paying for that window and anything else that breaks from now on."

"You're a real bitch, you know that?"

"Believe it or not, you're not the first"—*Whack!* Pain radiated through my ribs—"person to tell me that."

I sucked in a deep breath and cringed. She must have cracked a rib with that last one. I needed to do something before she did any more damage. The orb of anger pulsated in my center. I stoked the flame now, remembering Rhea's advice. Another ball whirled through the air. I focused on the sound, picturing the ball coming at me. Then I imagined sending a bolt of rage at it. The hair on my arms prickled, and electricity shot down my spine.

"Oh, shit!" Rhea shouted. A crash sounded, followed by a loud thump.

I cocked my head. "What happened?"

Rhea groaned. "You missed."

"Are you okay?" Another groan. I clawed at the blindfold. A tingle passed across my face and the cloth disappeared. I blinked a couple of times before I could focus. I looked around and found Rhea lying on the floor next to a hunk of twisted metal and broken glass. I rushed over.

"You're bleeding." I touched the smear of red at her temple. She winced.

"No shit, Sherlock. You shot down the light fixture."

"Rhea, I'm so sorry. I don't know what happened."

She stopped dabbing at her temple to look me in the eyes. "I'll tell you what happened. You used magic. Granted, we need to work on your aim, but this is a major breakthrough. You should be proud of yourself."

I shook my head. Guilt outweighed any sense of triumph. "I think we need to get you some medical attention."

She waved me away when I tried to help her up. I hovered nearby as she pulled herself to her feet. "Don't be silly. We need to keep work—oh." She wobbled and reached out. I grabbed her arm to steady her. "Okay, maybe I could use an aspirin or something."

I wrapped an arm around her, ignoring the bruises she'd put there. "Let's get you to your rooms and I'll have Maisie come take a look just to be safe."

Rhea swallowed. "Okay, but don't think this gets you off the hook. We're going to keep trying until your aim improves."

"Um, Rhea?"

She leaned against me as we walked. When she looked at me, her eyes were slightly unfocused.

"My aim wasn't off. I tried to focus on hitting the ball, but I was so frustrated with you I pictured your face instead."

Her steps faltered. She looked at me for a moment, her gaze unreadable. Then, finally, she nodded as if a decision had been made. "In that case, next time I'll wear a helmet."

19

Two nights later, we were back at Vein. As Rhea predicted, Giguhl's injury healed quickly, and he claimed his boys were good as new. I had my doubts about his readiness to fight but kept my mouth shut. Giguhl was a grown demon, and it wasn't my place to hover like an overprotective stage mother.

The fight pit was even more crowded tonight. I guess word of Giguhl's victory over the Defiler had spread. Dozens of dark-races spectators turned out to see Vein's newest champion fight. When Slade saw us walk in, he shot me an I-told-you-so smile but otherwise refrained from gloating.

This time it was a Gluttony demon. The thing was so massive it took up most of the ring. He looked kind of like Jabba the Hutt, only less attractive.

"What do you think?" Giguhl jogged in place with his gaze on the Glutton. I suppose he was trying to be intimidating, but his opponent was oblivious. He was too busy polishing off a bucket of fried chicken.

"I'd go for the tongue, personally," Slade said. He'd already done his song and dance for the crowd before joining us on the sideline.

Giguhl tilted his head and considered it. "I don't think I want to touch that thing."

"How about the eyes?" I offered. "That's always a good bet."

The bell dinged and Giguhl shot off into the ring. He then proceeded to ignore our advice completely. Instead, he ran straight forward like a ram and head butted the Glutton in its gelatinous stomach. He bounced off like he'd gone headfirst into a trampoline. His ass hit the concrete with a thud.

"The eyes!" I yelled. "Go for the eyes!"

Next, Giguhl did some sort of leaping attack maneuver and landed on the Glutton's head. The crowd went crazy. Giguhl hung on for dear life as the blubbery demon tried to shake him off.

"Hold on, Giguhl!" I tried to sound encouraging, but it wasn't looking good. The Glutton roared and shook harder, like an enraged bull trying to unseat a determined cowboy.

Then Giguhl reached up and grabbed a low-hanging rafter. He swung his body through the air and kicked a hoof into the Glutton's right eye.

An ear-piercing wail cut through the smoky air. The Glutton couldn't reach its eye with one of its short arms, and green blood sprayed the crowd.

I jumped out of the way. "Ha! Told ya!" Without thinking, I turned and gave Slade a high five. Then, realizing what I'd done, I cleared my throat and tried to recover my dignity. Slade smiled at me over the cigar he had clamped between his fangs.

The Glutton let out an unholy noise, forcing my attention back to the ring. I turned just in time to see Giguhl rip the obese demon's bulbous tongue from his mouth. Green blood spurted all over Giguhl. He hefted the tongue above his head like a trophy. The crowd screamed their approval.

Slade jumped in the ring then to do his song and dance. I turned to go, not having the stomach to listen to the tongueless demon beg for mercy. Plus, I needed another drink before I met with Slade in his office.

Slade slapped a stack of crisp bills in front of me. "That demon of yours is a gold mine."

I picked up the stack and did a quick count. Two grand. Not bad. Although I had to wonder what kind of cut Slade had taken. Not to be petty, but I needed to be making more than this to afford an apartment in the city. "He's something, all right," I said, referring to Giguhl.

"Why so glum?" Slade said. "You've got a good deal going here. Your demon's a monster in the ring, and you just get to sit back and rake in the cash."

"Believe it or not, I actually prefer to earn my money the old-fashioned way."

Slade's eyebrow lifted.

"Get your mind out of the gutter. I didn't mean prostitution."

"Right," he said. "Killing people is a much more noble profession."

"It pays the bills," I said. "Or it used to, anyway."

Slade sat his chair, watching me with a calculating stare. "I guess pissing off the Dominae's been pretty bad for business."

I sighed and leaned back in my chair. "You could say that."

Slade rose and went to the wet bar. He lifted a decanter, filled with something amber, in my direction. "Scotch?"

I nodded.

Slade made a production of pouring a couple of fingers of scotch into two glasses. He handed me one and clicked his glass in a toast. He sat behind the desk with his drink. Once his wingtips rested comfortably next to his leather blotter, he lit another cigar. He looked like a fat cat ready to pounce on a canary. "I don't suppose you've changed your mind about my offer."

I took a sip of the scotch. The amber liquid warmed my throat on its way down. I smiled. "You don't give up, do you?"

"Never." A slow smile spread across his full lips. My traitorous eyes enjoyed the sight.

"I still don't see why you need someone like me. I know you've been out of the game for a while, but it wouldn't take much to get you back into shape." I looked pointedly at his taut midsection. "You could try cutting down on the carbs. Maybe some jogging."

His smiled tightened at my jab. "Unfortunately, in my position, it would be . . . inconvenient to get my hands dirty, so to speak. No, I need someone I can trust to take care of certain delicate situations."

"My answer is still no."

He pursed his lips, as if trying to think of another angle. I saw the moment he realized it was time to retreat. "Okay.

I'll drop it. For now. But one of these days, when your defenses are down, I'll convince you."

I laughed. "See? You don't know me at all if you think I ever let my defenses down."

"Still playing the tough girl, huh?" he teased.

I sobered. "Don't fool yourself, Slade. I'm not playing at anything. You might have gone soft over the years, but I've only gotten stronger, faster, and smarter."

Slade smirked back, as if he wanted to challenge my assertions. I crossed my arms. Time to end this conversation. "The demon you can have because he wants to fight. But I'm not for sale."

He looked at me with a knowing smile. "Not yet."

While I waited for Giguhl to finish another celebratory round with the nymphs, I grabbed a beer at the bar. Luckily, I'd been smart enough to take my cut before he spent it all again.

While I drank, I thought about money. Even though I'd protested Slade's offer more than once, part of me wondered if returning to the dark side might be a viable option. Sure, the magic training was coming along. But the fact I had no long-term plans bothered me. Giguhl was making a nice bankroll from fighting, but I couldn't live off his winnings forever. Eventually, I'd need a job of some sort. From what I'd seen, a lot of the mages in the city held mundane jobs and blended into society for the most part. My skill set didn't exactly lend itself to legitimate work. The very idea of working in an office gave me the shakes.

So that left me with illegitimate options. I could always hire myself out as a contract killer, but I lacked the connections here to get started. Well, I had one, but at this point working for Slade was option Z. Maybe Rhea was right and I needed to work on my patience. Surely some other source of income would turn up.

I drained my pint of beer just as Earl came over with a fresh glass. He placed it on the bar in front of me.

"You read my mind," I said, impressed with the bartender's attentiveness.

He smiled. "Nah. The werewolf sent it over with his regards." I looked at him curiously, and he nodded toward a table at the back of the room.

Michael Romulus sat at the head of the table, surrounded by eight males. Judging from the way they watched him watch me, they were all members of his pack. Since he'd sent me a beer, I assumed I wasn't in danger of another challenge, but I knew better than to relax completely.

I met Michael's gaze for a tense moment. I hadn't seen him since our fight, and I wasn't sure how things stood. He didn't show any outward signs of lingering injury, but I guessed the bruise to his ego still stung. After all, even though Slade declared the fight a draw, we both knew I could have ended him. In my experience, most males don't enjoy the knowledge they'd been bested by a female.

He rose from the table, waving his companions to stay seated when they went to follow. I took a long draw of beer as he made his way over. I looked for signs of aggression, but he didn't bulk himself up or stare me down like an opponent. His shoulders were relaxed, and his eyes strayed just south of mine.

He stopped a respectful three feet back. "Sabina."

"Michael," I nodded. "Thanks for the beer."

"May I?" he motioned to the empty stool next to me.

His respect of my space helped me relax a tad, but my guard was still up until I knew the reason for this little chat.

"Sure," I said with a casual shrug.

He motioned to Earl for a drink before looking at me. "I hear that demon of yours is quite a sensation in the ring."

Ah, I thought, he wanted to ease in with small talk. I mentally shrugged and played along. "He's something, all right. Do you ever go to the fights? I didn't see you in there."

He nodded to Earl in thanks for the drink and took a sip before answering. "No, watching two demons beat the shit out of each other isn't what I consider entertainment. The world's violent enough without making it a spectator sport."

My eyebrows rose. Considering the last time I saw Michael he was trying to kick my ass, I found this stance ironic. But I guess he considered that necessary violence, as opposed to the recreational kind. "So if you didn't come here to provide me with color commentary on my demon's fighting skills, why don't you tell me what's on your mind?"

He'd been rolling the frosty mug between his palms, staring at it as if it held some sort of answers. Finally, he lifted his head and looked me right in the eyes. "You're right. I need to warn you about something."

I cocked my head. "Oh?"

"Someone's got it in for you."

My initial reaction was to laugh. After all, this wasn't news. But something told me Michael Romulus wasn't the kind of male to spread rumors. "Why do you say that?"

"Look, normally I'd shrug it off as not being my business. But since it's impacted my pack, I can't let this pass. The night you poached on our territory, my guys didn't just randomly stumble into you."

I shrugged, since I'd figured as much. "I figured they'd heard the gunshot when the human shot me."

Michael frowned. "A human shot you?"

I waved a hand, not wanting to get into it. "You were saying?"

He shifted in his chair. "Someone called me and told me you were poaching."

He had my full attention now. "Who?" I leaned toward him.

"I don't know. They just said there was a vampire threat in our territory. Since I had a few young scouts in the area, I called and told them to check it out."

I scrambled to think of an explanation. I hadn't told anyone where I was headed, because I just sort of ended up there when I'd left Maisie's place to clear my head. What's more, I hadn't seen anyone in the park that night before I ran into the human with the gun. "Someone must have followed me," I said half to myself.

"Any ideas who?" His tone told me this wasn't an idle question. The person who told Michael I was in the park had put his pack in danger. No wonder he challenged me to the fight. He probably felt responsible for his guys getting hurt.

"I'll admit there's a list of people who want me dead. But most of those would take a more direct approach than making an anonymous tip."

"Maybe they didn't want you dead."

"What do you mean?"

He placed his elbows on the bar. "What if they were trying to start problems? Rile up some racial animosity?"

"Hmm," I said, thinking it over. "It's possible. But that brings us to the question, why are you telling me this? After all, if that was their goal, it worked."

"Look, I'll admit when those guys came back beat up, I blamed myself. Then I blamed you, which is why I issued the challenge. But you had the chance to kill me and didn't take it. That tells me you're not making some kind of power play for my territory."

I shook my head. "Of course not. I had no idea about poaching rules when I went there. I just wanted some fast food."

His lips quirked. "Once I figured that out, I started thinking about that phone call. Someone played me. Us. And I want to know who."

"That makes two of us."

"Have there been any other attempts on your life lately?"

"You could say that." I told him about the assassins at the gas station and the demon attack on the subway platform.

Michael blew out a breath. "Have you considered the idea they might all be related?"

I shook my head. "Doesn't make sense. The assassin attack was courtesy of the Dominae. The demon was obviously a mage. The phone call? Who knows? But how could they possibly be related if I've got both mages and vampires after me? The two races are on the brink of war, so who has the power to unite them against me? And why would they bother?"

"Think about it, Sabina. The phone call tells me someone wanted the weres against you in addition to the vampires and possibly the mages. What if someone's trying to make sure you have no allies?"

"But to what end? I'm just an unemployed mixed-blood."

He tilted his head. "You're also the sister of the leader of the mage race and the granddaughter of the Alpha Dominae. Some people might consider you quite a threat."

I thought about that a minute. "Okay, for argument's sake, let's say someone considers me a threat and either wants me dead or without any allies. Who has the power to manipulate all the races?"

Michael took a long pull from his beer. He set it down slowly and looked me right in the eye. "I have a feeling when you can answer that question, you'll know who's out to get you. In the meantime, you better watch your back."

20

The next night, Maisie found me in the library. After another grueling workout with Rhea—who'd spent the entire session wearing a helmet—I'd gone there in search of books on Chthonic magic. I'm not much for book learning, but I was determined to do whatever it took to understand my new powers and how I could use them to my benefit.

"Am I interrupting?" Maisie asked from the threshold, her posture hesitant.

I looked up from the book I'd been reading. I'd been excited when I found a book titled *Blood, Sex, and Death: Chthonic Magic and the Modern Mage.* However, the dense writing and patronizing, academic tone didn't match the intriguing title at all. I put it down and shot Maisie a relieved smile. "Nope."

She took a seat in the armchair next to me. Her movements were slow, as if her limbs weighed her down. Dark circles shadowed the areas under her blue eyes. "I'm sorry I haven't been around much. All these meetings suck the life right out of me."

I set the book on the table between us and gave her my full attention. "I take it things aren't going well with the council?"

She grimaced. "Not just the council. Queen Maeve's emissary insists on daily briefings."

I frowned. "Why?"

She sighed and slid down a bit in her chair. "The queen isn't sold on the idea of war. The council is getting closer to a vote every day, and, with the exception of a couple of holdouts, it's looking like war is inevitable. But we need the queen's support if we're going to pull off a victory."

"But I thought faeries and mages were allies. I'd have thought her support was a foregone conclusion."

"We are allies. And in the past we could always count on the faeries to fight with us. But times have changed. Centuries ago, the human population was smaller and more spread out. But now they're everywhere and have the ability to communicate with each other quickly. If a battle breaks out and humans get injured or witness something, the entire world could know about it within minutes. Imagine what would happen if the humans' governments turned their weapons on us."

I hadn't thought about that angle. Not a surprise, since I never gave humans a second thought in general. But now that I thought about it, I understood the danger. Humans outnumbered all the dark races. If they found out we existed, infighting would be the least of our worries. During times of peace, all the dark races managed to stay under the humans' radar through various means. Since vamps were nocturnal, it was fairly simple to go unnoticed through subterfuge and careful leadership by the Dominae. Any vamps that got out of line were taken out of the picture. Mages and faeries had magic and human-friendly lifestyles on their sides. But war would mean the gloves were off, and the potential for total anarchy was huge.

"And you agree with her?" I asked.

Maisie nodded. "Like most of the council, I don't believe the Dominae should be allowed to get away with killing our own without repercussion. But I am worried about the bigger picture. The council is, too. That's what's held up the vote. We want to be sure we can contain the collateral damage if we go to war. And it's my job to convince the queen we'll be able to do that."

"How?"

"We have a few ideas. These days, it's possible to wage a war without two armies meeting on a battlefield. There's guerilla tactics and financial strategies that can cripple an opponent."

I nodded. "Go after the Dominae's business interests, destroy their resources."

She smiled. "Exactly. But the problem is we also have to ensure we're prepared for anything from the Dominae. They could use the same strategies against us. Or they could do it the old-fashioned way and attack us with everything they've got. That's the rub here. There's no way we can promise Queen Maeve that the Dominae won't expose us all."

"But why would they do that?"

She shrugged. "Who knows what they have planned? After all, they kidnapped dozens of mages to drain their blood. They obviously had a plan for it."

I sat back and digested all this. My gut clenched, thinking about all the angles and variables. I could only imagine the stress Maisie and the rest of the council were under right now. "With Adam working on her at court and you working on the envoy here, surely the queen will relent soon."

The skin around Maisie's eyes tightened. "Yeah, I'm just worried. I'll support whatever the council decides to do, but I'm not excited about the prospect of war."

I didn't say anything. What could I say? Sure, if the mages declared war on the Dominae, it suited my purposes. But there were other ways to get revenge against the Dominae. Ways that didn't threaten the destruction of both races.

Maisie shook herself and waved a hand in the air. "Anyway, I didn't come here to unload on you about all this. How are things with you? Rhea said lessons are going really well."

I shrugged. "I guess so. I'm just impatient."

She smiled. "She said that, too."

"I know you've been busy, but is there any word from the Pythian Guard on the attack?"

"Not yet. Unfortunately, the council's priority is having the Pythian Guard focus on shoring up our security. We've called in Guards from across the country, so we should have more manpower soon. But rest assured, we're committed to finding who sent the demon after you."

I tamped down my frustration over this news. It wasn't Maisie's fault the council had other priorities. "Any word from Adam?"

Maisie smiled. "That's one of the reasons I came to find you. Orpheus called him back from his assignment. He's expected back in time for the Blood Moon Festival."

My stomach gave a little jump. Rhea had told me the mages always had a big celebration for the full Blood

Moon, which was happening in four nights. Four nights until Adam returned to distract me.

"That's nice." I tried to make my tone sound nothing more than politely interested, but Maisie saw through it.

"The festival will be the perfect setting for your reunion, I think." She winked at me.

My cheeks heated. "I doubt it. He'll be busy with Pythian Guard stuff. Plus, Rhea mentioned something about me taking part in the rites since I'm the High Priestess of the Blood Moon." Whatever that meant. Thus far, all the title entailed was me wearing the necklace they'd given me when I arrived. I toyed with it now, looking down into the moonstone to avoid Maisie's shrewd gaze.

"You wouldn't be making excuses just because you're nervous, would you?"

I looked away from her knowing gaze. "Of course not. What's there to be nervous about?"

Maisie took my hand and forced me to look at her. "I really think you should take advantage of alone time with Adam while you have it."

The earnestness of her words surprised me. "Why? Is there something I should know?"

It was her turn to look away. "Of course not. I just think life's too short to let fear hold us back from grabbing what we want when it's in front of us."

"Maisie, we're immortal. Life being short isn't an issue."

"I hate to break this to you, sister, but I'd say immortality is the last thing you can take for granted given your lifestyle."

I frowned. "What the hell is that supposed to mean?"

"How many attempts have there been on your life in the last two weeks?"

I grimaced. "Okay, you got me there, but it's not like it's anything new. In my former line of work, someone took a shot at me almost daily."

"Look, all I'm saying is, if you're interested in Adam you should go for it. Given the current climate in our world, you never know when the winds are going to change and you'll miss your chance."

"I'll take it under advisement." I rose from my seat, feeling restless. As I did so, a painting over the fireplace caught my eye. "Who's that?"

Maisie's eyes widened. "That's our father. Tristan Graecus."

As I did a double take, Maisie rose to join me. I scanned the portrait with an eagle eye, looking for a resemblance. Now I knew where the black part of my hair color came from. And maybe there was a resemblance around the eyes. A familiar stubborn tilt to his chin. "I've never seen a picture of him before."

Maisie looked up at the image with a smile. "Not hard to image why our mother fell for him, is it?"

It was true. Our father was a handsome guy—for a mage. "Tell me about him."

Maisie pulled her gaze from the image to look at me. "He's considered a hero to all mages. A martyr of sorts. Did you know he was next in line to take over the Pythian Guard?"

I shook my head.

"According to Orpheus, he was one of the most talented Chthonic mages he'd ever met."

My stomach dipped. "Our father was a Chthonic?"

Maisie nodded solemnly. "I was surprised to find out it passed on to you. Chthonic mages are pretty rare."

I wasn't sure how to feel about this revelation. I never knew my father. Had never given his existence much thought past the trouble his decisions had caused my own life. My grandmother had talked about Tristan Graecus in venomous tones on the rare occasions she spoke of him at all. My mother was mentioned even less—her very name banished from my vocabulary because of the shame she caused my grandmother. Over the years, I'd overheard elder vamps whisper how I'd inherited my prideful ways from my mother. And now I knew I'd gotten my talent for death magic from my father. Maybe this news should have made me feel nostalgic or sad, but I mostly felt numb. Is it wrong to resent the dead? Because if I felt anything, that was it.

Maisie continued. "How much do you know about our mother?"

I paused, remembering Maisie was in the same boat. Since we'd been separated seconds after our vampire mother died in childbirth, the mages probably weren't too excited to tell her about dear old Mom. Especially since they apparently chose to believe our father was the victim of the whole scenario.

"Lavinia forbade anyone to speak about our mother in her presence. I overheard things, of course, but it's kind of fuzzy. So I didn't learn much from the vampire side. But back in California, Adam took me to meet Briallen Pimpernell. She's the faery who acted as midwife at our birth."

"That's right!" Maisie said. "What did she tell you?"

I briefly told Maisie the story of how the faery cared for Phoebe during her yearlong pregnancy. Lavinia and Ameritat—our grandmothers—had decided hiding Phoebe out in the woods would keep the scandal under wraps for a while. "Apparently, she was heartbroken when she arrived. Wouldn't speak to Briallen at all. Eventually, she opened up and told Briallen about Tristan. By that point, I guess he was already dead—or assumed to be," I corrected, remembering Briallen's assertion that his body had never been found, "and Phoebe was heartbroken and withdrawn."

Maisie was silent for a moment, digesting it all. "Did Briallen describe her?"

"Briallen said she had curly red hair and brown eyes. Said she was intelligent and earnest. Like I said, when she got there, she barely spoke. But I guess after she felt us move, she got excited and opened up to Briallen."

Maisie sighed. "It's all so tragic, isn't it? That she looked forward to our birth and never had a chance to know us and us her?"

I shrugged. "I guess so."

Maisie shot me a look for my lack of sentimentality. "At least we have each other now, right?"

I smiled. "Yeah."

Maisie blew out a breath, as if expelling the emotions built up talking about our parents' sad fates. "Let's change the subject. How's Giguhl doing in fight club?"

"Pretty good, actually. He's won two fights so far."

"That's great! I wish I could see him in action."

"Slade's got quite a setup there. Have you ever been to Vein?"

She shook her head. "I've never been to the Black Light District."

"Really?" I guess I shouldn't have been shocked. After all, the BLD was full of rough characters. Not exactly the type of place a spiritual leader of the mage race would hang out.

Something shifted in her expression, like a lightbulb went on somewhere. "When's his next fight?"

"Tomorrow night. Why?"

"Well," she said slowly, "I was just thinking. Maybe I could tag along. Would you mind?"

"I don't know, Maisie. I mean, it's kind of a rough scene. Besides, we still haven't figured out who's after me. If the mage takes another shot, I wouldn't want you caught in the cross-fire." I hadn't mentioned Michael's theories to any of the mages yet, and I didn't plan on doing so until I had more proof. Whether he was right or not, I assumed if another attack was coming, it would happen when I was away from the protection of the mage compound.

She waved away my concern. "We'll be in public, right? Surely they won't attack with witnesses. Besides, I'm not exactly defenseless. If the mage who attacked you tries again, I can help you."

"What if someone recognizes you? I have to imagine it's not exactly proper for someone in your position to be seen in a bar."

She raised that stubborn chin we'd inherited from our father. "I can use a glamour spell."

Dammit. With each argument I gave, Maisie appeared more determined to go. "I don't know, Maze."

"Oh, come on. It'll be fun. A girls' night out. I haven't had one of those in . . . well, never, actually. Please?"

I sighed. Even though I was worried, Maisie was old enough to make her own decisions. Plus, I kind of looked forward to the opportunity to hang out with Maisie away from mage central.

"I probably should be responsible and say no." I blew out a breath. "But what the hell?"

She smiled broadly, and her movements had a perkiness I hadn't seen in days. "I'm so excited."

I laughed, despite my misgivings. "We'll head out after my training session with Rhea tomorrow, okay?"

"Thanks, Sabina." She hugged me, and for once the move didn't make me squirm. "Okay, I need to get some sleep since it looks like tomorrow's going to be a late night. Sweet dreams, sister."

After she left, I picked up the book I'd been trying to read when she arrived but found it hard to focus. My conversation with Maisie had given my mind plenty to chew on. I kept telling myself I wasn't hungry enough to bite, but my brain had other plans. After I'd scanned the same page ten times without registering any words, I slammed the book shut and rose.

As I paced, the portrait of Tristan caught my eye again. It didn't take a psychologist to see the parallels between my parents and the situation with Adam and me. I'm sure there was some name for a daughter having an attraction to men like her father. Probably Freud had plenty to say on the issue. But I didn't care much for the whys. I had to figure out the whats. What did I want? What did Adam want? And what the hell was I going to do about it?

I took a deep breath and looked around, reassuring myself I was alone. I didn't want an audience when I admitted this to myself. I liked Adam. A lot. More than liked. Lusted after? Longed for? Lots of L words. Except for the big L. I doubted I was capable of that word. Still, where the mage was concerned, my feelings were stronger than I wanted to admit.

And since I was alone, I also admitted to myself that I was nervous about his return. Sure, he'd promised things when he left. But in my experience, males promised lots of things in the heat of the moment. Hell, maybe they even believed them when they said them. But distance and time are harsh on promises.

I looked up at my father's face again. Even if Adam truly wanted me, there was no guarantee things would work out. It certainly hadn't for my parents. According to Briallen, they were in love. Real love. They loved each other so much they'd ignored a centuries-old law against interracial mating, despite the risks. They'd loved each other so much they created two new lives together. Such a hopeful and optimistic act. And they were punished for it in spades.

I ran a hand through my hair and blew out a long breath. Stewing about it wouldn't make a solution magically appear. I wasn't some virgin who needed to follow a male's lead in a relationship, so seeing how he acted when he returned didn't appeal. As far as I could tell, my problem was one of my mind not agreeing with my emotions. I blamed Rhea for the fact I even paid attention to the emotional side. With all her insistence on opening myself to my emotions and instincts, she'd managed to make me an indecisive wreck.

I could just see what Adam had to say when he returned. But that wasn't my style. Instead of leaving it up to him, I decided to wait and see how I felt when I saw him. After all, absence made the heart grow fonder. So maybe when he wasn't absent anymore, the attraction would be less intense. Less urgent and confusing.

I hoped.

21

The shot slammed into the dummy's midsection. A wide circle burned for a moment before the entire straw man burst into flames.

"Good!" Rhea shouted. "What'd you do differently? You almost hit the target that time."

It helped to imagine myself as a weapon. A heat-seeking missile. A living, breathing instrument of destruction. Of course, I couldn't tell that to Rhea. To her, I shrugged and said, "I tapped into the universal energy."

Rhea smiled. "Bullshit."

I laughed out loud. The glow of accomplishment warmed my center. I'd been working on that maneuver for a couple of days. The two hours I'd already spent on the effort so far that evening left me dripping in sweat. But now, watching the dummy smolder and smoke, a surge of energy shot through me. "Does it really matter how I did it?"

Rhea cocked her head. "Guess not, as long as you can do it again."

I shook my arms and wiggled my fingers. "I'm ready if you are."

"Damara?" Rhea called, looking around the room for her assistant.

Damara sat cross-legged in the corner with white cords extending from her ears. A magazine lay open in her lap, and she didn't look up at Rhea's call.

"Damara!" Rhea shouted, waving her hands to get the girl's attention.

She looked up at Rhea with her eyebrows raised and a scowl on her face. The faint sounds of a guitar riff bled into the room as she removed the earbuds. "What?"

"Please retrieve another dummy from the storeroom."

Damara sighed and replaced the earbuds. I frowned, wondering what Rhea would do now that it appeared the girl was flat-out ignoring her. I glanced at Rhea, but she looked unconcerned. Suddenly, a tingle of energy crept up my spine. A second later, a straw dummy flew out of the storeroom and floated across the floor like a ghost. Damara kept the dummy afloat even as she continued to read her magazine. I blinked, surprised to see how easily she'd wielded magic. Just then, she looked up and smirked at me. Her expression said something along the lines of, "See how easy this is for me?"

I raised my eyebrows and pursed my lips, showing her I wasn't impressed—even though I was.

The dummy finally reached the opposite wall, and the ropes hanging from the ceiling tied themselves around its neck.

Damara rose then and brushed her hands together. I rolled my eyes, realizing she'd been showing off. *Whatever.* She might be able to move things easily, but I was

well on my way to being able to destroy them without lifting a finger.

Rhea turned back to me and opened her mouth.

"Can I go now?" Damara interrupted.

Rhea sighed, looking put-upon. "Yes."

Much stomping and squeaking ensued until Damara
disappeared through the door.

Watching the closed door, Rhea shook her head. "Why
do I put up with that child?"

I crossed my arms. "I was going to ask you the same
thing."

Rhea shrugged. "I feel bad for her, I guess. She doesn't
have anyone else. Her mom was one of the ones taken at
the vineyard."

My stomach lurched. Suddenly Damara's sullen ways
made a lot more sense. "That's horrible."

Rhea nodded. "She's also incredibly talented. She's already mastered several advanced areas of magic. But she's
impatient." She shot me a sly smile. "Like some other stu-
dents I know."

"What you call impatience, I call eagerness," I said
with a smirk.

"Smartass. You ready to go again?"

I nodded. "Just give me a sec."

I closed my eyes and focused on my breathing. Like
Rhea taught me, I visualized the energy surrounding
me—not hard, given I was in one of the largest cities in
the world. The air pulsed with it. I drew it up from my
feet, in from my fingers, and down from the top of my
head. I gathered it into a glowing ball in my diaphragm.
It beat there like a second heart, pulsing with power. On
my next exhalation, I imagined a thin stream of red rising

through my esophagus with the air. It climbed up until I could taste ozone in the back of my throat. My eyes flew open. The power surged through my pupils and shot like a laser across the room.

"Bull's-eye!" Rhea shouted.

I slammed my lids shut. The leftover power dispersed through my veins, making my arms and legs tingle. The rush of energy through my body made me dizzy. I swallowed against the rising nausea and focused on regaining my equilibrium. Rhea told me that in time, my body would adjust to the aftereffects of such an expenditure of energy, but for the time being it left me feeling wrung out. My shoulders sagged, and a bead of sweat trickled down my temple.

Once I felt more stable, I slowly opened my eyes. The dummy was the first thing I saw. It burned like an effigy for a moment until Rhea cast a spell to douse the flames. I limped to a nearby table and leaned on the edge, feeling worn-out but pleased.

Rhea came over and patted my shoulder. "Excellent work, Sabina. With a little more practice you'll be able to call up the power without concentrating so hard. Once you master that, we'll work on reversing the spell."

I frowned. "Reversing it?"

"Yeah, this is just a stepping stone on the way to being able to use your true power. Most mages can shoot energy, but only Chthonics can suck the life force out of living things. It's tricky and has some nasty side effects, but it's also quite effective."

My mouth twisted. "What kind of side effects?"

"Nothing you can't handle. But let's not worry about

that now." She patted my shoulder again. "You did really well tonight. I'm pleased with your progress."

"Thanks," I said. "This trick will come in handy if anyone takes another shot at me."

Rhea frowned. "Why do I get the impression you're hoping there's another attack?"

I considered lying, telling her I wasn't doing just that. But she'd see through that. "At least then I wouldn't be sitting around wondering when another attack was coming and who was responsible."

"Sabina, I get what you're saying, but I would caution you not to get too cocky. Any mage who could handle an Avenger demon will be able to block a simple power bolt. If I were you, I'd have Giguhl or another mage with you at all times."

As smart as her advice was, it rankled. The very idea of needing a bodyguard pissed me off. "I can take care of myself."

Her shrewd eyes narrowed. "We all need help sometimes, Sabina. Don't let your pride force you into a foolish and potentially deadly situation."

"I'm not an idiot," I said, my hackles rising.

"Yes, I'm aware of that. But I'm also aware you're itching to zap someone. I'm just saying, you need to keep a cool head and not get yourself in a situation you can't handle."

I jerked a nod. "Fine." Rising from the table, I worked my suddenly tense shoulders. "I need to grab a shower before I head to Vein."

"I hear Maisie's going with you."

I frowned. Was there anything this lady didn't know? "Yeah. It was her idea."

She nodded. "She told me. I think it'll do her some good. She's been so tense lately. Maybe getting away from here for a few hours will help her get her visions back."

I stopped, my earlier indignation dissolving. "I didn't know they left."

Rhea sighed and crossed her arms with a nod. "She hasn't had a vision since before you got here. It's the stress. Between the negotiations with Queen Maeve's emissary and the council pressuring her, it's no wonder she's blocked."

"How's the council pressuring her?" I knew there was some stress over the outcome of the vote, but Maisie hadn't mentioned the council coming down on her about something.

"Think about it. Maisie's an oracle. The council relies on her to foresee the potential outcomes of their decisions. Especially now, with so much riding on this war vote. But she hasn't been able to see a damned thing."

I chewed on my lip. "I hadn't thought of that. No wonder she's looked so worried every time I've seen her."

Rhea nodded. "Like I said, maybe a night away will help. Get her mind off things. Please promise me you'll keep your eye on her, though. If anything happens, Orpheus will have all our asses."

"He doesn't know?"

She shook her head. "Maisie told me because she needed some help with her glamour spell. The only reason I didn't argue was that no one will recognize her and you and Giguhl will be there to watch her back. But Orpheus would go apoplectic if he found out."

I gritted my teeth. If I'd known it would be this big of

a deal, I'd have flat-out refused Maisie's request the night
before. "Good to know."

When we arrived at Vein, Giguhl made a beeline for a
gaggle of nymphs. Squealing ensued as the girls fawned
over his arrival. I shrugged at Maisie and jerked my head
toward the bar. She followed close behind, almost tripping
over my heels. After the lecture I'd given her on the way
over about sticking close and not engaging anyone, this
wasn't a surprise. I just hadn't anticipated her taking me
quite so literally.

She and Rhea had done a good job with her disguise. At
first I'd been worried she'd decide to have a little fun with it.
But they'd gone with a few sensible, but effective, changes.
The red was gone from her hair, and the solid black tresses
were pulled back into a simple ponytail hanging down her
back. Her eyes were green now, instead of blue, and her
nose was a bit longer. She wore black jeans and boots with
a black shirt and leather jacket. She looked like Johnny
Cash's little sister, but I wasn't complaining. She'd blend
into the crowd in this getup much better than if she'd worn
her normal broomstick skirt and peasant blouse.

Slade came forward just as I motioned to Earl for two
Bloody Magdalenes. Maisie stood to my side, looking
around nervously. For me this type of place was like a second home, but for Maisie it probably looked full of trouble.
Which, come to think of it, was exactly why I liked it.

"Sabina," Slade said in his velvet voice. When he
smiled, he flashed a little fang—the vampire version of
a wink.

I nodded. "How's it hanging, Slade?"

He grinned. "Don't ask unless you really want to know the answer."

I felt Maisie shift behind me, offering the perfect opportunity to change the subject. I reached behind me and pulled her forward. "Slade, I want to introduce you to my friend Fiona." We'd decided to use Maisie's middle name, since it'd be easy for her to remember to respond to.

"Nice to meet you," she said quietly.

Slade barely acknowledged Maisie/Fiona at all. He glanced her way and nodded, but his eyes quickly returned to my face. "You going to hang around after the fight?"

I shifted uneasily. "I don't know." Probably Giguhl would want another celebratory session with the nymphettes after. But I wasn't ready to commit to hanging around any longer than necessary until I saw how everything played out.

Slade reached out and pushed a few stray strands of hair behind my ear. "Think about it, okay?"

I shrugged his hand away when it landed on my shoulder. Time to change the subject. "Who's Giguhl fighting tonight?"

Slade smoothly moved to the new subject, but the twinkle in his eye told me he knew he'd unsettled me. "We have something special for your demon tonight."

My eyebrows rose. "Oh?"

Slade nodded, glancing over at Giguhl. He had two nymphs in his lap, and a third whispered something in his ear that had his color high. "He's become a sensation. Demons are lining up to challenge him." He glanced at his watch. "Almost time. I need to borrow Giguhl for a few minutes beforehand, if that's okay."

I nodded. "It's okay with me, but good luck dragging him away from the groupies."

Slade laughed. "Watch and learn."

I leaned back against the bar and watched him prowl across the bar. As if he cast a spell, the crowd parted for him.

"That was interesting," Maisie said next to me. She'd been so quiet, I'd almost forgotten she was there.

"What?" I asked, keeping my eyes on Slade. He'd reached Giguhl and said something to the nymphs. They jumped up and moved away so fast, you'd think the place was on fire.

"You didn't tell me Adam had competition."

My head swiveled toward her. "Who? Slade?" I forced a laugh. "Been there, done that, don't plan on returning."

"Oh, please," Maisie said. "You were totally flirting with him."

My mouth fell open. "Don't be ridiculous. I don't flirt with anyone."

A single black eyebrow rose to her bangs.

I rolled my eyes. "Look, I'm not an idiot. I know Slade has debauchery on his mind. But I think I can manage to resist his manly charms."

She pursed her lips and watched as Slade led Giguhl through a curtain leading to the fight area. "Are you sure you want to? He's got a nice ass."

I choked on the swig of vodka and blood I'd been in the process of swallowing. When I finally caught my breath, I stared at my sister. "Shouldn't you be discouraging me? I thought you were on Team Adam."

She paused, her teasing expression going somber. "I'm on Team Whoever-Makes-Sabina-Happy."

I shook my head at her. "I appreciate your loyalty, but Slade isn't on the roster."

"If you say so."

Earl saved me from further discussion on the subject. He clanged a bell behind the bar. "Fight starts in ten!"

Excitement zinged through the bar. As one, the crowd flowed toward the back of the bar and the stairs leading down to the arena. I paid Earl and handed Maisie her drink. "You might want to pound that before we head down," I said over the din.

"Why?"

"Trust me. Drink." I tossed back my own glass and slammed it on the bar. Maisie hesitated for a moment. She chugged more slowly but managed to get the whole thing down. She whacked her glass on the wooden bar and squared her shoulders.

"Let's go watch that familiar of yours in action."

22

$\mathcal{W}$e had to push our way through an even larger crowd than before. I stopped short when I finally reached Giguhl and got a load of his getup. The boxing shorts were black with orange flames and the word *Killer* embroidered in red on the ass.

"Charming," I said.

"Cool, huh? Slade had them made for me."

"Yeah, that Slade's a real peach. Who's your opponent?" I glanced across the ring. He had the head of a jackal, and a thick black animal pelt was draped across his shoulders.

Giguhl sneered. "Chaos demon. Nasty fighters, the lot of them."

From the looks of the Chaos, I was relieved Slade insisted on the brass collars. Giguhl would have enough of a fight on his hand without magic entering the equation.

"Do you have a strategy?"

Giguhl shrugged his shoulders and stretched his arms across his chest as he spoke. "The thing with Chaos demons is they fight like berserkers. Look at him." Giguhl

pointed a claw across the ring. The Chaos danced in fren-
zied circles; with each pass, his muscles contracted and
bunched. A low rumble started deep in his chest and grew
in intensity until it was a full-on growl. Finally, he stopped
circling and clenched his muscles, widening his arms and
throwing his head back. A ferocious roar emitted from his
mouth, full of razor-sharp teeth.

"Someone's pissed," Giguhl said in a singsong voice.

"Again. What are you going to do?" I glanced at Maisie.
Her face had gone pale as an albino's ass. I'd deal with her
in a second. First I had to get Giguhl squared away.

"He'll come on strong at first, trying to intimidate me. I
just have to ride it out until he wears himself down."

The Chaos growled and snarled across the ring, his
glowing yellow eyes on Giguhl. "Good luck with that." I
patted Giguhl on the shoulder.

Slade jumped into the center of the pit and raised his
hands for silence. "Good evening, fight fans! Tonight we
have a special treat for you. Our new champion, Giguhl
'the Killer' from Gizal, has been challenged by two opponents." A roar of approval from the crowd.

I grabbed Giguhl's arm. "Did you know about this?"

He nodded, his eyes still on the Chaos demon. "Yeah,
the second challenge came in last-minute."

"This is bullshit," I said. "How can he expect you to
fight twice in one night?"

"I'm cool with it." Giguhl shrugged. "Plus, I told him
I'd only do it if he gave us a bigger cut of the winnings. He
was fine with it."

I'll just bet he was, I thought. Knowing Slade, he had
all the Black Light District bookies in his pocket. Giving

Giguhl a slightly bigger cut of the purse wouldn't affect Slade's bottom line too much.

Slade carried on with his showboating in the ring. I turned to Giguhl and made him look at me. "If you lose this fight, I'm going to kick your ass. You got that?"

Giguhl frowned. "You suck at this motivational-speech stuff. You know that, right?"

The bell dinged. I punched him in the shoulder, racking my brain for something more inspiring. "Go get him, Killer!"

Giguhl rolled his eyes and jogged into the ring like a boxer. Not to be outdone, Chaos performed some sort of crazy spinning entrance. Like a whirling dervish. Or the Tasmanian Devil. Giguhl jumped out of the way when a spin turned into a leaping kick. The Chaos turned and growled, spittle dripping from its jagged teeth. It pounced then, going after Giguhl with sharp claws. It slashed and snapped its teeth in a frenzy of movement. By the time Giguhl extricated himself, he was covered in red slashes across his chest and face.

He fell back, bleeding and bruised. I held my breath as the Chaos went in for another round. Only this time, Giguhl was ready. He punched Jackal Face right in the snout and followed that with a swift kick between the legs. The Chaos howled and fell to the ground. But Giguhl wasn't done. He grabbed the demon by his ears and pulled him off the floor. Giguhl's biceps heaved with the effort. He tossed the Chaos across the ring. The demon crashed into a group of spectators, who fell like bowling pins.

Giguhl turned to receive adoration from the cheering crowd. He absorbed their attention, inflating and expanding with it. A roar made the hair on my arms raise. Giguhl turned just in time to receive a punishing kick to the face from the livid Chaos demon. Blood spewed from Giguhl's mouth as he fell back, almost in slow motion.

The Chaos followed him down, going for the neck with his snapping teeth.

"Giguhl!" I shouted and moved forward. A hand caught my arm. I turned around to see Maisie frowning at me. I'd been so caught up in the fight, I'd forgotten about her.

"Let him handle it."

I opened my mouth to tell her to butt out, but she nudged me just as a cheer rose from the crowd.

"Look." She nodded toward the ring. I swung around to see the Chaos fly through the air again. This time, those standing in his path scurried out of the way. His body slammed into a cinderblock wall, cracking with the force.

Giguhl rose from the pit covered in dirt, blood, and sweat. He swiped a claw across his lips and stalked after the Chaos with murder in his eyes. This time, the Chaos didn't fight back when Giguhl dragged his ass off the ground. Giguhl punched until his claws were bloody and raw and the Chaos's teeth started raining down like hailstones. Giguhl moved to the midsection, savaging ribs and internal organs. The Chaos's broken jaw moved crookedly, spilling out blood and saliva. A faint yelp emitted from the shattered maw. "Mercy!"

An hour later, Slade stuck his head into the locker room. "Hey, Killer? You ready to kick some more ass?"

Giguhl sat on a bench with the hood of his red-and-black robe pulled down over his head. If Slade had come in five minutes earlier, he would have caught Maisie performing a quick healing spell to speed up Giguhl's recovery. I'd been worried about bringing my sister along, but now I thanked the goddess she was here to help. Even with Giguhl's healing powers, two demon fights in one night wouldn't be easy without some magical intervention.

I intercepted Slade and pushed him back into the hall.

"What can I do for you?" he said, seemingly unperturbed by my brusque interruption.

I crossed my arms. "What the hell were you thinking accepting two challenges in one night for him? I'm his manager—you should have asked me first."

"Calm down. The second fight is rigged."

My eyebrows slammed down. "What?"

He smiled, looking pleased with himself. "The demon's handler's in to me for a lot of money. I told him his debt would be cleared if he ensured Giguhl would win the fight."

"Why would you do that?"

Slade smiled. "Surely you're not that naive, Sabina."

"You bet on Giguhl."

He smiled. "I knew you were a clever girl." He moved closer. "So just relax. Giguhl will breeze through this next fight, and when he's done, we'll all be a little richer."

I sighed. "Next time, you talk to me first before you make decisions regarding Giguhl. As his manager, I have the right to veto these decisions."

"Yes, ma'am."

I moved back toward the door. "I'll send Giguhl out in a sec."

"Sabina?"

I stopped at the door and turned to look at him. "Yeah?"

"Any chance you can ditch your mage friend after the fight?"

I cocked my head. "No."

He shot me a heated glance I felt all the way to my undercarriage. "Pity."

23

I'd expected Giguhl to start shit talking the minute we reached the ring and saw his opponent. Instead, he stopped short, his gaze transfixed on something across the pit.

"Hey!" I complained when I bumped into his back.

He didn't say anything. I followed his eyes and realized the problem. A gorgeous chick stood in the other corner. She was about six feet tall, and her long, peacock blue hair shimmered in the overhead lights.

I felt Maisie lean around me and let out a low whistle. "Is she for real?"

Normally, I don't approve of catsuits. Very few females can pull off the skin-tight, one-piece garments. But I had to admit this chick was working it. The outfit clung to her generous curves from her collarbones down to her ankles. Something blue—almost like a train—trailed behind her, which seemed a tad overkill. But this chick obviously wasn't into subtlety.

"Man, Slade's going all out for this," I said. "Your

last fight didn't have a model to strut around between rounds."

Giguhl swallowed and nodded absently. Then he stopped. "Huh?"

I nodded toward the chick. "The model you're ogling. I'm surprised Slade is willing to lay out the cash for the talent."

Giguhl tore his eyes from the vision in gold. "Sabina, that's not a model."

I frowned. Giguhl looked at me with exaggerated patience, waiting for the lightbulb to click on. "Wait, *she's* your opponent?"

Before Giguhl could answer, the crowd gasped as a magnificent fan of peacock feathers unfurled behind her. Well, I guess that explained the blue train. And now that I took a closer look, I finally noticed the two small horns jutting from the sides of her head.

"Well, I'll be damned," I whispered.

Giguhl groaned and adjusted his codpiece. A snarky comment died on my lips as the vixen began to unwrap the golden chain from around her neck. She swung it around her head a couple of times before cracking it like a whip in Giguhl's direction. Once she made sure she had his attention, she blew him a kiss.

The seven-foot-tall demon at my side whimpered. "I think I'm in love."

I grabbed him by the shoulders and forced him to look at me. "Giguhl, get a hold of yourself."

He peeked out of the corner of his eye at her, but I grabbed his chin. "Listen to me, you can't let her psych you out."

"She's not psyching me out, she's making me horny."

I closed my eyes and repressed my gag reflex. "You're gonna have to focus if you're going to win."

"I can't help it. I've never seen a more gorgeous demon." He sighed like a lovesick teenager.

Of all the times for the demon to reveal his romantic side . . .

"You're going to have to fight her. You know the rules. Once a challenge has been issued and accepted, you have to fight."

Giguhl looked like he wanted to argue, but at that moment, Slade walked into the center of the pit. He went through his little spiel about the rules of Demon Fight Club, but tonight there was a twist.

"Tonight's match will be a little different, friends," Slade announced. "For the first time in the history of Demon Fight Club, we will be allowing the demons to use weapons!"

As a roar rose from the crowd, I glanced at golden demon's whip. "You're going to have to watch out for that whip," I whispered to Giguhl. "Do you have any weapons?"

He shook his head. "I didn't know he was changing the rules."

Yeah, I thought, nice of Slade to mention this wrinkle when we talked a few minutes earlier. I reached down into my boot and pulled out a knife. The six-inch blade wouldn't do much damage to a demon, but it might slow her down.

"If you can get close enough, you're going to have to cut her." He opened his mouth to protest, but I shushed him. "I know, I know, she's too beautiful. Slade said she's going to throw the fight, but we're going to have to make it look real."

He frowned but nodded. His claw curled around the handle of the knife.

Slade had finished his rule rundown by now and was introducing the fighters. "In the left corner, we have the prettiest killing machine this side of Irkalla. Don't let her good looks fool you; this Vanity demon is pure evil. Ladies and gentlemen, put your hands together for Valva!"

I choked. "Did he just say 'Vulva'?"

Giguhl rolled his eyes. "Vahl-va," he corrected.

I shook my head. "What were her parents thinking?"

Giguhl nudged me. "Hush."

Slade turned to our side of the ring. "And in the other corner, a demon who needs no introduction after his recent victory over Rargnok, the former champion of this fight club. The big, bad Mischief demon from the Gizal region of Irkalla—Giguhl!"

The crowd went wild. Giguhl stood straighter and pumped his claws in the air. Relief flooded through me. It looked like my demon's head was finally back in the game.

The bell clanged and Giguhl strutted into the pit. Valva sashayed toward Giguhl, who stood entranced by her shimmery curves. The demoness stopped in front of Giguhl and placed a manicured hand on her slim, gold-clad hip. Her other hand swung the necklace-whip back and forth, taunting him. Giguhl, gods love him, tried to hold firm. He swiped halfheartedly with his blade, narrowly missing her pert nose. She didn't even flinch.

At a loss, Giguhl took a couple steps back to regroup. Valva beckoned him with a finger. The move distracted him, so he didn't see the other wrist flick the whip like a lasso. The chain caught him around the neck, and she jerked it taut. Giguhl had no choice but to follow where she pulled. His claws worked at the whip, but before he could make any headway, Valva hooked her leg behind his. He fell hard on the concrete.

The demoness loomed over him and dug a heel into his chest. My heart pounded, thinking Giguhl was done for. But a slow smile spread on his black lips. He grabbed the chain and jerked Valva down on top of him. She gasped and scrambled, trying to dismount him. She dropped the end of the necklace, allowing Giguhl to unwrap it from his neck. He grabbed for Valva, but she moved too fast. As he jumped to his feet, her expression went from shocked to determined. The flirtatious vixen of a few minutes ago was gone.

Giguhl wrapped the end of the necklace around his wrist and swung it in an arc at his side. Valva stood on the other side of the pit, staring him down. They faced off. Each daring the other to make the next move.

Giguhl feinted a move to the right. Valva jumped into action, moving to her left. Surprisingly agile in her spiked heels, she performed a complicated series of leaping spins and kicks. Giguhl stood off to the side, watching her with wide eyes. Hell, even I wanted to applaud when she managed three back handsprings in a row.

She stopped a few feet in front of him, a challenge in her eyes. Giguhl raised his left arm and flexed his impressive biceps. Valva's full lips spread into an approving smile. Then, inexplicably, he performed a back flip. I gasped. Who knew Giguhl was so nimble?

He jumped up and landed on just his hands and walked

the perimeter of the pit. When he was back in front of
Valva, he flipped back over and picked her up. She giggled
as he spun her around his head. He tossed her in the air
and caught her in his arms.

I rolled my eyes. Maisie laughed next to me, enjoying
the show. But the rest of the crowd started booing. They'd
paid to see a fight, not some bizarre demon mating dance.

"No mercy! No mercy!"

Giguhl ignored them and set Valva gently on her feet.
Slade jumped into the ring and approached the pair. I ran
forward to play referee should the need arise.

Slade covered the mic with his free hand. "What the
fuck is going on here? You know the rules. Two demons
enter; one demon leaves."

"Screw the rules."

"Yeah," Valva said in a high-pitched voice. She re-
warded Giguhl's rebellion with a kiss on his cheek. His
green scales flashed red for a moment—the demon version
of a blush.

A few members of the audience booed. Others picked
up the chant. "Two demons enter; one demon leaves!"

Giguhl grabbed the mic from Slade, who looked like he
wanted to fight him for it but thought better of it. Giguhl
waved his hands for silence. "No one's going to the Pit of
Despair tonight."

Jeers and more boos greeted this announcement.
Giguhl ignored them and grabbed Valva. He dipped her
low, going in for a passionate kiss.

Slade turned on me. "Order him to fight!"

"Sorry, Slade. It's his decision."

He glared at me for a moment. "If he doesn't win, I'm
out a fortune."

"Sue me."

Just then, a male pushed past me and rushed into the ring. "Get off her!" He launched himself onto Giguhl's back. I grabbed the man by the scruff of his neck and pulled him off Giguhl.

The audience went quiet, holding their collective breath as they watched a new drama unfold. Maisie eased away from the crowd and came to stand next to me. "Who the hell are you?" I demanded.

He ignored me and jumped toward Valva. He grabbed her arm, inviting a low growl from Giguhl.

Slade stepped in. "That's Lenny. He's Valva's handler."

Lenny was a mage, judging by the scent of sandalwood coming off him. His lanky frame was covered in a bad suit, and his black hair looked like it had been slicked back using a pork chop. "You get your ass in gear and finish this fight," he yelled at Valva.

"Hey," I called. "I suggest you get your hand off the demon before Giguhl rips it off."

"Fuck that! She's going to finish this." He rose on his tiptoes and whispered angrily in Valva's ear. Giguhl shot me a look, begging me to let him take care of the mage. I shook my head.

"Calm down there, buddy," I said. "We can sort this out, but clearly, Valva doesn't want to fight."

He ignored me again and said to Valva, "You know the deal. You wanna stay with Lenny, you gotta earn your keep." He took a breath and changed tactics. His voice went from angry to sweetly threatening. "You don't want me to send you to the Pit of Despair, do you, sweetheart?"

Fear lit up Valva's golden irises. "No, Lenny. You can't send me there."

"What the hell's going on here?" I demanded to Slade in a low voice. "I thought she was supposed to throw the fight anyway."

Slade shrugged. "Lenny doesn't want to pay his debt, which just doubled since he didn't keep up his end of the deal."

"Whether she can fight or not, it doesn't sound like she wants to go home," Maisie said.

Lenny was sweating now. His eyes had a desperate glint. Too desperate. "I told you to kill that demon!"

"Hold on just a damned minute," I yelled. "What the hell do you mean by that? She was supposed to throw the fight!"

Shocked gasps rippled through the crowd. Slade cursed loudly. "Godsdammit, Sabina."

I was too concerned with figuring out what the hell was going on to worry about keeping Slade's racket a secret. "What did you mean she was supposed to kill him?"

Lenny's head jerked up, finally realizing he had an audience. "Fuck. She's gonna be pissed now."

I frowned. "Who is?"

Lenny shook his head. "Like I'd tell you. It's all your fault anyway, bitch."

I did a double take. "How the hell is this my fault?" I felt like I'd entered the Twilight Zone.

Lenny's eyes went unfocused and wild. "It's too late. Unless . . ." Lenny spun around toward Giguhl.

A prickle started at the base of my neck as I realized Lenny was drawing up his magic. My blood went cold.

Time slowed. I leapt forward, my hand going for my gun. Valva fell as Lenny pushed her down. Giguhl's eyes went red with rage. Behind me, I heard Slade yell.

The air shifted, crackling with energy. A bolt of something flew past me and slammed into Lenny. His body jerked, his own spell going wide. He froze like a statue.

The entire room went still with shock. I stopped with my gun aimed at Lenny's inert body. Glancing over my shoulder, I saw Maisie lower her hands. She saw my look and shrugged. "We can figure this out without anyone dying." Her voice held an undertone of steel I'd never heard before.

Slade burst into action, calling on his bouncers to clear the room. While they rounded up the confused crowd, I slid my gun back into my waistband. Adrenaline still singed through me, making my hands shake. Giguhl helped Valva off the floor. He wrapped his green arms around her while she quietly sobbed against his chest.

Maisie came to stand next to me. "Sorry about that."

"No, thank you," I said, realizing I really meant it. "Now we can get some answers out of him."

It took a few more minutes for Slade's men to clear the room. When the last patron exited, he came to join us. He ran a hand through his hair and blew out a breath. "Remind me why I shouldn't kick your ass out of here right now. Do you have any idea how much money you just cost me?"

I crossed my arms. "That's your own damned fault, and you know it."

"Children, do you think you can hold off on the blame game until we figure out why Lenny wanted Giguhl dead?"

Slade shot me a glare but nodded at Maisie. "You're right, Fiona. What do you suggest we do?"

I blinked. I'd forgotten the whole Fiona charade.

"First of all," she said and paused. A trickle of energy made my skin tingle. Sparkles of magic circled Maisie, morphing her back into her normal appearance as they traveled down her body. "My name's not Fiona. It's Maisie."

Slade's eyes widened and his mouth fell open. I smiled, enjoying the rare sight of Slade being caught off guard.

"What the hell is going on here?" he demanded, looking at me.

"Slade, this is my sister, the honorable Maisie Graecus."

He blinked and stared at Maisie. "Maisie Graecus, as in the leader of the Hekate Council? You're Sabina's sister?"

"Twin sister," she corrected, smiling.

"Excuse me, but if you're done with the introductions, we have a situation here," Giguhl said.

Slade schooled his features. "I apologize if anything I've said tonight has offended you," he said to Maisie. "I had no idea who you were."

She waved away his apology while I rolled my eyes at his ass kissing. "That was the point. I'd hoped to avoid revealing my identity, but since this situation involves both my sister and one of my constituents . . ." She trailed off, looking toward Lenny.

"Of course," Slade said. "If there anything I can do, just let me know."

She nodded dismissively, obviously lost in thought as she puzzled how to proceed.

I crossed my arms, trying to tamp down my impatience. If it was up to me, Lenny would already be dead. But Maisie was right. We needed to get to the bottom of this mess.

"Do you have any brass handy?" Maisie asked finally.

"Of course," Slade said. He walked over to Giguhl and pulled a set of keys out of his pocket. Giguhl glared at him while he unlocked the collar.

"Take off hers, too," Giguhl demanded.

Slade glanced at Maisie. She nodded. "By all means."

He clicked off Valva's collar next and brought both to Maisie. She shook her head. "Please place it on Lenny."

Slade smiled his apology at his lack of thought. Brass dampens magic. That's why all the demons in fight club had to wear brass collars. It prevented them from cheating and blasting their opponents with demon magic. They also worked on mages, which was why Maisie refused to touch them.

Slade clamped a collar around Lenny's neck. "Okay," he said.

Maisie's movements were economical as she switched into business mode. "I'm going to release the spell in a moment. Let's make this clear from the beginning: I'll be asking the questions. If any of you are unable to hold your tongue during this process, you will be asked to leave. Is that clear?"

The four of us nodded. Maisie took a step closer to Lenny and whispered something under her breath. The air popped as the spell released. Lenny stumbled forward, his previous momentum cut short. "What the hell?" he yelled. His hands moved to his neck. When he realized what was around his neck, he paused. His eyes closed. "Oh, fuck. I'm a dead man."

"Now, now, no one's going to kill you," Maisie said. "We just have a few questions."

Lenny shook his head. "You're wrong. When she finds out the demon's still alive, she's going to kill me."

"Who is?" Maisie said in a soothing voice.

Lenny was so distraught he didn't even realize Maisie had changed appearance. "I don't know!"

I clenched my fists against the urge to jump in and throttle the mage. Maisie moved closer, all soothing voice and calming movements. "What do you mean you don't know? How did you know someone wanted Giguhl out of the way?"

Lenny ran a hand through his greasy hair. "I got a phone call. Some chick told me that if I had Valva challenge the new demon fighting at Vein, she'd make sure all my debts were paid."

"She asked for Valva specifically?" When he nodded, she continued. "Why?"

"She said he'd beaten the other demons too easily. Maybe a hot piece of demon ass like Valva would distract him long enough so she could kill him."

I glanced over at Valva. She shot Giguhl a pained look, as if apologizing. He patted her arm to let her know he didn't blame her for Lenny's plan.

Maisie frowned. "But I thought you and The Shade had an agreement that if Valva threw the fight, your debt would be forgiven. Why agree to this mage's plan?"

"He offered me that deal after I'd accepted the chick's offer. She sent a wad of cash as a down payment. The note she sent with the money said failure would be really bad for my health."

"If she sent you money for the debt, why accept Slade's offer?" I said, unable to help myself.

"It was the only way I could guarantee Valva would

get in the ring with the Mischief. Shit! Now everything's ruined."

"Damned straight," Slade said. "Your debt just tripled to cover the money I lost tonight."

"Oh, gods!" Lenny's shoulders drooped.

"Lenny, I need you to calm down and focus. When did this female contact you?"

He gasped back a sob. "Two days ago."

"Did she give you a name? A number? Anything?"

He shook his head. "Nothing. The number showed up as unlisted. No name, either. I think she was a mage, though."

Maisie's eyes shot to mine. I nodded, acknowledging I caught the implication. Now we knew whoever sent Eurynome was female. Now the suspect list included only fifty percent of the mage population.

"Why do you think she was a mage?" Maisie asked.

"She said something about that one there"—he pointed at me—"being a threat to magekind."

The hair on the back of my neck prickled. I gritted my teeth against the questions that revelation brought up. Maisie was on top of it, though.

"If Sabina's the threat, why did she want Giguhl dead?" Maisie asked.

"She said she needed the demon out of the way so she could personally take out the mixed-blood."

A growl ripped through the room, echoing off the concrete walls. Lenny cringed, not so brave now that he couldn't hide behind his magic. I could practically smell Giguhl's anger. I couldn't blame him, since I was feeling pretty hot myself. Maisie shot the demon a warning look. Valva petted his arm until he stilled.

"I've heard enough," Maisie declared. "Lenny, you are under arrest for the attempted murder of a mage's familiar." She looked at Slade as Lenny's head drooped. "I need a phone."

Slade pulled his cell from an inner pocket of his suit coat. While Maisie called in backup, I went over to Giguhl.

"I'm not in trouble, am I?" Valva said.

I fought against the instinct to blame her for her part of this mess. It wasn't her fault she'd been summoned by an asshole. "No, it's not your fault." I smiled tightly. "G, can I talk to you for a sec?"

Giguhl nodded and kissed Valva on the forehead. When he pulled away, his body was covered in gold glitter. I pulled him far enough away that Valva couldn't listen in.

"This is some shit, huh?" he said. "Can you believe that douchebag?"

I swallowed, hating what I was about to say. "She can't stay, G," I blurted.

He paused. "Why the hell not?" he demanded finally.

"She's his property."

"Like hell!" he growled.

I sighed. "Listen, I know you like her, but he's probably going to jail or whatever the mages do to attempted murderers. He'll probably have to send her back when that happens."

"This is bullshit," he said. "It's not her fault!"

I placed a hand on his arm. "I know that."

He looked over at Valva. She had her golden arms wrapped around her middle as she watched Lenny beg Maisie not to turn him in. She looked vulnerable and lost standing there alone. "Can you talk to Maisie? See if there's another way?"

"I don't know—"

His eyes pleaded with me. "Please, Sabina. I love her."

I frowned at him. "How can you love her? You met her thirty minutes ago."

"I can't explain it." He sighed like a lovesick swain. "Valva completes me."

I rolled my eyes.

"I'm serious." And he was; I could see it in his eyes. My demon was in love.

I sighed. "Fine. I'll talk to Maisie."

Giguhl pumped a fist in the air. "Yes!"

I held up a hand. "But I'm not promising anything. Don't get your hopes up. She could very well send Valva back herself tonight."

He nodded eagerly as if he understood, but I could see he was already planning a demon wedding in his head.

With a martyred sigh, I walked back toward the ring. Maisie was talking softly to Valva. As I watched, she put her arm around the demoness. I paused, not wanting to interrupt. Maybe their bonding moment would soften Maisie up for my request. Of course, the wait also gave me time to think about the consequences of Valva staying. I didn't want two demons under my care. Hell, I could barely manage to keep Giguhl out of trouble.

Finally, Maisie gave Valva a final squeeze and came my way. When she reached me, she pulled me aside. "We need to talk about Valva."

"Actually, that's what I wanted to talk to you about too. Giguhl—"

Maisie interrupted. "I have to send her home, Sabina. I know Giguhl likes her, but Lenny's going to trial. We can't have a demon hanging around without someone taking responsibility for her."

"What if I take custody of her?" Not that I wanted a second minion, but I didn't want to let Giguhl down.

Maisie shook her head. "Sabina, don't you think you have enough on your plate without adding a second minion?"

I sighed. "Probably, but I can work something out."

Giguhl and Valva had been sidling closer as we talked, and now they were just a few feet away.

Maisie noticed them, too, and lowered her voice. "Are you sure?"

I looked at the demons. Giguhl pleaded with his eyes. Maybe having two demons at my disposal wouldn't be so bad. "It's the least I can do."

Maisie sighed. "If that's what you want. I'll have to have Lenny transfer control to you."

"He can do that?"

Maisie nodded. "Yeah, it's a simple transference spell. I'll tell him if he cooperates we'll take that into account during the trial."

"Okay," I said. "Let's do this."

Behind me I heard Giguhl whisper, "Yes!"

Maisie shot me a look like she thought I was crazy before she went to talk to Lenny. While they discussed the logistics, I went back to the demons.

"Well, Valva, looks like you get to stay." Then something occurred to me. No one had asked her opinion of this plan. "That is, if you want to?"

She looked up at Giguhl and smiled. "I do."

I barely managed not to roll my eyes. Who knew demons could be so sappy?

Over her head, Giguhl mouthed, "Thank you."

I nodded, suddenly feeling better about the decision.

"Okay," Maisie called. "We're ready."

The three of us went over to Maisie and Lenny.

"I'll remind you that any aggression on your part when I take off this collar will be added to your list of crimes," Maisie was saying.

Lenny nodded, looking broken. "Yeah, I know."

Maisie nodded to Slade, who unlocked the collar. Lenny took a moment to rub his neck. "I'm gonna need the salt from my backpack."

Slade went to the rumpled knapsack Lenny had dropped outside the ring. He found the box of salt and brought it to Lenny.

"Okay, everyone stand back," he said.

I cast a threatening glance his way to discourage any shenanigans. But he just went about pouring the circle in a businesslike manner. When he was done, he rubbed his palms together. "I'm ready."

Maisie nodded her permission, and we all stood silently while Lenny closed his eyes. Soon, a shimmering wall of magic rose around Valva.

"Enu Iddimu. Nadanu a Sabina Kane. Ana Harrani sa Alaktasa la Tara."

A laserlike beam of magic shot out from the circle and landed on Maisie, making her hair stand on end. After a moment, the light disappeared and the sheet of magic around Valva descended. I jerked, worried Lenny had figured out a way to harm Maisie. Since the spell was done in the Hekatian language, I had no idea what he'd just said. But other than a scowl and mussed hair, she looked fine.

Maisie's breath escaped her in a rush. "What the hell! I told you to transfer the demon to Sabina!"

"Oh, shit," I whispered, cluing in on the situation.

Lenny frowned. "I don't know what happened. You heard me say Sabina's name. It should have worked."

"Wait, what's going on?" Giguhl said, looking worried.

Maisie turned to him. "Lenny screwed up and transferred Valva to me instead of Sabina."

"I didn't screw up," Lenny muttered.

"Can't he just undo the spell?" I asked Maisie.

My sister sighed, looking annoyed. "No. Our only option is for me to transfer her to you myself." She shook out her hands and smoothed her hair. "Go stand by the circle and we'll try it again."

I went to stand next to the circle of salt. Valva stood inside, waiting patiently. "Okay," I said. "We're ready."

Maisie cleared her throat and raised her hands. She drew Valva's sigil in the air and repeated the spell Lenny had used verbatim—or so I thought. It certainly sounded the same to me.

I held my breath, waiting for the transfer spell to hit me. But nothing happened. After a few seconds of waiting, I grew restless. "Maisie?"

Maisie's mouth fell open. "It's not working."

Lenny snorted, looking superior. "Now who screwed up?"

Maisie rounded on the male. "I did the spell right. There's no reason the transfer shouldn't have worked."

Giguhl stepped forward. "Actually, there is one reason."

"What do you mean?" I asked.

He shrugged. "Maybe Valva's supposed to be with Maisie."

I looked at Maisie, gauging her reaction to Giguhl's theory. She looked shocked by the idea.

Giguhl continued. "Think about it. When I met Sabina, she wasn't looking for a familiar either. It just kind of happened without her really asking for it. Sort of like it was meant to be."

Maisie didn't look convinced. "I don't know, guys. Mages usually chose their familiars. With you it's different because you're a Chthonic. It makes sense you'd have a demon familiar."

"Yeah, but maybe the mixed-blood thing has something to with it," I said, playing devil's advocate. "Besides, you said before you've always wanted a familiar."

Maisie opened her mouth to respond, but three Pythian Guards flashed into the fight ring to take custody of Lenny. Maisie spent the next few minutes filling them in on what happened and handing out instructions. Once they left with Lenny, she turned back to us.

"Okay, I'm not convinced Valva's supposed to be my familiar, but until I can consult with Rhea and figure out what happened, there's not much I can do." She shot an apologetic look at Valva. "I'm sorry about all this."

Valva shrugged. "I don't mind. No offense, but anyone's better than Lenny."

Maisie smiled at the Vanity. "Thanks. We'll get this sorted out soon."

As she went to speak with Slade, and Giguhl and Valva began whispering to each other, I blew out a breath. What started as a girls' night out had ended in an attempted murder on Giguhl and my sister being stuck with a demon familiar she didn't want. I wasn't sure how the Maisie thing was going to shake out, but I did know one thing: No one messed with my demon. It was time to stop waiting for the council to find the mage behind all these attempts on my life. That bitch was going down.

24

The next evening, I was getting ready to head to the council meeting when my bedroom door burst wide open. Orpheus stood on the threshold looking like an enraged god.

"You!" he said, his voice low and menacing.

I frowned at him. "You were expecting someone else? This is my room, after all."

He pointed an accusing finger at me. "How could you take Maisie into that pit of iniquity?"

Ah, so that's what this was about. "Look, dude, she wanted to go. I tried to talk her out of it, but it was her decision."

Orpheus moved through the door and slammed it shut behind him. "I don't give a damn whose idea it was. You should have known better than to take the oracle to a seedy dive bar. I knew you were trouble the moment you arrived."

I crossed my arms. "You need to chill out. Nothing happened. Maisie's fine."

He sputtered for a moment, tripping over his tongue

in his rush to argue. "You call getting involved in an attempted murder nothing?"

I shrugged. "She handled herself well. In fact, she made sure everything worked out."

"If you call coming home with the stray demon of an attempted murderer working everything out."

I raised my chin. "I do, actually."

"I won't have this. You hear me? Maisie needs to focus on regaining her visions. She doesn't need to be wasting time consorting with the dregs of dark-race society." His tone implied he included me in that group.

"Look, buddy, I know you're used to calling the shots around here. But Maisie's a grown female. She makes her own choices. Maybe instead of treating her like some fragile doll, you should treat her like the intelligent, strong female she is. And just maybe, if you stop pressuring her to be a one-woman vision factory, she'll be able to relax long enough to start seeing the future again."

His eyes narrowed and his posture went all stiff and offended. "You think you know so much? You've been here a few days. I've known Maisie her whole life. Helped Ameritat raise her as if she was my own daughter, out of respect for your father's memory. So don't tell me how to deal with Maisie when you yourself have shown complete disregard for both her station and her safety. Your father would be ashamed of you."

I leaned forward, my jaw clenched and my stare icy. "I don't give a fuck what Tristan Graecus would think of me."

"And why doesn't that surprise me? You father was a hero. A mage of honor. How his genes managed to pro-

duce such a selfish and irresponsible brat like yourself is
a mystery."

My mouth dropped open at the venom in both his eyes
and his words. Before I could respond to his attack, however, he turned on his heel and slammed out of the room.

I went to the quivering doorframe and watched his
angry progress down the hall. The door next to me opened
and a horned head stuck out. Giguhl watched Orpheus's
retreat for a second. Then his head turned toward me.
"What was that all about?"

I blew out a breath. "Someone's not happy about
Maisie's night out."

Worry spread over Giguhl's face. "You don't think he's
going to make her send Valva back to Irkalla, do you?"

I shrugged. "I honestly don't know, G. He's not happy
about it, but I don't know if he has the power to make
Maisie get rid of her. I'll speak to her this evening and
find out what she's learned about the mix-up with the
transference."

Giguhl opened his mouth to say something, but just then
a golden arm snaked out from the door behind him. The
fingers tugged Giguhl's arm. "Come back to bed, my little
mischief maker." Valva's high-pitched voice was muffled
but unmistakable.

"Just a minute, my little peacock," he said. He turned
back to me. "Talk to Maisie."

I nodded. "I'm about to go to the council meeting. I'll
see if I can talk to her after."

"Thanks, Sabina." The golden hands pulled him back
into the room and slammed the door behind him. A few
seconds later, squeals and moans echoed down the hallway.
I sent a quick prayer of thanks to goddess I had somewhere

else to be. Giguhl and Valva's sex-a-thon kept waking me up all day, and I was going to stake myself if I had to listen to another round.

I grabbed my gun and hid it in a thigh holster under my chiton. The council didn't allow mundane weapons into the council chamber, but what they didn't know wouldn't hurt them. After Lenny's revelations the night before, I wasn't about to put myself in a room full of mages without a weapon. I might need more practice with my newfound magical skills, but I had plenty of experience using a gun. And I wouldn't hesitate to put that experience to use if someone came after me again.

From my vantage point in the front row of the audience, the entire council looked wound up tighter than concertina wire. In addition to the tension of the coming meeting, the fallout from the previous night's debacle was also clearly in play. Maisie kept shooting resentful looks at Orpheus. He steadfastly refused to even look at her, preferring instead to glare at me. I preferred to watch the small male sitting to Orpheus's left.

He had to be a faery with his knife's-blade cheekbones and luminescent skin. He filled out his green velvet coat and frilly white shirt with a muscular torso. His long brown hair covered his ears, but I'd bet cash money their tips were pointed. In short, he was gorgeous, but that wasn't why I watched him. Disdain twisted his cupid's-bow mouth and narrowed his almond eyes as he watched me.

Looked like the queen's emissary wasn't a fan. Since we'd never even met, his attitude surprised me. But before

I could ponder the whys, Orpheus banged his gavel on the table.

"This meeting of the ancient and venerable Hekate Council is now called to order."

The room fell silent except for the occasional shifting of bodies trying to get comfortable on the impossibly small cushions covering the floor. I caught Maisie's eye and sent her an encouraging smile. She tried to return it, but her lips formed a tight grimace instead.

Poor Maisie, I thought. Now that I knew about her vision problem, I could only imagine the intense performance pressure she must be feeling.

"As you all know, the council has been seriously debating the prospect of declaring war against the Dominae. We understand you're all invested in the outcome of our decision, but we ask for your continued patience as we weigh all the potential consequences." He paused and took a sip of water. I couldn't help but get the sense he was stalling.

"In addition to investigating the situation, we have also been in negotiations with Queen Maeve's special envoy, Hawthorne Banathsheh." He nodded toward the faery. "If the Council votes for war, the Queen's support will be crucial to achieving victory. To Mr. Banathsheh, we'd like to extend our welcome and our assurances the Hekate Council is committed to continuing our cherished alliance with all faekind."

Hawthorne nodded regally with a slight smile. "High Councilman Orpheus, Queen Maeve, may the Goddess protect Her, would like to extend her warmest regards to all members of this esteemed council as well as your honorable constituents. The queen is pleased we were able to come to a satisfactory resolution to our negotiations. If the Hekate Council, in its wisdom, decides war is the best course of action, the queen is prepared to offer her full support."

A ripple of excitement made its way through the mages. I sat up a little straighter at the news myself. I just couldn't figure out why Maisie didn't look more pleased by her success with the fae envoy.

Hawthorne smiled at the audience. "Together, our ancient and noble races will finally dispense with the scourge of all the dark races—the Dominae!"

As a cheer rose, the faery's eyes picked me out of the crowd. I shifted on my cushion uneasily. What was this guy's deal, anyway?

"Thank you, Envoy Banathsheh," Orpheus said. "Please send the queen our warmest regards upon your return to court tomorrow."

He shifted then to look at Maisie. "We will now hear from the Honorable Maisie Graecus. Maisie?" His voice was tight, as if he'd prefer not to talk to her. As it was, he barely managed to look at her.

Maisie, to her credit, rose with her shoulders back and her head held high. "I have nothing to report." She inclined her head respectfully in Orpheus's direction and sat back down.

Confused murmurs swarmed around me. Obviously, everyone was disappointed their oracle didn't have any new visions to report. Orpheus frowned and leaned over to Maisie, whispering. Maisie shook her head, her mouth tight. Orpheus stared at her hard for a moment. She met his gaze with her own, all but daring him to give her shit about her continued lack of visions. Finally, he sighed and turned back toward the mic. "This meeting is adjourned."

Outraged cries rang out over the crowd. The mages wanted more answers, but Orpheus stormed from the room. The envoy rose and went to speak with other members of the council, no doubt playing his diplomatic role to the hilt. I rose and went to Maisie. She was gathering paper and avoiding the glares of mages who walked by on their way toward the exit.

"Maisie?"

She looked up. "Hey, Sabina," she sighed.

I jerked my chin toward the door. "Someone's pissy. You okay?"

She sighed. "The only thing that will redeem me in Orpheus's eyes right now is being able to predict the outcome of the vote." She leaned in, whispering. "That's the real reason they're holding off now that we have the queen's support." She didn't sound happy about that bit of news.

"You'd figure they'd be happier about that."

A rueful smile spread on her lips. "Oh, the council's thrilled with the outcome. Queen Maeve has committed her army and resources to the war effort if the council declares."

I frowned, not understanding her bitter tone. "Isn't that a good thing?"

She shrugged. "In some respects. But I'm afraid of the price we'll all pay when this war happens."

I wasn't sure what I could say to ease her mind. The minute I found out the Dominae were angling for war, I knew it wouldn't end well for anyone. But with each passing day, war seemed inevitable. "Listen," I said, clumsily changing the subject, "I hope I didn't get you in trouble about last night."

"Don't worry about it. Orpheus wasn't happy, of course,

but he'll get over it. He's just tense about the vote right now." The corner of her mouth twisted up. "Besides, I don't really care if he's mad."

"Did you get a chance to talk to Rhea about the familiar thing?"

Maisie nodded. "Yeah, she agrees with Giguhl's theory. I didn't do the spell wrong, so there's no other explanation for why Valva is tied to me."

"I'm sorry."

"Don't be." She waved away my concern. "To be honest, I'm kind of excited to have my very own demon."

"Really? You're not going to send her back to Irkalla, then?"

"Nah, I'm going to keep her. For some reason, the universe thinks I need a familiar right now. Who am I to argue? Besides, turns out she's pretty cool."

I ignored the universe comment and focused on the second part. Other than her being a screamer during sex, I didn't know much about Valva. "How so?"

"Did you know she can turn into a peacock?" Maisie asked.

I shook my head. "No, but I guess it makes sense. If a Mischief demon turns into a cat, I guess it makes sense a Vanity would turn into a peacock."

Maisie laughed. "But that's not all. She's also a whiz at organization. While Giguhl took a nap today, she completely rearranged my workshop. I had no idea I owned twelve tubes of alizarin crimson. She even organized my canvases by size. She's going to save me a fortune in painting supplies."

Neither of us mentioned the fact that if Maisie didn't start having visions again, she wouldn't be needing any new supplies. Still, I was glad to see her excited about the prospect of having her own minion. "That's great, Maze."

She nodded absently. "Although we're going to have to figure out some sort of conjugal-visit schedule for those two. The minute Giguhl woke up from his nap, she disappeared on me."

I laughed. "You may be right. They kept waking me up all day."

"Maisie?" Damara interrupted, coming toward us. She didn't even acknowledge my presence as she gave me her back to talk to Maisie. "Rhea needs to talk to you about the Blood Moon Festival."

"Oh!" Maisie said. "Sabina, I'm sorry. I promised Rhea we'd go over plans for the festival right now."

I waved a hand. "No problem. I was going to hit the gym anyway."

Maisie waved. "Cool. I'll look for you there after my meeting. I've got a surprise for you."

I raised an eyebrow. "Oh? What is it?"

She smiled. "You'll have to wait and see. Bye!" She rushed off with Damara in tow.

As I made my way out of the chambers toward the gym, I felt pretty good. There were still storm clouds on the horizon, of course, but for the first time in a while I felt like maybe the glass was half full. Maisie and I were growing closer, my magic lessons were progressing nicely, and the council had finally snagged the support of the queen, which meant Adam would be back soon. Yep, life was definitely looking up.

25

The gym was empty, thank the Goddess. I'd been so anxious to get there, I'd forgotten to change out of my ceremonial chiton. But I didn't want to take the time to run all the way to my room now, so I shrugged. The skirt was loose enough I could still kick, and the sleeveless design wouldn't get in the way of punching. I pulled the gun from my thigh holster and set in on the table so it wouldn't get in the way.

I probably should have been practicing my magic, but with Rhea busy with Maisie, I decided to sneak in a physical workout instead. It had been so long since I'd had the freedom to really put my body through the paces and work up a good, honest sweat.

I threw on a pair of boxing gloves and made a beeline for the punching bag in the corner. Soon my punches and kicks fell into a soothing rhythm, allowing my brain to focus on other things. I realized it had been days since I'd thought about my grandmother. When I'd arrived in New York, I'd been driven by the need for revenge. And while I still wanted to make her pay, I found that the edge of that need had dulled. One of these days, I'd meet her again face-to-face, but in the meantime, there were more pressing concerns. Like Maisie's prophecy, and a looming war, and finding out who was trying to kill me and why.

I hadn't told Maisie, but I resented how little the council had done to track down the mage who sent Eurynome after me. I hadn't mentioned it because, well, they had bigger issues to deal with. But I hoped that Lenny's attempt on Giguhl's life would light a fire under their asses. According to Maisie, Lenny was sitting in a cell in the basement of the building awaiting trial. But whoever sent him after Giguhl was smart. A trial wouldn't reveal the real culprit.

I imagined a female mage's face stamped on the front of the bag. Whoever the bitch was would pay for going after Giguhl. Coming after me was one thing, but no one threatened my friends.

My knuckles started to bleed, but I kept punching. The pain eased some of my frustration. My breath came in quick pants now.

My mind shifted back to my conversation with Michael Romulus. He seemed to think the mage who tried to kill me might be working for someone else. But who?

Wham, wham, wham—I punched faster.

If Michael was right, why would someone want to make sure I didn't have any allies?

Whack! I side-kicked the bag twice. I jogged around it now, hitting it with jabs and kicks, punishing it for not giving me answers.

Finally, the bag surrendered under the force of my

blows and split open. Sand spilled to the floor like blood from a wound. My breath heaving, I lifted my hands. My fingers throbbed hotly. The knuckles looked like someone had taken a mallet to them.

I sighed. Violence was so simple. Kill or be killed. Wound or be wounded. There was a pleasing symmetry in the black and white of it. Mages seemed to prefer shades of gray. And the longer I stayed with them, the more that gray creeped into my brain. The more I felt like I was groping my way through a dense fog.

"I think it's dead."

I spun into a crouch, hissing in surprise at the intruder.

Hawthorne Banathsheh stood in the doorway, his hands raised. "I apologize for catching you off guard."

I rose and forced my muscles to relax. My heart still pounded, but I forced a casual shrug. "I didn't hear you come in."

He pushed away from the door. "Not surprising." He nodded toward the ruined punching bag.

I crossed my arms. "No offense, but I'm not really in the mood for a chat."

Hawthorne ignored that and moved farther into the room. "I haven't had a chance to properly introduce myself."

Remembering his disdain during the council meeting, I raised my chin. "I know who you are, and let's not pretend you don't know who I am. Just tell me what you want and leave."

"As you wish." He pulled a sword from the scabbard at his side.

I should have felt surprised or angry. Instead, I felt a healthy dose of irony and weariness. "Put the blade away, Peter Pan. You might accidentally cut yourself."

You'd think a faery facing down a seasoned assassin might look a little anxious. Instead, Hawthorne Banath-sheh had the calm countenance of a professional killer. "This is faery steel," he said in a conversational tone. "Did you know these swords are specifically designed for decapitating vampires? That's one of the reasons the council wanted the queen's support so badly."

For the first time since he drew the blade, my heart picked up a notch. He flicked the blade so it caught the light. The metal had an iridescent glow that implied it held some sort of magic.

I shifted my weight to the balls of my feet. "That's interesting." From the corner of my eye, I gauged the distance to my gun. "But I'd be more interested to know why you're pulling it on me?"

He moved to the right, tracking my movements with the blade. "It's simple, really. You're a threat to our plans."

"Whose plans?"

He laughed, sidestepping to the right, putting himself between me and the gun. "I'm afraid that's classified information."

"Fair enough," I said. "How are you going to explain murdering me to the council?"

He tilted his head to the side. "Sabina, let's not be naive. Your temper is well-known, as is your murderous background. Do you really think anyone here is going to question me when I tell them you attacked me? Not when they're all counting on the queen's support."

He was smart, I'd give him that.

I considered just rushing him and ending this. But blades are tricky. The minute something stabby enters a fight, someone's getting cut. Since he was the one with the sword, it didn't take a leap to figure out who'd be bleeding. I wasn't sure exactly how the faeries crafted their steel, but I was pretty sure it held some sort of nasty spell. I didn't want to chance getting nicked to find out for sure.

Instead, I feinted left and rolled right. Hawthorne took the bait but recovered quickly, overcorrecting to give chase. The blade whistled through the air just above my head. I came up with my back to the table. If I could avoid Hawthorne's parries and thrusts for a few more steps, I'd grab the gun and end this.

But with his next swing, something shiny fell free of his frilly shirt. Normally, seeing a necklace wouldn't have distracted me, but when I saw the gold eight-pointed star pendant, I hesitated.

In that split second, moving fast as lightning, Hawthorne slashed my left arm. The wound was shallow but hurt like hellfire. I'd been right about the sword being spelled. The flesh tingled painfully for a split second before going completely numb.

I dove for the gun with my left hand. At that moment, Hawthorne's sword slashed viciously at my arm, knocking the gun from my hand and slicing a gash down my forearm. The gun dropped to the floor and the feeling raced out of my arm.

My heart slammed into my ribs, and cold sweat covered my body. I went limp, dropping to the floor. Hawthorne's blade slashed the air in front of my neck. I hit the floor hard and rolled. I cursed and rolled again as the faery bastard came back for another swipe. Obviously, I couldn't just roll around the floor praying for help to arrive. Time to call on the only other weapon available to me.

Hawthorne's boot slammed into my ribs. "Lie still and accept your fate."

Time slowed. Hawthorne's sword cut a slow, wide arc through the air. The energy exploded through me hard and fast. I screamed with the force of it. The faery's eyes widened a split second before the spell blasted out of my eyes and right into his midsection. His green jacket ignited immediately. His mouth gaped mid-swing, and a gasp escaped his mouth. The sword clattered against the hardwoods.

His screams raised the hairs on the back of my neck. Flames licked Hawthorne's body like hungry mouths, consuming him. He ran in circles, as if it was possible to escape the agony. But his movements only encouraged the fire to burn hotter, brighter.

It was one thing to watch a dummy burn. But watching the faery jerk and wail as he burned alive was truly horrifying. The scent of burnt flesh stung my nose.

I crawled to my knees, watching helplessly. My conscience kicked in, realizing what I'd done. Yes, he'd tried to kill me, but no one deserved to die like this. He finally collapsed into a mewling heap by the windows. Still, the fire burned. Pink scalp showed through the smoldering remains of his hair. His lips were burned off, leaving his mouth nothing but a mass of teeth. The grotesque facsimile of a smile made bile rise in my throat.

By this time, I'd begun to get feeling back in my arms. Without allowing myself to think too hard about what I was about to do, I picked up the gun. I limped slowly toward the windows.

I stood over the smoldering body and listened. A soft wheeze escaped his charred mouth. His lidless eyes were open, the pupils shot through with red. I crouched down and placed my ear next to his ruined face. The skeletal face groaned, making me jump. That one pathetic noise made my decision for me.

I pulled the trigger.

26

They found me sitting next to the body. The gun still in my hand and my eyes on the golden pendant.

I heard Maisie's gasp first, followed by a male curse. Footsteps pounded across the wooden floor. I looked up slowly and then blinked.

"Adam?"

His handsome face was creased with worry as he knelt in front of me. "Sabina? Talk to me." His hands ran over my face, checking for injuries. When he reached my arms, his eyes narrowed. The skin had closed but remained hot and angry red.

"Oh, my gods!" Maisie groaned, covering her mouth at the sight of the faery's ruined body. "Sabina, what happened?"

"I-I don't know. One minute I was working out, and the next thing I knew he pulled a sword on me."

"What? Why would he do that?" Maisie said.

"I don't know. He was too busy trying to chop my head off to explain himself. But I think I know who he was working for." I pointed to the amulet. "And it wasn't just the queen."

Maisie tried to look, but her eyes skittered away from the gruesome display. Adam, made of stronger stuff, rose and frowned down at the body. "Is that what I think it is?"

"What is it?" Maisie asked.

"It's supposedly an amulet worn by members of the Caste of Nod," I said. "I saw one once in a magic store in L.A. When I asked about it, the clerk got all agitated. Told me a faery whose mother worked for the Caste pawned it. He begged me not to tell anyone he had it, because he didn't want that kind of attention."

Maisie looked at Adam, who nodded solemnly. "I've never seen one in person before, but I've heard the same thing."

"Even if he is a member of the Caste, why would he want to kill you?" she said. Her face looked like it had aged years. "Sabina, this is bad. Really bad."

"Tell me about it," I said. "It's not like I asked him to try to kill me, Maisie."

She hesitated. "Are you absolutely positive he struck first?"

I looked at Adam and saw the same question lurking in his eyes.

Seeing their suspicion, something inside me broke. I suppose on some level, I knew they'd never believe me. Hell, I wouldn't have believed me, either. They'd literally found me holding a smoking gun—next to a smoking body. Still, the doubt in their eyes cut me deep.

Before I could defend myself, Orpheus burst into the room. "What the hell is going on here?" He stopped short when he saw the body. His face contorted into a mask of rage. "How could you do this?"

"Orpheus—" Maisie began, only to be cut off.

"Lazarus, arrest her."

Adam hesitated. At that moment, a dozen other mages, including Rhea, Damara, Giguhl, and a few guards, spilled into the room. How word traveled so fast, I had no idea.

"Lazarus! I told you to take this murderer into custody!" Orpheus shouted over the shocked gasps of the newcomers.

Adam stepped forward. "Sir, I think we need to let her explain."

Orpheus glared at Adam. "Are you questioning the leader of the Hekate Council, boy? I gave you an order."

Adam's chin came up. "She claims it was self-defense, sir. Surely she deserves a chance to explain."

"I don't give a damn who struck first. Someone with her training should be able to subdue a faery without lethal force. From the looks of that body, she not only tortured him with magic, she also shot him point-blank in the head. That's not self-defense."

"Sabina wouldn't have done this without a reason," Giguhl said, breaking into the argument.

"Giguhl," I said quietly, with a warning clear in my voice. I appreciated his defending me, but I didn't want him in the middle. If Orpheus got his way and they locked me up, Giguhl might be considered guilty by association.

Two guards had taken my arms during the argument. I allowed the restraint because fighting them would only worsen matters.

Through the gathering crowd, I spotted Rhea standing near the door. Her gaze met mine, but instead of disappointment or condemnation, her expression was thoughtful and maybe a little sad.

"The demon's right," she said, calling out to be heard over the raised voices. "Sabina might have a temper, but I don't buy that she'd kill the faery in cold blood without a damned good reason."

Orpheus turned toward Rhea. At her defense, some of the wind came out of his sails, but he didn't change his course. To back down now would make him look indecisive and weak. "Regardless of her reason, she just murdered a high-ranking member of Queen Maeve's court," he said. "I have no choice but to lock her up pending an investigation." He nodded to the guards holding my arms. "Take her to the holding cell."

"Orpheus, no!" Maisie pleaded. Tears streamed down her face.

He looked at Maisie with regret on his face. "If the queen finds out I made an exception just because she's your sister, things will only be worse for all of us."

A muscle worked in Adam's jaw. "I'll take her down."

"You're lucky I'm not throwing you in a cell for insubordination as it is," Orpheus snapped. "You two," he nodded to the guards holding me, "lock her up."

Rough hands pulled me up and led me out of the room. I went along willingly. More than anything, I craved silence. A private moment so I could fall apart without an audience.

As I passed Adam, he shot me a look full of longing. I shook my head imperceptibly. I didn't want him getting into more trouble over me. I wasn't worth it. I'd screwed up everything he and Maisie had worked for by killing the faery.

He nodded and went to put an arm around Maisie, whose body was shaking with loud sobs.

As I passed Giguhl I said, "Stay close to Maisie. And whatever you do, don't do anything stupid."

The demon's claws worked like he wanted to punch something, but he jerked a nod. He'd obey me on this. I shot him a forced smile and allowed the guards to lead me through the room. Just before we went through the door, Rhea held up a hand to stop the guards.

"Stay calm and have faith," she said.

I nodded to let her know I appreciated her support. But faith and I weren't on speaking terms, and I highly doubted spending time in a cell would change my opinion.

Ten minutes later, metal bars shot through with brass slammed shut in my face. I slid down the walls of the cramped cell. I wrapped my arms around my stomach. I worried if I didn't, I'd literally break into pieces.

There was a crack in the wall a few feet away. Just a small fissure. I stared at it for a long time.

It's not that I'd given up. More like I'd just accepted the truth. I'd fucked up big-time. I knew how much was riding on the queen's support, and now I'd compromised everything Maisie had been working for. Orpheus wasn't right, though. If I hadn't killed the faery, he would have killed me. No doubt about it. I'd seen the murderous intent in his eyes. But the fact I had no choice didn't make the situation less volatile. Even if I could convince the council the faery had forced my hand, they'd still blame me for screwing up their chance of getting the queen's support.

A roach crawled out of the crack then. As it scurried

across the floor, I thought about Hawthorne's necklace. Instinct told me I was right about his connection to the Caste of Nod. I turned that over in my head, looking at it from every angle. But hard as I tried, I couldn't figure out why the Caste would want me dead. I'd never even met a member of the Caste—that I knew of. And even if I had, what threat could I possibly pose to them?

A crackle of energy sounded outside the cell. I didn't feel it since I was behind brass, but I heard it. I finally blinked and looked away from the crack in time to see Maisie materialize on the other side of the bars.

"We have to hurry," Maisie said. Reaching into a hidden pocket of her skirt, she produced a key. I watched as she unlocked the cell door. Didn't move as it swung open.

"Sabina? We have to hurry."

I blinked again.

She snapped her fingers in my face. "You have to snap out of it. You have to get out of here."

I tilted my head to the side. "Why?"

"If they hand you over to the queen, she'll have you executed."

"No," I said slowly. "Why are you helping me?"

She sighed. "Because you're my sister. And I know you wouldn't have killed the faery unless you had to."

"Don't fool yourself, Maisie. I'm an assassin, remember? I don't need a good reason to kill."

She grabbed my arms and shook me. "Stop it. I know you were defending yourself. And I'm not going to allow Orpheus to hand you over to the queen as some sort of sacrificial lamb."

"I burned him, Maisie." My voice cracked.

Her face was grave. "And then you put him out of his

misery. You did the right thing, Sabina. So stop punishing yourself. He was going to kill you." She grabbed my hand. "Adam and I are going to keep working on Orpheus, but you need to disappear for a while. Just until the heat dies down."

I closed my eyes. How had things gotten fucked up so fast?

"What was Adam doing back, anyway? I thought he wasn't coming until the festival."

"When I wrapped up the negotiations with Hawthorne"— her voice cracked on his name—"I convinced Orpheus to let Adam come back early. That was my surprise."

I opened my eyes and looked into my sister's watery blue gaze. She'd thought she was playing Cupid, organizing a reunion between me and Adam, and I'd fucked it all up. "I'm sorry."

"No, I'm sorry. You deserve better than this." Another tear slid down her cheek.

I huffed a humorless laugh. "No, I don't. But I appreciate your support, no matter how misguided it may be."

"I figure the best thing to do is send you to Slade. Do you think he'll put you up for a few days? I'll send a message when it's safe to return."

Her suggestion made sense. Slade already wanted me to work for him. Surely he'd put me up for a few days if I agreed to do a couple of jobs.

"What about Giguhl?" I asked, trying to cover all the angles.

"I'll keep an eye on him."

I nodded. That was for the best. I didn't want to tear him away from Valva because of my fuckup.

"Tell Adam—" What could I say? At this point, he was

probably regretting ever bringing me to New York. "Just tell him I said good-bye, okay?"

Maisie swallowed hard. "There's no need. When you get back, you two can say everything that needs to be said to each other."

I forced a smile. "Okay."

I didn't have the heart to tell her I wouldn't be coming back.

Pins and needles exploded on every part of my body. Freezing wind whipped at my face and hair, making my teeth chatter. A high-pitched whine pummeled my eardrums. So intense I felt close to madness. My brain struggled to make sense of these sensations. But my thoughts shifted like quicksilver.

The wind stopped suddenly. My ears popped, and every nerve ending on my body sizzled in the silence.

I blinked and looked around. Vein's familiar urban decor surrounded me. Behind the bar, Earl paused in the process of drying a pint glass. His mouth hung open in shock.

"Hey, Earl."

He set the glass down slowly. "Hi."

"Slade around?"

He shook himself and nodded. "In his office."

Leaving the surprised barkeep staring, I turned toward the stairs. As I moved toward them, I realized Maisie had sent me away in my own clothes. The goddess bless my sister. If I'd shown up in Slade's bar wearing a blood-splattered chiton, it would only invite questions I wasn't prepared to answer. I squared my shoulders, not allowing myself to think too hard about what I had to do.

When I opened the office door after a quick knock, Slade looked up from his desk. He'd been frowning at an open ledger when I came in, but when he saw me, his face cracked into a surprised smile.

"Sabina?" He rose and came forward. "This is an unexpected pleasure."

"I just came to tell you I've decided to take you up on your offer."

Slade stopped midstride and frowned. "What?" His keen gaze swept over me. I'm not sure what he saw, but something shifted in his expression, moving from confusion to concern.

I swallowed, hating him for making me say it out loud. "Yes, I'll work for you."

"You look like hell." He put an arm around my shoulders. "Let's sit down and talk about it."

I shook my head and shrugged off his sympathy. "There's nothing to talk about. Either you want me to work for you, or you don't."

Slade watched me silently for a few moments. I wondered if I looked as broken as I felt. Finally he said, "I take it things didn't work out with the mages?"

I closed my eyes. "I said I didn't want to talk about it."

"I'll take that for a yes, then." He paused, his eyes warm with sympathy. "I might be able to scrounge up some work for you."

I opened my eyes again. This time, as I looked at Slade,

the backs of my eyes stung. Whether from relief or regret, I didn't know. Probably both. "It's just for a couple of days. So I'm ready to start immediately."

"Sabina, I don't think—"

I waved a hand to quiet his protest. "If that doesn't work for you, I'll figure something else out."

He blew out a breath. "Do you need money? Is that it?"

"I need to get out of town ASAP."

He frowned. "That bad?"

I nodded.

He leaned back into the couch and blew out a breath. "Look, I know it's none of my business, but maybe you shouldn't be making any hasty decisions right now."

"You're right," I said. "It isn't any of your business."

"Sabina—"

I gritted my teeth. "I'm fine, dammit." But the crack in my voice gave me away.

"Sure you are," he said with a knowing look. "Look, I'm not going to push you to spill your guts. Just know if you need to talk, I'm here, okay?"

I didn't want to talk about it. In fact, I was done talking about anything. Exhaustion clung to me like a parasitic vine. I stifled a yawn.

"You're beat. Why don't you crash here? There's a room behind the office with a futon. It's not much, but it's private and safe."

Leave it to Slade to understand that safety would outweigh comfort. "Thanks, Slade."

The corner of his mouth lifted. "Hey, what are friends for?" He patted my knee. "C'mon, the sun's almost up. I'll help you get settled and then head home."

I followed him across the office to a bookcase on the

far wall. He felt around for a hidden switch. The shelves slid aside smoothly, barely making a sound. Behind them, a steel door was set into the wall. "Nice," I said.

He shrugged and used a key to open the dead bolt. "I set it up as a panic room years ago. I sleep here when I get word some new blood decides they want to take over my turf."

"That happen often?"

He shook his head. "Not anymore."

He motioned for me to go first into the dark room. He flipped a switch and light bathed the small room. He was right. It wasn't much to write home about. A futon took up most of one wall. A small dorm fridge hummed in the corner. An out-of-date TV was hooked up to an old-school VCR with a few tapes piled next to it on the floor. Another door across the room probably led to a bathroom.

"What changed?" I asked. There was no use commenting on the room, so I focused on what he'd said.

"About twenty years ago, things were different. Turf wars were pretty common. The Hekate Council was worried the tensions would expose us all to humans. So they came to me and struck a deal. I'd get exclusive rights to sell their cash crops with a hefty commission. In return, I agreed to clean things up and keep the vamps and weres in line." He shrugged. "Every now and then some new blood comes to town and tries to challenge my control, but they usually don't get too far. I've made sure it's in everyone's best interest to keep me in charge."

I looked at Slade with new eyes. Sure, he was no altruist, but his accomplishments were impressive. He'd also managed to escape the Dominae's hold and build a new life for himself. If staying in New York didn't mean I'd risk running into mages everywhere I turned, I'd almost consider staying and working for him on a more indefinite basis.

"Anyway, I better head out before the sun rises. My apartment's a few blocks away." He grabbed a cell phone from his jacket. "This has my number programmed. Just hit 'one.' If you need anything, let me know."

I took the phone and stuck it in my pocket. "Thanks."

He looked around as if trying to think if there was anything else I needed to know. "Oh, there's bagged blood in the fridge. I have Earl restock it regularly, so it's fresh. Help yourself."

I grimaced. Bagged blood. Ugh.

"Okay, I'm off. Try to get some sleep, okay?" He put his hand on the side of my face, and his thumb stroked my cheek. I considered being offended by the presumptuous contact, but truth was, it was comforting. After weeks among mages and their fucked-up customs and rules, being around Slade felt comfortable. Easy. Like putting on a favorite pair of broken-in jeans.

Only Slade stepped closer. The look in his eyes told me his thoughts had taken a less platonic direction. In my exhaustion, my reflexes were muted. He leaned in, and I was still processing the fact he was about to kiss me. But just when it clicked I needed to stop him, he changed path and kissed my cheek. "Good night, Sabina."

I watched him walk out and shut the door. I heard the bookcases slide back into place. And a few minutes later, I listened to the sounds of him and Earl closing down the bar. Only when I was sure I had the building to myself did I collapse on the futon. I was out a few seconds later.

That day, I dreamed about being burned at the stake. As

I screamed in agony, I looked out over the crowd. Maisie was there, sobbing as she clung to Orpheus. Adam and Slade were punching each other while Giguhl cheered them on. And Stryx sat on Lavinia's arm as she danced around my funeral pyre.

28

To Slade's credit, he'd patiently ignored me for an hour before he broke.

"All right, dammit." He slammed his pen down on his desk. "Stop pacing before you wear a rut in my carpet."

After being plagued by strange dreams all night only to wake up to a bag of cold blood, I'd woken in a shitty mood. I'd spent an hour in the bar spoiling for a fight before Slade demanded I go to his office.

I stopped and smiled. "You got something for me, after all?"

When I'd asked earlier, he'd said it was too soon. Probably he was right, but I didn't care. I needed to do something before I went crazy.

"Yes, but don't get too excited. It's a small job. There's a vamp who owes me some back blood taxes. I need you to go convince him bringing his account up to date is in his best interest."

I'd spent a few years being an enforcer for the Dominae out in L.A. The job involved delivering a bunch of broken noses and shaking down the scum of the earth for over-due tithes. Before I got promoted to full-fledged assassin, I knew every vampire club owner, porn peddler, and pimp in the City of Angels. So I knew a little something about convincing reluctant debtors to pay up.

"How persuasive do you want me to be?"

"Very. This guy's a real asshole. By the time I figured out he was cooking his books, he'd been underpaying for years. And now he's two weeks late on his payment."

My hand curled into a fist, itching to be put to use. "I'll take care of it."

In addition to his role as professional pimp, Tiny Malone also owned a strip club called The Fang Bang. Located in Alphabet City, the club catered to horny vamps. Upstairs, Tiny rented out rooms to the nymphs he kept on staff for clients who preferred their blow jobs fang-free.

The club consisted of one large cave-like room drenched in red light. On a stage toward the back, a female vampire gyrated her hips in time with "Blood Sugar Sex Magik." Her tits were real—implants never took in vamps—and covered in silver glitter that matched her G-string. Another chick lay on the bar, dripping blood from a bottle onto her rack. A few horny male vamps watched mesmerized as she licked the blood from her nipples.

I headed straight for the bar on the opposite end from the blood show. A male vamp eyed me from a nearby stool. His greasy red hair hung limply to his shoulders, and his right hand was busy in his lap. I avoided his leer as I tried to get the bartender's attention. The three-hundred-pound barkeep stood next to the female on the bar, making sure none of the onlookers helped themselves to a free grope.

When he finally noticed us, he held up a finger. I took the opportunity to get the lay of the club. Several males were clumped in front of the stage watching the female in the silver G-string rub her crotch against the pole. Around the perimeter of the room, other girls gave lap dances to males with shadowed faces. Other than the front door, I saw only one other exit, which seemed to lead to a hallway—probably the "blood rooms." They were like champagne rooms you'd find in mortal strip clubs, only instead of bubbly, customers got blood with their private shows. Typical setup for this type of club.

The bartender finally pulled himself away and approached me. "What?"

Tiny needed to talk to his staff about customer service. I smiled at the asshole. "I'm looking for Tiny Malone."

He jerked his head toward a dim corner of the club. "Over there."

I squinted through the haze of cigarette smoke and pheromones. Sure enough, an obese vampire surrounded by strippers sat in a corner booth, puffing on a cigar. "That's *Tiny*?"

The bartender shot me a look. "It's called irony. Look it up." With that, he turned to yell at a male who was getting grabby with the girl dancing on the bar.

I took a deep breath and made my way toward Tiny. Surrounded as he was, I tried to think of some way to get him alone. Then it occurred to me I was the only female in a strip club not wearing pasties and a G-string. I pulled the bodice of my tank top lower and adjusted my bra to show a little more cleavage.

When I reached the table, I stood across from Tiny. He looked up, his eyes bored. I preferred to believe this was a side effect of looking at bare tits all day, and not a commentary on my own assets. "Are you Tiny?" I asked, putting a little flirt into my voice.

"Who wants to know?"

"My name's Candy. I heard you were looking for some new girls." I'd heard no such thing, of course. But in my experience, even if guys like Tiny weren't hiring, they wouldn't pass up a chance for a private audition from some new talent.

Tiny heaved his bulk forward, leaning his elbows on the table. "You got any experience?" His eyes assessed my boobs as he talked.

"Yeah, I used to work at the Tit Crypt in L.A.," I said, rattling off the name of a club I'd actually been to.

His eyes narrowed. "Your tits are kinda smallish."

Gods, this guy made my skin crawl. I made a mental note to demand a few hundred extra from Slade for my suffering. I forced a casual shrug. "Never had any complaints."

"Well," he said, "let's see 'em."

I tilted my head. "Excuse me?"

"Your tits, honey. Need to see the goods."

Cold sweat broke out on my chest. I should have expected this. The idea of baring myself to this pig made me want to puke. However, if I refused, I'd have no chance of getting the pig-man alone.

"How about I give you a private show instead?" Bile rose in my throat. I choked on it as I said, "I'd love to show you my moves."

"That can be arranged." Tiny's eyes lit up. "Why don't we go back to my office?"

Tiny shoved one of the strippers out of the way. She whined, but a glare from her boss shut her up. He tried to heft his massive proportions out of the booth. The stripper grabbed his hands and pulled until Tiny's belly became un-wedged. His body flew forward, nearly knocking the strip-per on her ass. I bit my tongue to keep from laughing.

Until he put his arm around my shoulders. Then I had to concentrate on not punching him right there in the mid-dle of the club.

Tiny's hand brushed my breast as he ushered me through the black curtain next to the stage. My skin crawled, but I gritted my teeth. Soon the charade would be over and I'd finally get to show Tiny my real skills.

The dark hallway smelled of stale beer and illicit sex. A curtain to my right was open just enough to see a cherry-red head bobbing in a guy's lap. The customer had one hand on the chick's head as he drank blood from a cham-pagne flute with the other. Classy.

Tiny made no attempt at small talk. Instead, he led me to a door at the end of the hall next to a heavy metal door with an exit sign glowing above it.

I'd never seen an office with a bed in it before. The room was barely big enough to contain both the bed and Tiny. He walked right over and lowered himself onto the edge. He lit a cigarette and tossed the lighter aside. "Well"—he patted his crotch—"come on. I don't got all night."

I smiled at him and went to lock the door. He leaned back. When I turned back toward him, I got an unfortu-nate glimpse of his member. Looked like I'd finally dis-covered the real source of his name. Irony, my ass.

Tiny grabbed himself and waggled his dick like bait. "Hit me with your best shot."

I sashayed across the room, a teasing smile on my lips. "I can't wait."

I grabbed him by the lapels and hauled his ass off the bed. My fist finally got its wish and slammed into his fat mouth.

"Ooh, someone likes it rough." A trickle of blood smeared the corner of his grin.

"Shut up, asshole." I punched him in his gut. "The Shade sends his regards."

Tiny seemed to catch on then. He shoved me hard. I slammed into the table. Dildos scattered across the floor. I jumped over them and grabbed the back of Tiny's shirt before he could reach the door. Wrapping my arm around the bulk of his neck, I jerked him back.

"Your payment's late, Tiny," I whispered in his ear. "The Shade's not happy."

"The check's in the mail!" His voice went up an octave. "I swear."

I delivered a jab to his kidneys. He grunted and tried to pull away. I grabbed his left arm with my free hand and twisted it up high behind his back. "Not good enough, Tiny."

He was panting now. A sheen of sweat covered his moon face. "What do you want?"

I had no idea how much Tiny owed Slade. The fact Slade hadn't requested any broken bones told me it wasn't huge money. Slade hadn't asked me to come back with a good-faith deposit on his debt, so I decided to just scare him a little. "You've got twenty-four hours. If The Shade isn't holding cash in his hand this time tomorrow, I'm gonna come back." I jerked his arm a little higher. He hissed against the pain. I leaned in to whisper. "You don't want that. 'Cause if I have to step foot in this shithole again, they'll be calling you No Dick Malone."

He whimpered.

"Do we understand each other, Tiny?"

He swallowed audibly. "Y-yes."

"Good boy." I released his arm and patted his shoulder. I'd planned on making him sit on the bed so I could make a quick exit. But now that he wasn't being subdued, Tiny freaked. He swung around and clocked me in the chin. My teeth clacked together painfully, and I fell back onto the bed. Tiny's girth slammed on top of me, pinning me to the mattress. He put his sausage fingers around my neck and squeezed.

"No one threatens me in my own club!"

Pinpoints of light danced in my vision as he cut off my air supply. I grabbed hold of his pinkie and bent it back. But Tiny was pissed and pumped full of adrenaline. If he felt the digit snap, he didn't react. If anything, his grip tightened.

"I'm gonna cut off your head and send it COD to The Shade."

My hands groped the bed for something—anything—I could hit him with. A sharp sting on my palm broke through the haze of asphyxiation. The cigarette Tiny dropped earlier. I grabbed the smoldering butt and jabbed it into Tiny's left eye. The pressure on my neck disappeared, and air rushed into my lungs. Tiny writhed on the floor, his hands covering his ruined eye. I jumped off the bed, ready to get the hell out of Dodge.

That's when the scent of burned flesh hit me. Combined with Tiny's cries, the scent took me right back to watching Hawthorne burn. Bile rose in my crushed throat, making me gag. Suddenly, wanting to get out of the room became a desperate need to get out. I tripped over Tiny and stumbled to the door. My fingers clawed at the dead bolt. Finally, the lock turned and I burst into the hall. Two steps later, I slammed through the exit and into the alley behind the building.

Warm spit filled my mouth. I made it ten feet before I doubled over next to a Dumpster. All the bagged blood I'd forced down that morning now forced its way back out onto the filthy pavement. And when it was all gone, bitter bile and dry heaves followed. I felt to my knees and wiped the back of a shaking hand across my mouth. The urge to lie down was strong. But I didn't have the luxury of indulging my body's need to rest. It was only a matter of time before Tiny's men found him and came looking for me.

Using the Dumpster for leverage, I pulled myself off the ground. I took the cell phone Slade had given me out of my jacket pocket as I limped down the alley.

He answered on the first ring.

"Slade? I need help."

29

$\mathcal{H}$e picked me up a few blocks away from the club. When I got in the car, he frowned as his gaze scanned over me. "Are you injured?"

I shook my head and slammed the door. He looked at me hard for a few seconds before deciding I was telling the truth. He eased his black BMW into traffic.

The ride back to Vein didn't take long, but tension hung thick in the air. I could feel Slade's unanswered questions pushing against the barrier I'd erected. But he'd kept his mouth shut, and I appreciated him not pressuring me to spill my guts.

But by the time we reached his office, my head felt like a pressure cooker. I went to the bookcases and slammed through the door into my room. Slade hung back. As I closed myself in the tiny bathroom, I heard ice hitting glasses in his office.

In the mirror, my face stared back at me with a stranger's eyes. Instead of the usual blue, now my irises were almost black with the shadow of fear. I blinked and rubbed my eyes with shaking hands. Refusing to look in the mirror again, I splashed some water on my face and rinsed the sour taste from my mouth.

What was happening to me? Too many half-formed thoughts and troubling memories bumped against each other until I felt like I might go crazy trying to figure it all out myself. Suddenly, the privacy I'd sought in the bathroom became oppressive. I made my way back to Slade's office.

He leaned against the desk, looking pensive when I returned. When I sat in a chair in front of his desk, he pushed a glass of whiskey in my hand. I lifted it, and the smoky scent made my stomach churn. But I felt cold inside. So cold I felt like I might never be warm again. Ignoring the scent, I tossed back the drink in one gulp. It scorched a path down before it spread its hot fingers through my stomach.

Slade sipped on his own drink and watched me refill the glass. "Do you want to talk about it?"

I shook my head. Something told me once I opened the floodgates, I'd drown.

Slade nodded, seeming unsurprised by my refusal. "Should I assume something went wrong with Tiny?"

I shook my head. "No, not really." It wasn't a lie. I'd accomplished what Slade sent me to do. The message was delivered.

He nodded, absorbing that. "Okay. Do you want me to leave so you can be alone?"

My head jerked up. The idea of being alone scared the shit out of me. Then I'd had nothing but my own black thoughts to keep me company. Slade waited patiently for my decision. He'd shucked the suit coat and now leaned against the desk in slacks and a white dress shirt with the collar open and the sleeves rolled up. The picture of casual confidence. Confidence so in opposition to my own shaky insecurity and fear. As I watched him, something shifted like mercury inside me. Suddenly, wanting him to stay became needing him to stay. Needing him, period.

He seemed to sense the change and held out a hand. I watched him for a moment. The gold flecks in his hazel eyes glowed with something warm. I placed my cold fingers in his hot hand. When he tugged gently, I went with the momentum, right into his arms. I tried to convince myself it was just a friendly, supportive hug, but I knew better. We both did.

His neck was next to my nose, and I inhaled the coppery scent coming from his skin. After weeks surrounded by the sandalwood scent of mages, Slade smelled like coming home.

I had two choices. I could pretend that somehow everything would magically work out and I'd return to mage life. In this scenario, maybe Adam and I would stand a chance. But part of me wasn't sure I wanted that. Not anymore. The truth was Adam wanted me to be someone I wasn't. Ever since I'd met him, he'd been nagging me to change, to embrace my mage side. But clearly mage life wasn't a fit for me, and pretending it was hadn't done me any favors.

That left me with scenario two. The vampire holding me wasn't demanding I become someone else. And he was so warm. So solid and vital. I tried to absorb some of that into myself, but I couldn't get close enough. Not this way.

Slade whispered my name. I lifted my face to look into his hot eyes. He hesitated a split second, as if he expected me to laugh or run. I met his gaze steadily. It was time to start moving on.

His lips warmed mine a second later. I closed my eyes and savored the whiskey taste of his mouth.

Why are you doing this?

Call the voice in my head conscience or self-preservation. Call it plain old common sense. Either way, I ignored it. And when my traitorous brain tried to call up Adam's face in my head, I slammed the door shut and locked the dead bolt.

Something deeper inside—the raw, throbbing, vulnerable part—craved this. The scent, the feel, the taste of Slade soothed the restlessness that had been squirming inside me for weeks. Letting him take the lead felt good. I'd spent so such time fighting, it was a relief to surrender.

He groaned and deepened the kiss. He slid his hands through my hair, yanking painfully against my scalp.

Yes. Punish me.

I nipped his lips with my fangs. The metallic taste of blood bloomed in my mouth. The potency of his vampire blood gave me a small boost of adrenaline. It fueled the small spark waking in my belly—and below.

The introduction of blood play changed the game. Slade pushed me back against the edge of the desk. He pulled off my tank top, exposing the black lace bra underneath. Soon the bra joined the shirt on the floor. And then his hot, wet mouth was on me. The nipple swelled and tightened. The sharp pain of fang to sensitive skin. I clenched my teeth and grabbed a fistful of his auburn hair. The pleasure–pain sensation of him pulling on the wound almost made me come.

Need's claws dug into me. This would be no sweet reunion of bodies. No earnest search for mutual fulfillment. I was no longer capable of worrying about right or wrong. My nerves felt exposed and raw, and the only thing that could soothe them was release.

Slade took the hint and grabbed my hips, lifting me onto the desk. Fitting himself between my thighs, he pressed himself to my core. Layers of clothes combined with his hardness and my wetness to create delicious friction.

He nuzzled my throat, breathing deeply at the jugular. "I want to eat you alive."

Not an idle threat from a vampire. I pushed him away roughly. "No veins. Just fuck me already."

His swollen lips lifted into a smile. "With pleasure."

His warm palm pushed against my collarbone. Pushing back with my hands, I shoved the papers behind me off the desk and lay back. Overhead, the lights crowned his head like a halo on a fallen angel, casting his face in shadow.

Good.

His hands at my zipper. The scrape of jeans at my hips. Lifting my ass to accommodate their trip south. I spread my knees without shame. Cool air tickled my hot flesh, heightening the anticipation.

He'd taken off my pants but left my panties in place. Not out of any concern for my modesty. But because he wanted to rip them off me. As they fell to the floor, I watched his hot eyes caress me. I should have felt exposed and vulnerable, but instead I felt powerful. Filled with the sacred feminine knowledge I could control this male with my body.

Slade pulled my ass closer to the edge of the table, positioning me for easy entry. Then, thank the gods, the head of his cock pressed against my opening. He rubbed it there once, twice, coating himself with the slick. The pressure increased, and then, finally, he was inside. I arched my back and wrapped my legs around his waist, urging him on. He complied, his hips pistoning faster, harder, deeper.

His head was thrown back, the muscles in his neck corded with exertion. His jugular throbbed there, begging for my fang. The scent of warm blood and hot sex rose around us like vapor. My fangs throbbed in my mouth. My hunter instincts urged me to drink from him as he pounded inside me. To complete the circle. But I didn't want that kind of connection with Slade. For a vampire there is no greater intimacy.

To distract myself from the bloodlust, I unwrapped my legs from his hips and perched them on the edge of the table. Coming up on my elbows, I used the newfound traction to give as good as I was getting. We slammed together like tectonic plates. Soon, the seismic shift began, a quaking somewhere deep in my pelvis. It radiated outward, growing in intensity as it spread.

I closed my eyes and surrendered myself to bittersweet oblivion.

30

I woke up in a cold sweat, my heart pounding. It took me a second to remember where I was. I didn't remember the dream, but the panic I'd woken with told me not to chase the shadowy images hovering on the edges of my mind.

As consciousness slowly rose, I felt a warm body under me. Raising my head, I looked up into Slade's sleeping face. We must have passed out after our last workout on the couch. I swallowed and laid my head back on his chest.

The clock on his desk was in my line of sight. My heartbeat slowed to match the ticking of the seconds. I closed my eyes, not wanting reality to intrude.

Slade shifted under me. His arms came up around my back, and he sighed contentedly. Soon I felt the pressure of his lips on my hair.

I looked up. His eyes were open, and an intimate smile pulled at the corners of his mouth. "Hi," he whispered.

"Hey." I accepted the squeeze he gave me before I climbed off him in search of my clothes. He watched me get dressed with his arms behind his head.

"I owe you a pair of panties."

I zipped my fly before responding. "You can make it up to me by waiving the blood tax so I don't have to drink cold bagged blood for breakfast."

As soon as I said it, guilt sparked as I remembered my promise to Maisie, but I tamped it down. I'd only promised I wouldn't feed from humans as long as I was under the protection of the Hekate Council. That wasn't an issue anymore. Besides, I didn't have to kill anyone to feed. There were ways to do it that left the prey disoriented enough not to remember what happened.

He came up on one elbow. "Oh, I see how it is: You seduced me just so you could score a hot meal."

I laughed out loud. His easy humor broke the lingering tension. "Yes, I've often found males can't resist a hungry female in the midst of an existential crisis."

He chuckled and rose. His hair stood up in tufts around his head. "Either way, of course I'll waive the tax. It's the least I can do after weakening you with my furious love-making skills."

I snorted and sat down to pull on my boots. Of course, he was partially correct. A night of sex always left me famished. But the stress I'd been under was the real reason I needed to feed.

He took his time pulling up his pants before he paused. "I have to say, I never thought we'd be sharing postcoital banter again after all these years."

I smiled, remembering the flirtation and heated glances he'd sent me since the moment we reconnected. "Liar."

The corner of his mouth lifted. "Okay, I thought about it. But after you clocked me in the jaw, I knew better than to hope."

"You deserved that."

"Probably." He inclined his head, conceding the point. His teasing expression disappeared and he hesitated before saying, "Should I assume you want to feed alone?"

The subtext to his question was clear. And the answer was, yes, I needed to be alone. I'd never enjoyed the awkward phase that followed sex. If he came with me, we'd be dancing around the subject all night. Plus, I never hunted with a partner. Too distracting. "Yeah."

He smiled, but it was forced. "Try Times Square. The tourists make for easy pickings. Just make sure you don't leave a trail."

My fangs already throbbed in anticipation. I hadn't had fresh blood in weeks, and the prospect made my adrenaline surge. I nodded. "Gotcha." I finished zipping on my boots and rose.

"And Sabina?"

I turned and looked at him. "Be careful, okay?"

My stomach clenched. Already, things had changed. When he'd sent me off to Tiny's, he'd said, "Don't fuck it up." But now I was just running out to feed and he was suddenly worried about me. On some level, his concern warmed me. Who didn't like having someone give a shit about whether they came back? But on another, it put my guard up a little. When someone worried about you, it meant there were expectations. Ones I wasn't ready to deal with. So I just smiled carelessly and said, "Don't wait up."

Times Square at night can blind a person. My sensitive eyes squinted at the swirling neon lights and flashing bulbs that invited worshippers to pray to the gods of consumerism. The area isn't just rough on the eyes; it's hell on all the senses. The scent of exhaust mixed with hot, putrid steam rising from sewer grates. Taxi horns and shouts mixed with blaring radios. Tourists who stopped to watch the lights on Broadway found themselves bumped and jostled by an erratic river of humanity.

I loved it.

I'm sure natives avoided the tourist-trap vibe, but to me, the place hummed with energy. The high was almost as good as the one I got from blood. Almost.

Sex with Slade had sent me over the edge, unleashing the hunger. But the truth was, I didn't need just blood. I needed space. Slade and I made a lot of sense on paper. Common backgrounds, similar outlooks on life—we each understood how the other ticked. But if we were so right for each other, why couldn't I muster any of the sweet anticipation that always accompanied finding a new lover?

If I was being honest with myself, I'd admit that sex with Slade had a lot more to do with running from my problems than with running toward a relationship with Slade. A slight prick of guilt accompanied that admission. Slade had been there for me when no one else was, but I didn't believe he was looking for more than a few nights of mutual pleasure any more than I was. I still hadn't changed my mind about leaving. Whether Slade agreed with that decision or not didn't really matter. I had to look out for myself now. And right then, I needed blood more than I needed air.

I stalked through the crowds, past the megastores and chain restaurants. Underneath the urban stench, the perfume flowing through mortal veins teased me. My fangs throbbed at the promise of fresh blood. I wove my way through the crush, looking for an easy target. The problem was there were too many to choose from. I felt like a kid in a candy store, faced with the task of finding the perfect sweet.

The choices seduced me. Did I crave the teenyboppers dancing outside the MTV studio? Too young, I thought. Their blood needed time to mature. The guy with the "Repent" sign standing on the milk crate? I shook my head. His blood probably tasted bitter—like guilt.

Ah, there. Right there.

He had his eyes on a tourist's purse. I had my eyes on him. He was young, built, rough. He'd be wasting away in jail within two years, tops. As I watched, he snatched the middle-aged woman's wallet from her purse. She'd been too busy arguing with her husband to notice.

The mark took off running like a gazelle through a sluggish herd. I took off after him. He took a right on Forty-eighth Street and ducked behind a building. I found him in a dark corner, going through the wallet. Amateur.

"Whatcha got there?" I could have just taken him without the banter. But I enjoyed drawing out the anticipation.

He dropped the wallet and pulled a knife with a wood-and-brass handle. "Back off, bitch."

I snorted. "Put that toothpick away."

He jabbed the knife in my direction. "I'll cut you."

"Not if I stab you first." I sank my fangs into him before he could blink. He struggled, of course. But the sound of metal hitting concrete told me he'd dropped the knife.

He smelled of desperation. It mixed with the scent of smoke in his hair and the cheap cologne he'd applied by the bucketful.

Oh, his blood was a potent brew—hot and rich. Young males always offered the biggest high. Of course, the spliff he'd smoked before heading out for the night also helped. I'd be craving snack cakes and pizza within the hour, but I didn't care. My cells greedily consumed his vitality. My nerve endings buzzed from the high.

Eventually, his body went limp, and I let it slide to the pavement. I hadn't killed him, but he'd need more than cookies and juice when he woke up. Grabbing some discarded boxes, I covered him. By the time he woke or someone found him, I'd be long gone. I grabbed the paring knife and stuck it in my boot before I walked away.

After feeding, I walked in the opposite direction of Vein. I told myself I just wanted to enjoy the night a little longer, but the truth was I wasn't ready to face Slade or reality. Not yet. For a little while longer, I wanted to enjoy the blood surging through my veins. I wanted to roam the night like a real vampire again. The sun wouldn't rise for several hours, bringing with it a new day and tough decisions to be made.

For several blocks, I was content to just experience the pulse of New York beating around me. The blood had heightened my senses, and with every step there was a new scent, a new sight, and new sound to experience.

After a while, though, the shadows of Central Park loomed up ahead. My steps faltered. I looked around, trying to get my bearings.

Now that I'd escaped the dense forest of skyscrapers, I could see the sky. To the west, the full moon was a heavy crimson orb. The Blood Moon. My stomach dipped. With the chaos of the last couple of days, I'd forgotten all about the festival.

It didn't matter, really. Not anymore. What did matter was that I didn't have to worry about running into any mages in this part of the city. They'd all be up in Sleepy Hollow for the festival.

I turned right on West Fifty-ninth instead of heading into the park. With the trees of the park whispering in the breeze on my left and the cacophony of the city on my right, I felt pulled in two directions. I kept my eyes straight ahead, not giving in to the tension on either side.

About a block later I heard flapping wings, followed by a screech. I stopped and looked into the shadows. A pair of red eyes blinked at me from a tree just inside the park. I hadn't seen Stryx in days. So much had been going on, I hadn't even noticed his absence, to be honest. Seeing him now made the hair on the back of my neck prickle. But then I remembered Maisie said she'd send me a message. Had she sent Stryx?

As I neared his tree, Stryx took flight, leading me farther into the woods. I followed but pulled my gun just in case. There'd been too many surprises since I'd come to New York not to take the precaution.

Finally, the owl stopped on top of a bridge arcing over the trail. The park was quiet. A curfew kept most normal people out this time of night.

Approaching footsteps sounded behind me. I spun into a crouch, my gun ready for action. Damara stopped short at the mouth of the tunnel, her hands raised. "Whoa, chill out. It's just me."

I frowned. "Damara?" Relief over seeing a familiar face was mixed with confusion. Damara seemed like an odd choice for Maisie to send with a message. "How'd you find me?" Maisie had sent me to Vein, so she would have sent Damara there first.

She nodded behind me toward Stryx. "I used the owl to track you down."

Sounded reasonable, so I nodded, but I was still tense. If Maisie had sent Damara it meant something had changed. "What's going on?"

Damara waved a hand. "Maisie wants you to meet her at the Crossroads tonight."

I frowned. "Why?"

"Orpheus worked everything out with Queen Maeve. Convinced her you were defending yourself. The council has dropped all charges against you."

I frowned. "If everything's fine, why didn't Maisie come and tell me this herself?"

"The festival. She's been really busy getting everything ready."

While I absorbed that, Damara fidgeted impatiently. In fact, she seemed downright agitated. I hadn't noticed it at first, since she caught me off guard. My instincts told me something wasn't right.

"So why not send Adam? Or Giguhl?"

She looked to the left. "I don't know. Look, we need to hurry."

I lowered my eyebrows. "Why the rush?"

"It's a surprise." She crossed her arms. The move made her shirt gape and exposed a glint of gold between her breasts.

"I don't like surprises." I crossed my arms, mirroring her. "Nice necklace, by the way."

She looked down and released her arms. Then her eyes

shifted, going hard as she looked at me again. "Thanks. It belonged to my mother."

My eyes narrowed. "Did it, now?"

She pulled the necklace from her shirt and toyed with it. "She gave it to me on my eighteenth birthday. One week before she disappeared."

I stilled. Rhea had told me Damara's mother had died at the vineyard. Even though my instincts told me something was off here, a trickle of doubt crept in. Maybe the girl didn't know the significance of the necklace. "Does that symbol mean anything?" I asked, playing dumb to see if she knew.

Damara laughed, the sound bitter. Her posture transformed from the drooping slouch of a teen to the tight, hard stance of a pissed-off woman. "Sabina, let's not patronize each other," she said, her voice dripping with scorn. "We both know what this symbol means."

"What does the Caste have to do with all this?"

"All you need to know is they want you dead, and I'm going to make sure they get their wish."

"Be careful, little girl." I lifted my gun. "You're playing a dangerous game here."

She crossed her arms, unruffled by the weapon aimed at her chest. "The only one in danger here is you. Who do you think manipulated the weres into attacking you? Who do you think summoned Eurynome? Who do you think forced Lenny to go after that annoying demon of yours? You think you're so tough, but you're really just an idiot who doesn't know when you're not wanted."

I raised my eyebrow. "If you're so dangerous, why am I still alive?"

She gritted her teeth. "I'll admit it was a mistake to

send others to do my dirty work. But now I'm going to finish the job I started the night you arrived."

"Well, you can certainly try," I said, raising the gun.

She smiled wickedly at the gun. Suddenly, the static of rising magic made the hair on the back of my neck prickle. Before I could pull the trigger, a stun spell slammed into me. My limbs went cold and heavy.

She laughed and plucked the gun from my frozen hand. "Too bad your demon isn't here to save you this time. He proved incredibly hard to kill, and I wasn't sure how I'd manage to get you alone after he survived the attack at Vein. Of course, then you fucked up and got the council to turn against you, which made it a lot easier to get you alone tonight." Her fist cracked into my jaw. "That's for killing Hawthorne, you bitch."

I couldn't move, but I could feel. And right then my blood felt like lava in my veins. The muscles in my jaw ached from both the blow and from wanting to scream at her. To demand answers.

"Ooh, you're mad, aren't you?" she said with a fake pout. "You haven't figured it out yet, have you? You're dying to know why and how." She whistled low, and a second later Stryx landed on her shoulder. She raised her free hand to pet the owl. "Did you know several human races consider owls harbingers of death?"

I racked my brain, trying to remember if Damara had ever been around when Maisie and I discussed my immunity to the forbidden fruit. I prayed she hadn't been. Because if she shot me, I'd survive and get a chance to teach this little bitch a thing or two about harbingers of death.

She moved closer now, crowding me. I couldn't see the

gun, but I sure as hell felt the cold steel digging into the skin over my heart. "Who's going to mourn you, murderer?"

Knowing you're about to get shot is strange. Several things happen at once. Normally, you brace yourself for impact, but frozen as I was, I could only watch and wait. You hear the explosion. Feel the punch of the bullet. The scent of gunpowder singes your nose. But it takes a few seconds for the pain to register. In this case, because she'd shot at such close range, the bullet seared a path through my chest before forcing its way out my back.

Despite knowing the bullet couldn't kill me, my body still freaked out as pain overrode reason. My heart pumped like a piston in overdrive. Cold, clammy sweat covered my skin. I panted and grabbed at my chest.

A second of panic passed before I realized I was able to move again. The alloy used to make my special apple bullets contained brass, which dampened the spell. It wasn't enough to outright cancel the spell, though, so each movement was like wading through quicksand. Thank the goddess I'd fed so recently. If this had happened before I replenished my blood, I'd probably have passed out for a couple of hours.

Despite the red haze of pain, I knew I didn't have the luxury of writhing around. Pretty soon, Damara would start to wonder why I hadn't combusted. I could sense her standing over me, enjoying the pain she'd inflicted. Somewhere nearby, Stryx screeched, clearly agitated as he flew away. Reaching into my boot without her noticing took effort—more effort with the dampened spell making my movements sluggish. But soon enough I gripped the handle in my fist.

Severing her Achilles tendon was like slicing through

a rubber band. Before she realized what happened, her leg collapsed out from under her. My muscles screamed with exertion, but I managed to grab her ruined ankle and squeeze. She screamed and writhed against the pain.

The urge to kill was strong. I wanted to punish this little bitch for all the problems she'd caused me. I wanted to make her understand that no one fucked with me and lived to brag about it. But I leashed the primal need in favor of reason. Killing her now would be a mistake. She had information I needed. And I'd already learned the hard way that killing first and asking questions later didn't work for me anymore.

I left her writhing on the ground and felt around the dark tunnel for the spent shell casing. While the bullet itself had brass in the alloy, the casing itself was pure brass. It was my only option for ensuring Damara couldn't use magic against me while I got my answers.

Finally, my fingers closed around the shell. I crushed the metal in my fist until it was a small clump instead of a cylinder. Holding the brass helped release the lingering spell, quickening my movements. I climbed on top of the screaming mage and pinned her hands under my knees. Then I shoved the brass into her gaping mouth. She sputtered and choked, but I pinched her nose and covered her mouth. Her eyes widened in panic. Her face went blue and then green before she finally swallowed.

I released her and fell back on my ass. My breath heaved in and out, each labored breath bringing a shock of pain in my chest. Tears streaked Damara's face, but her eyes shone with hatred instead of fear. I didn't feel an ounce of guilt. She was lucky I'd let her live—for now.

I grabbed the cell out of my pocket and called Slade. I

gave him a Cliffs Notes version of the situation and told him where to meet me. "I'll be there in ten," Slade said before disconnecting.

I slapped the phone closed and shoved it in my pocket. Behind me, the sounds of flapping wings signaled Stryx's departure. Stupid owl.

"Now," I said, jerking Damara off the ground. She whimpered and limped against the pain in her ankle. I shoved her forward, holding her hands behind her. "You're going to tell me everything you know about the Caste of Nod."

31

Thirty minutes later, Slade pulled the BMW up to a warehouse in a seedy section of the city. A sign on the building read "Romulus Imports." Slade and I had debated where to conduct the interrogation when he picked us up. My vote had been Vein, but he'd vetoed that idea, claiming the bar wasn't private enough. So he'd called in a favor from Michael Romulus, who offered the use of one of his warehouses.

The bay door opened, and Michael waved at Slade to pull the car into the loading area. I sat in the back with my gun nuzzled up against Damara's ribs. She'd been quiet the entire ride, but when she saw the four massive werewolves waiting inside the warehouse, she tensed for flight.

"Don't even think about it," I said.

Slade turned off the engine and exited. He opened the back door and pulled Damara out, leaving me to follow. I shook Michael's hand. "Thanks for this," I said.

He nodded, his eyes on Damara. "Anything you need."

"Where should we do this?" I asked.

"Follow me," Michael said, motioning for Slade to bring Damara along. He led us into a storeroom off the main warehouse area. Rex came forward with a pair of brass cuffs and made quick work of binding the mage into a chair. Damara's chin was high during the entire process. I'd give her points for bravery, but I didn't expect it would last long.

"You can torture me all you want," she said. "I'm not telling you shit."

I approached her slowly, letting her wonder what I had in store for her. Despite her brave front, her body trembled so hard the chair's legs squeaked against the concrete floor. "I already know you're working for the Caste. I also know you summoned Eurynome and tried to have Giguhl killed in Slade's club."

Beside me, Slade hissed and flashed his fangs at the mage. Her eyes widened.

"I also know," I continued, "that you called the Lone Wolves on my ass in the park that night."

A low growl came from behind me. Damara cowered in the chair.

"It's a full moon tonight, right, Michael?" I asked, my eyes still on the mage.

"Yep," he said.

"What do you guys normally do to celebrate?" I asked in a casual tone.

He came to stand next to me, looming over Damara with his arms crossed. "We all change into our wolf forms at midnight and then have a big hunt."

I looked at him. "Have you ever hunted a mage?"

He shrugged, playing along. "No, but we'd be willing to make an exception in this case." He looked around at his buddies. "Right, boys?"

Four growls filled the small room. Even though I knew they were playing it up to help me out, the sound made the hair on my arms prickle.

Damara's eyes widened as she looked around the room. A trickle of sweat rolled down from her temple. "You're bluffing."

I smiled. "You willing to wait an hour for these guys to change and prove you wrong?"

She swallowed convulsively. "But I didn't do anything to you," she whined to Michael.

He leaned down into her face. "You put my pack in danger." He sniffed her hair.

She shied away. "Wh-what are you doing?"

"Memorizing your scent for the hunt."

She whimpered. "I didn't mean for your guys to get hurt. I just wanted her dead."

My eyebrow quirked. "Why?"

Realizing she'd slipped, she clamped her mouth shut and shook her head.

"Okay, why don't you tell me how? You didn't follow me to the park. I would have smelled you. How'd you know where to tell him to look for me?"

She smiled then, some of her bravado returning. "The owl. You were so stupid you didn't even know he's been spying on you for the Caste for weeks."

I gritted my teeth together. "Adam told me Stryx was a spy for Lilith."

"An old wives' tale. Stryx has worked for the Caste for centuries."

"That fucking owl. I always thought he was creepy."

"I wouldn't have had to use him at all if you'd died that first night like you were supposed to."

I frowned at her. "What are you talking about?"

"The cleansing potion."

My mouth fell open. Memory of the cleansing ceremony flashed in my head. Now I remembered how it had been Damara who handed Rhea the potion. "What did you put in it?"

"Apple juice and strychnine."

I smiled evilly at her. "Nice try, you little bitch. I'm immune to the forbidden fruit." Without the apple to remove my immortality the poison hadn't killed me, but that certainly explained my violent reaction to the brew.

As Damara's eyes widened, Slade gasped beside me. "You are?"

I looked at him. "Later."

He nodded, but I could tell he was dying to ask more about it.

"Okay, Damara," I said. "I'm growing bored here. I suggest you start giving me some useful answers before I let the vampire here go to town on you. What do you think, Slade? Have you ever fed from a mage?"

He pursed his lips, thinking about it. "I'll admit I've been curious. She's young, too. I bet her blood tastes like cotton candy."

Damara's eyes went hard. "You killed my mom."

I frowned. Rhea had told me Damara's mother had died at the Dominae's vineyard, but I hadn't killed any mages. "No, I didn't. Clovis Trakiya killed those mages."

"Because you led him there. Without you, my mother might still be alive."

Memory of dozens of mages hooked up to life support while their blood was slowly drained from their bodies intruded. No doubt about it, the Dominae had no plans to release those mages. Once their bodies stopped producing blood, their bodies would have been discarded like yesterday's newspapers.

I laughed humorlessly. "Don't fool yourself, little girl. If Clovis hadn't killed them, the Dominae would have. I went to the vineyard to save your mother and the other mages, not kill them."

She frowned. "You were working for Clovis."

I shook my head. "I was sent to kill Clovis. I was only pretending to work for him. When I found out about the Dominae's blood-farm operation, I tried to save the mages. The truth is Clovis screwed all of us over. He said he wanted to save the mages, but he killed them to frame the Dominae."

Her face fell. "But they told me—"

"They lied."

The tears fell then. Her shoulders slumped, making her look like a pitiful child. My conscience kicked in. Obviously, the Caste had manipulated her, but that didn't let her off the hook for trying to kill me or my demon.

I kneeled next to her. "Look, I know you're angry. You wanted revenge for losing your mom. Believe me, I understand wanting to punish someone for the pain. But I didn't kill your mom. Tell me why the Caste is after me, and I'll make sure they pay."

She sniffed and shook her head. "You can't stop them."

"Let me try."

"What does it matter?"

"Because I need to know who I'm up against."

She shook her head sadly. "It's already too late. They told me if I didn't deliver you to them by eleven-thirty, they would attack the mages at midnight."

"What?" I raised my voice. "Why are they going to attack the mages?"

"It's too late!"

I shook her shoulders. "We have forty-five minutes to warn Maisie and the council. It's not too late. Tell me, Damara! Help me save them."

She became hysterical, sobbing and shaking. I smacked her face. "Tell me!"

"They'll do anything to make sure the war happens."

"Why?"

"Because they want Lilith to return."

The room went absolutely still in the aftermath of that bomb. Goose bumps broke out on my skin, and my stomach felt like I'd swallowed cement. "What?"

"The *Praescarium Lilitu* prophesied that if one of the dark races ever wipes out another, Lilith will return. The Caste knows about Maisie's prophecy that you're going to unite all the dark races, so they need you out of the equation. When you killed the faery, we thought everything would be fine. No one would listen to you anymore. But when the queen withdrew her support, the council voted against going to war."

A million questions rushed to the tip of my tongue. But at that point, all I needed to know was what was going to happen in forty-five minutes at the Crossroads.

"So they're going to attack the mages? How will that force a war?"

Damara's face went hard. "You don't get it, do you? The Caste itself isn't attacking the mages. The Dominae are."

My veins froze. "What?" I whispered.

Damara's voice filled with acid. "If I'd known when I joined that the Dominae were so involved, I never would have agreed to help them. But by the time I found out, it was too late. I begged them not to attack the council." Her voice cracked. "That's when they said they'd give me one more chance. But since I failed to deliver you to them, they're going to wipe them out." A sob racked her body, but I was beyond sympathy.

"How'd they convince the Dominae to attack?"

"Easy. One of those bitches is a member of the Caste."

"Which one?" I demanded, my voice as icy as my blood.

"Lavinia Kane."

Adrenaline kicked into overdrive. I turned to Slade. "I need your car."

He shook his head. "If you think I'm letting you go in there by yourself, you're crazy."

"Slade, I don't have time to argue with you. This could be a suicide mission."

"So be it. If she's right, then this affects all of us."

Michael spoke up. "He's right. We're going, too."

I looked around the room at the six determined male faces. "Fine. Bring her along."

Michael frowned. "Why not just kill her?"

Damara whimpered and tried to break free from the were who held her.

"Two reasons. First, considering I cost them the support of the queen, my credibility is for shit with the council. Showing up at their sacred festival with a pack of were-wolves and a vampire probably won't change their minds. So Damara's our insurance policy. They may not listen to us, but they'll listen to her."

Slade nodded. "And the second reason?"

"I'm out of the justice-dispensing business. Let the council decide what to do with her." I paused. "Assuming any of us are still alive after tonight, that is."

32

Thirty minutes later, I sat in a van filled with five pissed-off werewolves, a former vampire assassin, and a quietly sobbing mage. The mood inside the van was tense. Each of us sat still and quiet, as if bracing ourselves for what was to come.

Finally, Slade's curse broke the silence after another call to the council went straight to voice mail.

Michael spoke up then. "Sabina? We need to talk about something."

"What's up?" I asked, leaning forward through the seats. My stomach churned with each passing mile. Even if we got there in time, I wasn't sure the council would actually listen to me. Hell, I didn't even know if Maisie would listen to me.

"In twenty minutes, we'll all change to wolf form. It may actually work in all our favor, but I wanted to warn you so you don't get distracted."

I nodded and looked up at the full moon. It hung like

a red wound in the sky. Or was it a celestial stop sign, an omen of doom?

The lull in excitement and the heightened anticipation of more to come put me in a reflective mood. Not an hour earlier, I'd been thinking about how I needed to look out for myself. Funny how life can do a one-eighty on a dime. Damara's admissions had changed the game. I couldn't walk away with everyone I cared about in danger. Some lone wolf I turned out to be. But as worried as I was, part of me felt good to have a purpose. Something other than my own self-interest to focus on. Of course, my reasons for rushing back to the Crossroads weren't completely altruistic. Knowing my grandmother's role in this whole drama had reminded me of the reason I came to New York to begin with. Now I had more reason than ever to seek her out and make her bleed.

Of course, I knew better than to expect my grandmother to show up at the battle. She and the other two Dominae wouldn't deign to get their hands dirty with an ambush. But knowing she was behind all this made me determined to send as many of her vampire goons to Irkalla as I could before I joined them there. And if I survived, nothing would keep me from making good on my promise to see her destroyed.

The headlights glinted off the exit sign for Sleepy Hollow. Time to get my mind back in the game. "When we get there, I want you all to wait out front while Slade and I talk to the council. If you see trouble coming, howl your ass off and we'll come running."

Michael nodded. "We'll be ready."

I leaned back with a noisy exhale. Slade grabbed my hand and held on. "We'll make it in time."

I looked at him, wishing I felt as optimistic. "I'd feel a lot better if I knew what the Dominae were planning."

He nodded solemnly, giving my fingers a squeeze. "We'll find out soon enough." He nodded toward the windshield. I looked up to see the black gates of the compound illuminated by the van's headlights.

"Sabina," Michael said.

He leaned out the window and punched a button on the security pad. I leaned over his body so the camera would get a clear shot of my face.

"State your name and purpose," a voice demanded from the intercom.

"This is Sabina Kane. I need to speak to Orpheus immediately."

There was a drawn-out pause. I leaned forward to push the button again when the voice finally responded. "Miss Kane, you are forbidden on the premises by decree of the Hekate Council. Please back your vehicle away from the gate."

I didn't have time to argue, so I made my play. Damara sat in the passenger's seat, so I yanked her forward toward the windshield. Shoving my gun to her head, in full view of the camera, I shouted, "I have Damara Crag as a hostage. Open the gate or I will put a bullet in her brain."

My heart pounded in my ears during the unnatural silence that followed my threat. Everyone in the van held their breath as we waited for the mages' response. Then, finally, the gate buzzed and slowly yawned open.

I lowered the gun and released Damara. She curled into herself on the passenger seat as Michael put the van in drive.

"Okay, everyone, look alive," I said. "It's showtime."

*   *   *

A greeting party waited for us in front of the manor. Six Pythian Guards stood with machine guns and magical weapons trained on the van. Orpheus stood at the front of the group, his face darker than a thundercloud. Michael stopped with the headlights trained on the group.

"Exit the van with your arms raised!"

I looked at Michael. "Everyone out. Slowly. They'll probably take me into custody, but I'm pretty sure I'll still get a chance to talk to Maisie. You guys try to look as un-threatening as possible."

"We'll try," Michael said. "But the minute the clock strikes midnight, things are going to get pretty hairy."

I shot him a lame attempt at a smile and opened my door. "Do your best."

I held up my hands and jumped out. Slade held Damara's arm with one hand beside me. The weres lined up behind us.

Immediately, the guards came forward with their weapons trained on us. Adam moved to stand next to Orpheus. His face was hard, completely void of recognition. I couldn't blame him. After all, as far as he knew I'd gone shit-house crazy and kidnapped his aunt's protégé.

I kept my hands up, allowing another guard to pat me down for weapons. The weres and Slade got the same treatment. When they nodded the all-clear to Orpheus, he came forward. He jerked a nod for one of the guards to take Damara. Looking totally defeated, the girl went willingly, shooting me worried looks as they led her a few feet away.

"You have a lot of nerve showing your face here," Orpheus said finally.

"Believe me, I know I'm not welcome," I said. "But in about ten minutes, this compound is going to be under attack."

Orpheus's eyes scanned my bloody clothes, left over from my fight with Damara earlier. "By you and what army?"

Realizing he'd misunderstood my warning, I regrouped. "Not by me. I came to warn you that the Caste of Nod got tired of waiting for you to declare war. They've convinced the Dominae to bring it to you instead."

Orpheus tossed back his head and laughed. "You almost had me going. The Caste of Nod? That's ridiculous."

I looked him in the eye. "Ask Damara how ridiculous it is."

Orpheus paused and looked at the girl. "Damara? What's she talking about?"

Damara opened her trembling mouth to speak, but at that moment, the front door burst open. Maisie ran out with Rhea on her heels.

Maisie stumbled to a stop when she saw the guns trained on me. "Sabina? What's going on?"

Orpheus stopped her when she moved to approach me. "I'll tell you what's going on. Your sister kidnapped Damara."

Maisie's eyebrows slammed down. "What? Why?"

Rhea glared at me. "You little bitch!"

"I only claimed she was a hostage to get inside the gates. The truth is, she's the one who's been trying to kill me. Tell them, Damara."

All eyes turned on the girl. Her mouth worked as tears spilled down her cheeks. "I-I didn't know it would come to this."

Rhea's anger fell and betrayal took its place. "Damara?" her voice broke. "How could you?"

Damara's head bowed in shame. "They told me she killed my mom."

Orpheus's eyes widened. He hadn't recovered by the time Maisie's voice cut through the silence. "I think we need to go inside and sort all this out."

I shook my head. "There's no time."

"Someone better start explaining what in the hell is going on!" Orpheus bellowed.

"Damara," I said with a command clear in my tone.

"It's true. The Caste of Nod has been manipulating everyone to force a war. They wanted me to kill Sabina so she couldn't fulfill Maisie's prophecy, and when I failed, they decided the Dominae should ambush. The Alpha Dominae is in their pocket."

Maisie rubbed her forehead. "I'm lost. Why would the Caste want to force a war, and what does all this have to do with Sabina?"

"Sabina," Slade said in a low tone. "Two minutes till midnight."

My heart leapt. "Look, we don't have time to explain. We need to get your people out of here now!"

Orpheus crossed his arms. "Even if the Caste tries to attack, they won't make it inside the gates. We've doubled our wards and our security. The only beings getting inside are mages."

I raised an eyebrow. "Then how did I just get in with a pack of werewolves and a vampire?"

He paused, the first hint of doubt showing in his eyes.

Maisie opened her mouth, but whatever she was going to say was cut short by an explosion behind the building that left my ears ringing. Everyone jumped, turning toward the sound. Behind the house, a plume of smoke rose and screams ripped through the night.

"Godsdammit!" Orpheus shouted. "What the hell was that?"

A low snarl made the hair on the back of my neck raise. I turned slowly. My eyes widened when I saw Michael, Rex, and the three other werewolves in midchange. Their faces contorted, their noses elongating and their mouths filling with razor teeth. Their clothes shredded and dropped to the ground as their muscles bulked and their skin sprouted coarse fur. As the Alpha, Michael's fur was silver, while the others had varying shades from black to brown. As I watched with wide eyes, Michael threw his massive head toward the sky and howled. The rest of his pack followed suit. Then, without warning, the group took off running with the massive silver werewolf in the lead.

The Guards who'd been holding the weres stumbled back and raised their guns.

"No," I yelled. "They're with us."

"Leave them!" Adam shouted.

I shot him a grateful look.

I turned to Slade. "Get the weapons." Before we headed to the Crossroads, Michael had the weres turn the van into a mobile arsenal. For a race that usually kept out of politics, Michael and his pack had an impressive stash of vampire extermination supplies. Now Slade jumped toward the van and started distributing guns. Orpheus was shouting instructions to the Pythian Guards, who ran in the same direction the weres went.

I ran to Maisie. Adam was yelling at her to get inside,

but she was resisting. "Maisie, he's right. You need to hide."

"No! I need to help."

I shook my head. Maisie wasn't a warrior. She'd never survive whatever waited for us behind the house, and I couldn't afford to be distracted by protecting her. I turned to Adam. "Is there a safe room in the house? Someplace she can hide?"

"Yeah. There's a hidden room on the second floor."

Maisie ripped her hands from mine. "I'm not hiding."

Rhea stepped in and shot me an apologetic look. With that one glance, all was forgiven. "Sabina's right, Maisie. You're too important. Especially now that your visions have returned."

I looked up quickly. "Really?"

Maisie nodded solemnly. "Yes, but not soon enough to foresee this, apparently."

That made up my mind. I grabbed her hand and started running toward the house.

"I said no!"

"Come on," I said. "I want to show you something."

We ran into the house and up the stairs. Adam, Slade, and Rhea followed.

As we ran, I did hasty introductions. "Adam, this is Slade." I paused. "He's an old friend," I said after a moment's hesitation. Next to me, I saw Adam's eyes shoot to Slade. "Slade, this is Adam. He my—"

"I'm her new friend," Adam cut in. "And we've already met. Although I thought everyone called you 'The Shade.'"

Slade grunted. "Everyone but Sabina."

I almost stumbled on the stairs but, given the situation,

I figured now wasn't the time to freak out about either the awkwardness of seeing the mage I sort of loved next to the vampire I'd recently had sex with. Not to mention the fact these two males apparently already knew each other.

We reached the top a second later, and I pushed Maisie toward the windows and pointed. "Do you see that?" I demanded. She gasped when she saw what was waiting for us below. "That's not a game, Maisie."

Chaos reigned. Figures in black descended on the masses like bloodthirsty crows. Magic zinged through the clearing like lightning. And from a distance, the howls of several werewolves added their dark music to the violence. A flash of green caught my eye, and I caught my breath. Giguhl was down there, fighting a trio of vampires while Valva attacked a fourth.

Maisie's eyes didn't leave the grisly scene. "I'm not hiding. I can't expect my people to die while I hide like a coward. Now give me a gun and let's go help them!"

I sighed. Maisie might not be a warrior, but she was no coward. I looked at Adam. He shrugged reluctantly. "She knows how to use one. I taught her years ago just in case."

I sighed. Now that I'd seen what we were up against, I understood we'd need every able body fighting if we were going to survive. I handed her a Glock. "It's got apple bullets."

Maisie surprised me by flipping the safety off like a pro. I raised an eyebrow.

"Sabina," Slade said. "We need to move."

I cocked my gun. "Let's go."

33

I thought the bird's-eye view of the battle was bad. But running into the thick of it, I knew the real meaning of hell. I charged into the smoky, blood-soaked clearing, leaping over bodies.

Rhea broke off early on to help heal the mages who'd already been injured. Slade and Maisie ran behind me. But seeing the magical fireworks up ahead, I shouted for Slade to split up and help a group of mages surrounded by magic-wielding vampires. I grabbed Maisie's hand and started pulling her along behind me.

"Sabina!" Adam called. I stopped and turned. He ran toward me, his face expressionless. Then he grabbed me around the waist and pulled me to him. His lips slammed into mine for a brief, hard kiss. When he pulled away, he smiled. "I'm glad you came back. Now make sure you stay alive."

A little dazed, I nodded stupidly. "You, too."

With a last, heated glance he ran into the fray.

"Sabina, watch out!" Maisie yelled.

I turned just as a vamp jumped me with a flash of fangs. I didn't recognize him. Didn't matter. I shot him between the eyes. I paused, expecting nausea to strangle me. Only my fickle conscience didn't rear to life. Instead, laser-sharp resolve overcame me. I couldn't let these bastards kill everyone I cared about in the world.

I grabbed Maisie's hand and ran toward a clump of three vamps ganging up on a female mage. She was holding them off with zaps of magic, but she was outnumbered.

One of the vampires raised his hands and shot a bolt of energy at the mage. I paused as she fell back, knocked unconscious from the blow. Now I knew what the Dominae did with all the mage blood they'd drained. When vampires feed, they absorb the essence of the creature they feed from. That's why the Black Covenant had forbidden vampires from hunting mages or faeries. The access to their magical blood made them too dangerous.

The three vampires descended on her like a pack of jackals. Screaming with rage, I ran at them. I threw one a few feet away and shoved the gun into the back of another's skull. His face exploded all over the mage's pink chiton. The third guy—the one who'd used magic—rounded on me.

He raised his hands to throw a bolt at me, but I ducked and rolled. As I came up, I swept my leg under his. He fell to the ground and Maisie shot him the chest. I left Maisie to help the mage up and moved ahead.

Through the chaos, I saw Giguhl up ahead. I started to follow him in case he needed backup, but a screech caught my attention. Stryx circled overhead. I raised my gun and took aim. That fucking owl had been spying on me for the Caste all along. I closed one eye and pulled the trigger.

The owl screamed as the bullet ripped through one of his wings. I cursed as his body fell. I didn't have time to hunt him down and finish the job.

A familiar scream ripped through the clearing. Through the haze of smoke—the by-products of so many spells shooting around—I saw Maisie was in trouble. A vamp had her in a headlock while two others grabbed for her feet.

I went on autopilot. Reaching my sister was my only focus. I pushed my way through the crowds of fighting mages and vamps trying to get to her. On some level, I was aware of Slade's pounding footsteps behind me.

"Sabina!" he warned a split second before someone tripped me. I fell forward, face-first into the ground. The impact knocked the wind out of me and the gun from my hand. I scrambled forward to retrieve it, but my attacker grabbed my legs and pulled me back. I scissored my legs and flipped over awkwardly.

The demon could have been Giguhl's brother—a Mischief demon. Same black horns, same black lips and goat eyes. Only this one had green-and-black-striped scales. My heart sped up. How the hell did the Dominae get demons to fight for them?

Vamps I could handle, but I still had no idea how to best a demon. Even one as low on the danger scale as a Mischief. I kicked, dodging its sharp claws. Over his head, I saw Slade fighting two vamps as he tried to get to me.

The demon grabbed me, pulling me off the ground. Suddenly the world shifted and I crashed back down to the dirt. I flipped over in time to see Giguhl heft the thing and throw it several feet away. Relief flooded through me. I'd never been so happy to see my demon. But the enemy

Mischief was up in an instant, running at Giguhl. Before I could jump in to help, Valva came flying at them looking like a Valkyrie. She jumped on the Mischief's back while Giguhl tossed bolts of demon magic at him. She wrapped her diamond chain around the demon's throat while Giguhl blasted his midsection.

"Go help Maisie!" Giguhl shouted.

A vamp got in my way, and I pulled a knife from my boot and threw it at his back. He ignited as soon as the apple-wood handle pierced his back, but I was already past him. Heat from the explosion warmed my back while I took another one down.

Nearby, I heard a bloodcurdling scream. I looked over in time to see Damara fall under the fangs of a vampire. My chest tightened. The poetic justice of the situation was lost among sympathy for the naive girl. Her need for revenge had blinded her to the dangerous game she'd been pulled into until it was too late.

"Sabina! Help!" Maisie's cry forced Damara from my mind. I cursed as I noted the eight-to-one odds my sister faced. I pumped my legs and used my weapons to clear a bloody path to her. She didn't pause to look at me, just turned her back so we formed a two-headed defense machine.

Beyond the shoulders of the vamps attacking us, I saw the bodies of dozens of mages littering the ground. Small groups held their own against their fanged and horned attackers. A few mages had summoned their own demons to fight. The entire area had broken out into bloody pandemonium.

I stabbed a female vamp in the neck. As she fell and went up in flames, I saw Adam fighting his way toward us.

I didn't have time to worry about him, because ten demons suddenly appeared in the clearing and headed toward us.

"Sabina?" Maisie called over her shoulder as I kicked a male in the stomach.

"Yeah?" I heard a zing of energy fly behind me.

"If we don't make it out of this alive—"

"Kill first, talk later," I interrupted.

She was too busy fighting to come back with a retort. I couldn't blame her. For every vamp I killed, five more took his place. Where were they all coming from?

I called out. "Giguhl!"

In a flash he appeared behind the female vamp I was fighting. With one swift move, he zapped her with some demon magic.

"You called?" His chest and claws were covered in blood. Ash smeared his green face.

"How many of these assholes have you taken out?"

"'Bout twenty. But they seem to be multiplying."

"Go find Slade."

"I saw him a few minutes ago fighting with the weres."

I hadn't seen the weres yet, but I'd kind of had my hands full. I shot a vamp who chose that moment to rush us. He ignited at our feet.

"Giguhl," Maisie yelled over her shoulder. "You and Valva go find Rhea."

"Aye, aye, captain," he said before disappearing into the crowd.

Five more vamps flashed into the clearing not twenty feet from us. My heart kicked up a few more notches.

My muscles screamed from exertion. My bloody hands ached. My stomach clenched. They just wouldn't stop coming. Still, Maisie and I fought. She'd stumble and I'd help her up. I'd fall back and she'd support me. We were an outnumbered team, but a team nonetheless.

I glanced over and saw Slade and five weres holding their own with the demons. It looked like we were finally making some headway.

As more mages joined us to fight, I felt Maisie pull away from my back. We were finally making a dent. I shot one of the few remaining vamps in the chest. As he exploded, I took a deep breath, but when another horde flashed into the clearing it changed into a gasp. Suddenly, the area was swarming with vampires and demons again.

Rhea ran up with Giguhl and Adam. "Everyone circle up!"

Everyone nearby—about twenty mages and demons— fell into a circle, our backs toward the center of the circle. Rhea grabbed my left hand in a tight grip and Adam took my right.

I jerked my head toward her. "What are we doing?"

"We need to combine our magic if we're going to defeat them."

"Rhea I don't—" I began, panic gripping me. I wasn't sure if I could handle zapping anyone anymore. Just the memory of zapping Hawthorne had made me puke.

Rhea's intense gaze burned into me. "You can do this."

"But —"

She squeezed my hand and turned to address the circle. "Tap the line!"

A low hum of energy pulsed up from the ground. I wasn't sure exactly what we were doing, but I concentrated on trying to pull the force up through my bones. I closed my eyes and focused. My hands burned as Adam's and Rhea's hands filled with magical energy. Pressure built in my chest, my lungs, my throat before condensing into my diaphragm.

"Now!" Rhea yelled.

The force jerked my eyes open and pushed a scream out of my mouth. A blinding burst of light exploded from our circle. A wide band of energy radiated out of all of our bodies in a ring of power. The force of it tore through the vampires and demons surrounding us. The ones closest exploded instantly. Those farther back weren't killed, but they were knocked back, writhing on the ground.

Every nerve in my body felt raw and exposed. Tremors shook my limbs—magical aftershocks. Someone bumped into me. I looked around, feeling drunk and disoriented.

"Sabina?" I recognized the movement of Adam's lips but was having trouble hearing.

I blinked and tried to focus. He grabbed my shoulders. "Sabina?"

I swallowed against a wave of nausea.

Orpheus ran over, covered in blood. "Lazarus, you take several guards and comb the area for survivors."

Adam nodded. "Yes, sir." He squeezed my shoulder before he ran off.

Orpheus rounded on me. "Where's Maisie?"

"She was just here." I frowned and looked around, not seeing her familiar form anywhere. "Rhea? Have you seen Maisie?"

Rhea knelt next to a mage with a wicked-looking neck wound. "No. I thought she was with you."

My heart slammed against my ribs. "Giguhl!"

"Yeah?" He and Valva were helping Orpheus look for surviving mages among the wreckage.

"Did you see Maisie?"

He frowned. "Not since right before we circled up."

I cursed. "Help me look for her!"

We split up, combing the area and calling for her. When I ran into Adam near the Sacred Grove, dread had spread through my veins like venom.

"Sabina, what's wrong?"

"I can't find Maisie anywhere."

He paused, his face morphing into a mask of worry. "She has to be here somewhere. I'll help you look." His face and hands were covered in blood from staking vamps who'd survived the magical blast.

"No, you need to be sure none of those assholes live. I'll find her." I forced a smiled. "Maybe she went inside the house or something."

He looked unconvinced. "Okay, I'll ask the weres to sniff around, see if they can pick up her scent."

I paused. With all the craziness of the fighting, I'd totally forgotten about Michael and his pack. Once I found Maisie, I needed to check and make sure they were all okay.

"Good idea," I said. "I'll let you know if I find her."

The lights from the manor's windows created macabre spotlights on the battlefield. I ran toward the glow inside, hoping to find Maisie there.

I ran through the rooms, screaming for Maisie until my voice went hoarse. Finally, I made my way up to the Star Chamber, drawn there because it was the room she loved most in the house. I threw the door open and walked in with my gun drawn. But the room was empty except for Maisie's lingering scent and her art supplies. I slammed my fist into the wall.

"Godsdammit, where are you?"

I walked deeper into the room, fear for Maisie knotting my stomach. Then I saw the canvas propped up on an easel next to a window. My heart stopped.

Against the stark white of the canvas, the rust-colored medium was unmistakable. In blood, someone had written: "Checkmate."

34

*A*dam found me a few minutes later. I was sitting on the floor, panting. All around me, splintered easels and art supplies littered the floor like assault victims. My hands were sticky with drying paint and stung from the splinters I'd collected during my brief freak-out.

But now that the anger had passed and fear took its place, I couldn't rip my eyes from the canvas to acknowledge his arrival. "Sabina?" He knelt beside me.

"She has her."

Despite my unclear statement, he seemed to get I was talking about Maisie. "Who has Maisie?"

I pointed a trembling finger at the canvas. "Lavinia."

His eyes turned to look at the canvas. When he saw the message, he cursed under his breath. I could smell his anger rising, intensifying his sandalwood scent. "How do you know?"

I didn't tell him that this one simple word had told me everything I needed to know. I didn't tell him that even before I'd sniffed the canvas, I'd known it was Maisie's blood. And I didn't tell him that even before I'd found the canvas painted in blood, my gut told me that Lavinia had somehow managed to take Maisie.

Checkmate. The word banged around in my brain like a stray bullet.

"I just know," I said, finally.

He nodded, seeming to take my word as proof enough. "But why take Maisie? If she could manage to kidnap her under our noses, surely she could have gotten you instead."

I turned my face on my knee and looked at him. His tone was calm, but his eyes burned with the same mixture of fear and rage boiling inside me. "That would have been too easy. This is punishment. She's wants me to know she's running the game now."

A muscle worked in Adam's jaw. His fists clenched so hard his knuckles turned white. "Like hell she is. We'll figure out how to get her back."

I shook my head. "There's only one way to get Maisie back now."

"Sabina," Adam said in a warning tone. "Don't say it."

I raised my head. "It's the only way."

"Bullshit. You think Lavinia will just let you trade places with Maisie? They'll never let both of you out of there alive. It's bad enough Maisie's life is in danger. I won't risk you, too."

I threw up my hands. "What other choice is there?"

He ran a hand through his hair. "We'll figure something out. But first we need to break the news to Orpheus."

He held out a hand and helped me stand. His arms wrapped around me. This wasn't a romantic gesture, but one of comfort. I accepted the strength he offered, absorbing it into my skin along with his sandalwood scent.

"Am I interrupting something?"

I pulled back to see Slade standing at the door. Adam turned, too, but kept an arm around my shoulder. "Lavinia has Maisie," I said.

Slade's face went hard as he cursed out loud. "Gods, I'm sorry."

"We were just about to go let Orpheus know. We've got some decisions to make now."

"Actually, that's why I came to talk to you." He looked pointedly at Adam.

Adam took the hint. I missed the weight of his arm as he withdrew. "I'll just go tell Orpheus." He shot Slade a look. "Will you be okay?" he asked me.

I nodded. "Thanks, Adam. I'll be down in a minute."

Slade watched Adam as he crossed the room. Earlier, when we'd been rushing into battle, I hadn't had the luxury of comparing them side by side. But now I was struck by how different they were.

Slade, even covered in the detritus of battle, looked like he belonged more in a boardroom than a battlefield. The years had polished off his rough edges, leaving him lean and distinguished-looking. Adam, with his muscles and goatee, looked tougher—more like a street brawler. But the truth was, each man was dangerous in his own way. Slade with his fangs and assassin background. And Adam with his magic and his experience as a special-ops mage. Looking at both of them now, I realized they were each dangerous to me in different ways, too. But where Slade was dangerous because he knew me so well, Adam was dangerous because he knew who I had the potential to become. But none of that mattered now. Not with my sister missing and my grandmother waiting for a showdown.

Adam shot me one final look before exiting. Slade shut the door behind the mage with a click. "Should I assume I have some competition there?"

I shook my head. I so was not going there right now. "What did you want to talk about?"

He sighed and came forward. "From the looks of things, the mages will be on the move soon."

I nodded. "I assumed they wouldn't stay now that the compound is compromised."

"Will you go with them?"

I shook my head. "I have other business to take care of."

"You're not seriously considering going after Lavinia by yourself, are you?"

I crossed my arms. "I haven't decided yet," I lied.

Slade raised an eyebrow. He knew me too well to believe that. "Don't be an idiot, okay? Take someone with you. I'm sure the mage"—he nodded to the door to indicate Adam—"would love to help you."

I noticed Slade hadn't offered to help. Maybe I should have felt hurt or at least surprised, but I wasn't. "You're staying." It wasn't a question. What was the point of pretending I didn't know he'd already made up his mind?

His expression didn't change. No guilt crept into his eyes. "You know this isn't my fight."

I raised an eyebrow. "If that's true, why did you fight tonight?"

"Because it was on my turf." He shrugged. "But I'm not going to tuck tail and run like the council's planning. I put too many years into building a life here to leave."

I understood his reasons, but part of me was disappointed. This wasn't the Slade Corbin I'd come to know. Now he was The Shade. And The Shade looked out only for himself. I crossed my arms. "Fine. See ya."

"Sabina, don't be like that."

"Me?" I laughed humorlessly. "Like it or not, this war is going to affect all the dark races. It's only a matter of time before it comes right to your door. I thought you were a fighter, Slade."

His eyes narrowed. "A smart fighter chooses his battles. And I'm afraid this isn't one I think I can win. Better to cut my losses now and try to survive."

"Fine, you go look out for your self-interest. While you're doing that, the rest of us will be fighting the battles for you."

"Spare me the self-righteous indignation, Sabina. I have a responsibility to the dark races in this city. The mages might be leaving, but there are still thousands of vamps and weres here who need leadership. I've already talked to Orpheus and promised to help any way I can from here."

That took some of the wind out of my sails. "Oh."

He smiled. "The same applies to you, by the way. If you need help, all you have to do is call."

I smiled ruefully, embarrassed that I'd jumped to conclusions about his motivations. "Thanks."

He moved closer, taking my hand. "I don't suppose I could convince you to come back here after you find your sister."

The subtext of his casual request glowed like neon. He wasn't asking if I'd come back and work for him. He wanted to know if I intended to continue what we'd begun

last night. I shook my head. "If I manage to survive rescu-
ing Maisie, the council will need my help."

The corner of Slade's mouth twitched. "I suppose I
should be happy you didn't use the whole 'it's not you, it's
me' line. Thanks for sparing my ego."

I laughed. "I highly doubt your ego was in danger where
I'm concerned, Slade. We both know it would never work
out between us."

"I suppose you're right." He sighed dramatically.
"But if you ever need to use my body again, it's at your
disposal."

I grinned and pulled him in for a hug. He dropped the
teasing and squeezed me back. As we hugged, he whispered into my hair, "Don't get yourself killed."

I smiled against his chest. "Ditto."

With that, I pulled away. He let me go and smiled one
last time before he walked away. Part of me wanted to call
him back, but I didn't. Slade and I had our own paths to
follow now. Maybe they'd intersect again somewhere down
the road, but for now I was just happy we'd parted ways on
better terms this time than the last time we met.

It's funny how someone you thought was an enemy can
turn out to be an ally.

I glanced at the canvas—a parting gift from my
grandmother.

It's funny how someone you thought was an ally can
turn into your greatest enemy.

Halfway back to the grove, I heard a howl rip through the
air. The mournful sound made the hair on my arms rise.
Looking toward the west, I saw five hulking, shadowy

forms silhouetted against the Blood Moon. I watched Michael and his pack sing their night song for a moment, my heart heavy with the sound.

Unlike Slade, I knew Michael's decision to leave wasn't motivated by self-interest. The pack came first for Michael. I smiled, thinking for the first time in my life, I finally understood that drive. Turning my back on the werewolves in the distance, I made my way toward the Sacred Grove. Deep down, I knew I hadn't seen the last of Michael Romulus. But in the meantime, I had decisions of my own to make.

I found Adam near the altar in the grove, surrounded by the surviving mages. Seeing how few survived made my chest tighten. When the battle started, I estimated three hundred mages had turned out for the festival. But now fewer than one hundred remained.

"We have to go to the queen," Orpheus was saying when I reached them. He stood in the middle of a small circle made up of Adam, Rhea, and the few surviving members of the council. "She won't be happy to see us, but we have to warn her about the Caste's plans."

"Adam, you were there. Do you think she'll change her mind about the alliance now?" a councilwoman asked Adam.

He looked grim. "I don't know. Hell, the Caste could very well have her in their pocket, too. After all, Hawthorne Banathsheh was working for the Caste."

I looked away at the mention of the faery I'd killed.

"Sabina," Orpheus said, "I'm sorry we didn't listen to you sooner. If I hadn't been so—" his voice cracked.

I took pity on the leader. He wasn't to blame for losing so many of his people. That blame rested firmly on

Lavinia's shoulders. "There's no sense rehashing what happened. We have to move forward."

He nodded curtly. "You're right. In addition to warning the queen, we'll put the call out to the rest of the race. If we're going to rebuild, we're going to need every able-bodied mage we can find. Rhea?"

She stepped forward. "I'm on it. When you guys head to the queen's court in North Carolina, I set out for the colony in Massachusetts. They can help me get in touch with the others."

Orpheus turned to me. "Adam said you're prepared to go after Maisie?"

I nodded grimly, waiting for him to argue. But he surprised me. "Honestly, it's for the best. If you show up at the court, there's no way Queen Maeve will listen to us. And if anyone can get Maisie back, it's you." He crossed his arms. When he spoke again, his voice was gruff. "But if you think we're willing to sacrifice your life by sending you in alone, you're crazy. Lazarus will go with you. All three of you better come home alive."

I shook my head. "No, this is my fight."

"You're wrong," Rhea said. "Whether you like it or not, you're one of us. Just like Maisie is one of us. We won't let you go on a suicide mission because you're too stubborn to accept help. Maisie deserves more, and so do you."

I glanced at Orpheus, who nodded solemnly.

"Besides," Adam cut in, "If I don't go, who's going to high-five you when you finally teach that bitch grandmother of yours a lesson?"

"Me!" Giguhl said.

"Me, too," Valva said, coming to stand next to Giguhl. The Vanity demon's eyes were hot with determination.

"Plus, as Maisie's minion, I have every right to help save her."

Looking at the determined mage and the two loyal demons standing by me, my eyes started to sting. "Thanks, guys."

"Then it's settled," Orpheus said. "I want daily reports on your progress. If you need anything, I can't promise I'll be able to get it, but I'll try."

The gravity of the situation weighed heavily over the clearing. It was hard to believe that just a few days ago, the council was debating whether to go to war. And now the war had come to them, and they'd lost so many in the first battle. I didn't envy the task ahead of Orpheus, but I had to admit the prospect of my own mission felt pretty daunting, too. Somehow, I had to figure out how to save Maisie and make sure that Adam and the demons made it out alive.

"I don't like the look in your eyes," Adam said. "You're considering ditching us and doing this alone, after all, aren't you?"

I shook my head. "No. I'm just wondering how we're going to pull this off. We don't know where they're keeping Maisie. And even if we find out, they'll be expecting us. You guys sure you don't want to back out now?"

Giguhl grinned and threw an arm around Valva's shoulders. "You're joking, right? You're stuck with me whether you like it or not."

Valva smiled wickedly and nodded. As Maisie's familiar, she had a right to come, too. Of course, I was sure Giguhl might have had something to do with her easy agreement.

I looked at Adam. His face was somber. For a split second, I thought he'd be the voice of reason and back out. But then his trademark grin returned. "We're a team, Red."

A spark of guilt ignited in my gut. I didn't deserve Adam's loyalty. In fact, I didn't deserve Giguhl's or Valva's, either. But, I decided, I sure as hell needed them. And now that I'd gotten my head out of my ass, I planned on doing everything in my power to deserve it from here on out.

"All right," I said, a second wind of adrenaline warming my insides. "Let's go get my sister back."

Acknowledgments

*I*t may come as a surprise to many people, but I am not known for my patience. Nowhere is this more evident than when I'm dealing with myself. Fortunately, I am quite lucky to be surrounded by so many patient and supportive souls who endure my irascibility with the calm of saints (at least to my face).

Jonathan Lyons, my intrepid agent, endured numerous drafts of this book. He deserves a medal for that alone. But even more, I am forever in his debt for telling me to embrace my creative neurosis. I have to say, I'm enjoying the hell out of it.

Devi Pillai also suffered through many drafts. She also managed not to laugh, yell, or curse at me. Instead, she got me drunk and then gently applied the thumbscrews until I got it right. Well played, madam.

The amazing team at Orbit US continues to rock it out. Tim Holman, Alex Lencicki, Jennifer Flax, Lauren Panepinto, the sales and marketing gurus—everyone has been so supportive and cool. Thanks, guys!

A huge thanks also goes to my beta reading champs, all

amazing writers in their own right: Sean "Numb" Ferrell, Suzanne "Cold Kiss of Death" McLeod, and Mark "Battle of the Network Zombies" Henry. Buy their books, people.

A special shout-out for Lee Smiley. When I sent out the call for help titling this book, Lee suggested the title "Black Light District." In the end, it didn't fly as a title, but I loved the idea so much it became an element of the story. Thanks, Lee!

To Mark and Leah, thanks for brightening my life with snark and filth. To Zivy for the pep talks in New York, for the years of friendship, and for making me laugh all the time. To Emily, thanks for becoming my No. 1 book pimp even though you'd never read a vampire novel in your life. To the members of the League of Reluctant Adults for always making me laugh and the great advice.

A huge thanks goes to Mr. Jaye, who is my advisor, my best friend, and my love. You and Spawn are the foundation of joy in my life. I'm a lucky woman, and it's all because of you.

extras

www.orbitbooks.net

about the author

Raised in Texas, **Jaye Wells** grew up reading everything she could get her hands on. Her penchant for daydreaming was often noted by frustrated teachers. Later, she embarked on a series of random career paths before taking a job as a magazine editor. Jaye eventually realized that while she loved writing, she found reporting facts boring. So she left all that behind to indulge her overactive imagination and make stuff up for a living. Besides writing, she enjoys travel, art, history, and researching weird and arcane subjects. She lives in Texas with her saintly husband and devilish son. Jaye Wells has her own website at www.jayewells.com.

Find out more about Jaye Wells and other Orbit authors by registering for the free monthly newsletter at www.orbitbooks.net

if you enjoyed
THE MAGE IN BLACK

look out for

THE IRON HUNT

by

MARJORIE M. LIU

CHAPTER 1

I was standing beside a former priest in the small secondary kitchen of a homeless shelter, trying to convince an old woman that marijuana was not a substitute for sugar, when a zombie pushed open the stainless-steel doors and announced that two detectives from the Seattle Police Department had arrived.

I listened. Heard pans banging, shouts from the other kitchen; the low, rumbling roar of voices in the dining hall, accompanied by classical music piped in for the lunch hour. Tchaikovsky's *Sleeping Beauty*. My choice for the day. Sounded pleasant with the rain pounding on the tin eaves, or the wind sighing against the cloudy window glass.

I heard no sirens. No dull echoes from police radios. No officious voices grumbling orders and questions. Some comfort. But on my skin, beneath the long sleeves of my leather jacket and turtleneck, the boys tossed in their sleep, restless and dreaming. Today, especially restless. Tingling since dawn. Not a good sign. When Zee and the others slept poorly, it usually meant someone needed to run. Someone, being me.

'Impossible,' Grant muttered. 'Did they say why they're here?'

'Not yet. Someone could have called.'

'Any idea who?'

'Take your pick,' Rex said, the demon in his aura fluttering wildly. 'You attract busybodies like gravity and a 34DD.'

The old woman was still ignoring us, and had begun humming a complicated melody of show tunes from *South Pacific*. A tiny person, skinny as a scrap of leather, with a nose that had been broken so many times it looked like a rock-slide. Pale, wrinkled skin, long hair white as snow. Wiry arms scarred with old needle tracks and covered in thick plastic bangles.

Mary, one of the shelter's permanent residents. A former heroin addict Grant had found living in a gutter more than a year ago. His special project. An experiment in progress.

I watched her lean over a red plastic bowl, filled to the brim with brownie mix and chocolate chips. Her right hand stirred the batter, a pair of long, wooden chopsticks sunk ineffectively into the mix, while her other hand held a glass jar packed with enough finely crushed weed to make an entire city block high for a week.

She peered through her eyelashes to see if Grant was looking – which he was, even though his back was slightly turned – and we both flinched as she dumped in another lump of the green leaves and started stirring faster.

'You need to get rid of that stuff,' I said. 'Split it between the garbage and the toilet.'

Grant's knuckles turned white around his cane. 'It could be a coincidence the police are here. Some of them stop to chat sometimes.'

'You willing to take that risk?'

'Flushing evidence won't take care of the basement.'

I looked down at the old leather of my cowboy boots, pretending to see past them into the cavernous underbelly of the warehouse shelter. Furniture used to be manufactured in this place. Some of the big sewing machines and leatherworks still gathered dust in those dim, dark spaces. Lots of places to hide down there. Rooms undiscovered.

One in particular, hidden behind some broken stairs. Found by accident, just this morning. Filled with heat lamps. Packed wall to wall with a jungle of carefully cultivated, highly illegal plants. A makeshift operation. And one old lady hip deep in the middle of it, singing to her green babies. Knitting little booties for real babies.

Crazy, charming, sweet old Mary. I had no idea how she had managed to pull off an underground farm. She might have had help. Or been manipulated. Maybe she was just resourceful, highly motivated. Either way, there was a mess to clean up – and not just for Grant's sake, because he owned this shelter.

He liked Mary. He liked her enough to bend his

moral backbone and risk his reputation – hold her hand and try to make things better. I felt the same. The old woman needed someone to make things better. No way she would survive jail. I knew it. He knew it. Not even handcuffs. Not a glint of them. Mary was like a butterfly wing. Rubbed the wrong way, and it would be scarred from flying.

'Sin is in the basement,' she warbled sweetly, oblivious. 'Turn on the light, Jesus. Shine, Lord, shine.'

The zombie laughed. It was an ugly, mocking sound, and I stared at Rex until he stopped. He tried to hold my gaze, but we had played this game for two months. Two months, circling each other. Fighting our instincts.

Rex looked away, leathery hands fidgeting as he adjusted the frayed red knit cap pulled low over his grizzled head. The high collar of his thick flannel coat hugged his coarse jaw. His host's skin was brown from a lifetime spent working under the sun. Palms callused, covered in fresh nicks and white scars. He wore his stolen body with ease, but the old ones, the deep possessors, always did. Wholly demon, in human flesh.

He was afraid of me. He hid it well, his human mask calm, but I could see it in the little things. I could taste it. Made the boys even more restless on my skin, but in a good way. We liked our zombies scared. We liked them better dead.

Grant gave the zombie a stern look and swayed close to my elbow, leaning hard on his carved wooden cane. Tall man, broad, his face too angular to be called pretty. Brown hair tumbled past the collar of his flannel shirt and thermal. His jeans were old, his eyes intense, brown as an old forest in the rain. He could be a wolf, another kind of hunter, but not like me. Grant was nicer than me.

'Maxine,' he rumbled. 'Think you can handle Mary?'

Sunset was still two hours away, which meant I could handle a nuclear blast, the bogeyman, and a vanful of clowns – all at once – but I hesitated anyway, studying the old woman. I grabbed the front of Grant's shirt, stood on my toes, and pressed my mouth against his ear. 'She likes you better.'

'She adores me,' he agreed, 'but I can deal with the police.'

I blew out my breath. 'What do I do with her?'

His hand crept up my waist, squeezing gently. 'Be kind.'

I pulled away, just enough to see his mouth soften into a rueful smile, and muttered, 'You trust me too much.'

'I trust you because I know you,' he whispered in my ear. 'And I love you, Maxine Kiss.'

Grant Cooperon. My magic bullet.

And it was going to kill me one day.

'Okay,' I told him weakly. 'Mary and I will be fine.'

He smiled and kissed my brow. Mary's singing voice cracked, and when I glanced around Grant's broad shoulder, I found the old woman glaring at me. She was not the only one. The zombie looked like he wanted to puke.

Whatever. My cheeks were hot. I cleared my throat and glanced at the flute case dangling over Grant's shoulder. 'You going to use your voodoo-hoodoo?'

'Just charm,' he said wryly, kissing me again on the

cheek before limping from the small kitchen, his bad leg nearly twisting out from under him with every step. Rex gave me a quick look, like he wanted to say something, then shook his head and followed Grant past the swinging doors.

Faithful zombie, tracking the heels of his Pied Piper. My mother would turn in her grave if she had one. All my ancestors would. They would kill Grant. No second thoughts. Cold-blooded murder.

Stamping him out like any other threat to this world.

I glanced at Mary. She was licking brownie mix off her chopsticks – watching me warily. I tried to smile, but I had never been good at holding a smile, not when it mattered, not even for pictures, and all I managed was a slight twitch at the corner of my mouth. I gestured at the jar in her hand. 'Probably ought to put that away.'

Mary continued to stare. Zee stirred against the back of my neck – a clutching sensation, as though his tiny clawed heels were digging into my spine. It sent a chill through me; or maybe that was Mary, who suddenly stared with more clarity in her eyes, more uncertainty. As though she realized we were alone and that I might be dangerous.

She had good instincts. It made me wish I was better with words. Or that I knew how to be alone with one old woman and not feel homesick for something I could not name, but that made my throat ache as though I had been chewing bitterness so long, a lump the size of my heart was lodged like a rock behind my tongue.

'Mary,' I said again gently, and edged closer, wondering how I could get the jar out of her hand. I did not want to scare her, but I had to hurry. No matter what Grant said, I did not believe in coincidence. Odds were never that good. Not when it mattered.

Zee twitched. I ignored it, but a moment later my stomach started churning, like my bowels were going loose, and that was odd enough to make me stop in my tracks and listen to my body. Except for nerves, I never got sick. Not a single day in my life. Not a cough, not a fever, no vaccinations needed. I had an iron gut, too. Give me a food stand in Mexico with local water, old meat, some questionable cheese – and I would still walk away without a burp.

But this felt like the beginning of something. I rubbed my arms, my stomach. Zee shifted, tugging on my spine, then the others joined him – all over my body – and every inch of me suddenly burned like I had been dipped in nettle oil.

I swayed, leaning hard on the table. Mary flinched. I could not reassure her. I could not think. I was too stunned. And then I could do nothing at all, because pain exploded in my eyes, like a razor shaving tissue from my eye sockets. I bent over, pressing my fingers hard against my face. Digging in. Breathing through my mouth. My knees buckled.

Then, nothing. Pain stopped. All over my body, just like that. No warning.

I huddled, breathless, waiting for it to return. All I felt was an echo, burning through my skull and skin like a ghost. My heart hammered so hard I wanted to vomit. I was light-headed, dizzy. My upper lip tasted like blood. My nose was bleeding.

I sensed movement. Looked up, vision blurred with tears, and found Mary staring, chopsticks pointed in my direction like chocolate hallucinogenic magic wands. Her blue eyes were sharp. My knees trembled. Blood roared in my ears.

'Devil always comes knocking like a bastard,' she whispered.

I heard footsteps, the rough click of a cane. I snatched the jar of weed from Mary's hand, and ignored her squeak of protest as I hurried to the sink and dumped its contents down the trash disposal.

I turned on the faucet, flipped the switch – and while the disposal rattled, I dashed water on my face. My gloves were still on. I grabbed a paper towel to swipe the blood from my nose and crumpled it in my fist, turning to face the swinging doors just as Rex pushed through.

His aura sang with a dark crown so thick and black it pulsed like a cloud of crude oil. Amazed me, again, that anyone in this world could be misled by his kind, that demons could take hosts and move so freely amongst their human prey and not one person blink an eye. I could not fathom such blindness. The danger of it.

Or why I let Grant continue his experiments with them.

He was just behind Rex. His eyes were wild, fierce, edged in shadow. Something had happened. When he walked in, his gaze slipped immediately to the crown of my head, searching. I knew he could tell from my aura that I was hurting. Grant started to speak, but I heard more footsteps, and he gave me a warning look just as two men walked in after him.

The detectives. I recognized them, even if I did not know their names. They were in their thirties, with close-shaven hair and neat suits. I was familiar with their faces because they stopped by the Coop every now and then to see Grant. Checking up on people. Using him as a sounding board. Once a priest, always a priest. Folks still trusted him to lend an ear.

The men stood a moment in silence, studying Mary and Rex. Then me. I tried to stay calm even though I felt like a deer caught in headlights. I disliked most police. Not on principle. Most did good work. That was the problem. I had broken too many laws over the years to be comfortable around anyone with a badge.

I hoped I looked appropriately docile. I had cleaned up that morning, and my hair was pulled back. A bit of lipstick, some mascara. Nothing heavy. Not that I was trying to impress. I thought they had come for Mary. I was almost certain of it. I was scared for her. And Grant.

But I got a surprise.

'Maxine Kiss?' asked the detective on the left, a slender black man who kept his thumbs hooked lightly over his belt. He looked too by-the-book for such a relaxed posture, which made me think he wanted his hands near his gun and Mace. 'My name is Detective Suwanai, and this is my partner, McCowan. We have some questions for you.'